"Who do you think did it?"

Instead of answering, I pulled a paper napkin out of the dispenser, jotted down the names of some possible suspects and handed it to Jerry. He looked it over and nearly did a spit-take when he saw his name there.

"Why me?" he asked, looking genuinely hurt.

"You know why. And if you'll notice, my name is a lot higher on that list than yours is. The only person who heard you bitch about Jana is me. On the other hand, I can think of at least five people right off the top of my head who've heard me say that Jana's driving me crazy, that I hate her, that I want to push her out a window, that kind of thing. I don't think I ever actually threatened to strangle her, but you get the idea."

"O.K. then, did you do it?"

"Did you?" I shot back.

Other Marti Hirsch Mysteries by
Miriam Ann Moore
from Avon Twilight

LAST DANCE
STAYIN' ALIVE

Avon Books are available at special quantity discounts for bulk purchases for sales promotions, premiums, fund raising or educational use. Special books, or book excerpts, can also be created to fit specific needs.

For details write or telephone the office of the Director of Special Markets, Avon Books, Inc., Dept. FP, 1350 Avenue of the Americas, New York, New York 10019, 1-800-238-0658.

I WILL SURVIVE

A MARTI HIRSCH MYSTERY

MIRIAM ANN MOORE

This is a work of fiction. Names, characters, places, and incidents either are the product of the author's imagination or are used fictitiously. Any resemblance to actual events, locales, organizations, or persons, living or dead, is entirely coincidental and beyond the intent of either the author or the publisher.

AVON BOOKS, INC.
1350 Avenue of the Americas
New York, New York 10019

Copyright © 1999 by Miriam Ann Moore
Published by arrangement with the author
Library of Congress Catalog Card Number: 99-94815
ISBN: 0-380-79120-X
www.avonbooks.com/twilight

All rights reserved, which includes the right to reproduce this book or portions thereof in any form whatsoever except as provided by the U.S. Copyright Law. For information address Avon Books, Inc.

First Avon Twilight Printing: October 1999

AVON TWILIGHT TRADEMARK REG. U.S. PAT. OFF. AND IN OTHER COUNTRIES, MARCA REGISTRADA, HECHO EN U.S.A.

Printed in the U.S.A.

WCD 10 9 8 7 6 5 4 3 2 1

> If you purchased this book without a cover, you should be aware that this book is stolen property. It was reported as "unsold and destroyed" to the publisher, and neither the author nor the publisher has received any payment for this "stripped book."

Dedicated to Jennifer Lubach—friend and inspiration.

The author wishes to acknowledge Jose David for invaluable information and Tommy Nuedling for invaluable life experience.

1

Take care of it.

How many times had Jana Crowley said that to me? Did she need a limo booked? "Take care of it." Was there a stack of correspondence she didn't want to deal with? "Take care of it." Did she need excuses made for a social no-show or help doing a sneak-away from a boring party? How about a little cocaine for a long night?

"Take care of it," she would say with whatever emotional shading it took to accomplish the goal. It could be a sweet request, a cajoling plea, or an outright order worthy of her soldier father. I'd taken care of all of it. I was her best friend. Besides, I was on the payroll.

Well, Jana, I thought, how the hell am I supposed to take care of this?

This was Jana's dead body.

I knew it was Jana because I'd seen her twenty minutes earlier in the same laundry room, wearing the same dress. It was black, slinky, and sparkly, with long arms, a tight bodice, and plenty of décolletage. It was nearly identical to the one I was wearing. She was lying facedown in the dust and it still looked better on her.

When I left her there just before 10 P.M., she'd been

1

sitting on the table where people might have folded their laundry, if the inhabitants of such a posh address could be bothered to wash their own clothes. Jana and I used it as a private clubhouse, knowing we were unlikely to be bothered by anyone, certainly not our respective, disapproving spouses. Jana had been chewing gum so that her husband wouldn't know she'd been sipping Chivas Regal from a hip flask, which I was going upstairs to ditch.

At 10:50 P.M., I came back down the hall from the elevator singing a holiday song. "Chanukah, oh Chanukah, come light the menorah. Let's have a party . . ." I stopped singing and started giggling. Singing wasn't my strong suit and the weed wasn't helping.

"Come on, Miss Crowley. The multitudes await and your husband is being a pain in the ass."

I expected a snappy comeback, but there was nothing. Only the stillness of the basement and my voice echoing against it. I kept talking so I wouldn't have to listen to the silence.

"Let's go, Jana. Chew the damn Juicy Fruit and—Oh shit!"

That was when I walked in and saw her lying on the floor, facedown with her arms in front of her.

"Oh my god! Jana, get up. What's the matter with you?"

She didn't move. Even without medical training, I had the feeling she wasn't going to. I had never believed that old story about your life flashing before your eyes when you die, but for a second I couldn't breathe and I did see flashes of my life, my life with Jana anyway. I saw the adventures and the parties and the fights and the really bad fights and the last reconciliation. When I caught my breath and stopped feeling dizzy, I looked down and she was still there on the floor.

Take care of it.

How was I supposed to do that? Think, Marti, think.

I WILL SURVIVE

If I'd known I was going to find a dead body, I'd have thought twice about smoking the joint. Maybe I'd have taken a Valium instead. At least I hadn't used anything psychedelic. Mescaline before a party was a definite no-no.

Wait a minute. How do we know it's a dead body?

A lifetime of reading murder mysteries told me not to touch her, but I had to be sure. My imagination was already galloping ahead, looking for some answer besides the obvious. Just because she was on the floor didn't mean she was dead, and even if she was dead, I didn't necessarily have a murder on my hands. She could have just keeled over from natural causes.

Yeah, Marti, keep telling yourself that.

Jana Crowley was one of the most intriguing women in New York City, at least according to *New York Magazine*. She was able to wrap most men around her finger, which meant she didn't have many female friends. Aside from alienating most of the competing beauties, she'd managed to piss off many of her fellow artists, several art critics, more than one of her Upper East Side neighbors, and, for a while, her best friend, namely me.

I crouched down next to her, which wasn't easy in two-inch heels. I put out a hand tentatively, as if I were putting it into a cage with a snake and had to be able to snatch it back quickly. Her wrist was cold to the touch, colder than the chill of the unheated laundry room. I didn't feel a pulse.

I could feel myself starting to panic and I knew I didn't have time for it. I took a deep breath the way I do when I'm about to read tarot cards. That reminded me of a reading I'd done for Jana the day before. My ability with the cards had been one of the things that bound us together. She liked to check in with the occult before making major decisions.

I once joked that if I'd been able to read for her before

she got married, the cards could have stopped the wedding. She didn't think that was funny.

Her questions were about the future. She expected to see symbols of wealth and happiness. Instead the reading had started with the Devil and the images had been death and destruction. There were enough swords to equip a medieval army.

She'd lit a Dunhill, flared her nostrils and stomped into her studio without asking me to join her. At the time of the reading, I'd assumed the cards reflected my own feelings, rather than any trouble in Jana's future.

The window into the occult didn't prove anything, I told myself. Maybe she'd had a heart attack, or alcohol poisoning, or anything besides what I thought had happened. I wanted to get out of there, get some oxygen, get a tranquilizer, get some help, but I couldn't leave until I looked at her face. I lifted her head slightly. I wanted to scream but all that came out was a gasp.

"Oh god," I whispered.

It didn't take a professional to recognize the puffed cheeks, bugged eyes, and lolling tongue. Jana Crowley had been strangled.

This was some major trouble and taking care of it wasn't going to be easy.

2

December 18, 1981, was the coldest day of the year so far, the first night of Chanukah, and a good day for a murder. By the time the party started I'd had my share of bloody-minded thoughts, both homicidal and suicidal. I'd spent the morning decorating for the evening's soiree and thinking that one way or another, someone was going to die. Then I went to my hairdresser and things really went downhill.

"Marti, we need to talk."

I groaned at the words. They'd always been a red flag for trouble ahead, and the last person I wanted to hear them from was the man I trusted with my hair.

It was another brutally cold day in the coldest winter anyone could remember hitting New York. I'd wrapped myself in a sealskin coat and come to East 51st Street to escape the frigid temperature and my inner gloom by having my usual quarter inch taken off the bottom and hearing some good dish from Marc, my prima donna hairdresser.

Instead of proceeding to the hot water and hot gossip, he was looking at my hair critically.

"Your hair isn't doing anything for you," he continued in tones usually reserved for "I think it's malignant."

"What's it going to do, write a best-seller?"

"I have an idea," he said in a coy singsong, like a parent luring a child to something too healthy to be fun.

"Uh-oh."

"Come on, Marti, you'll love it."

"But I've always had long hair."

"Exactly," he said decisively, as though that settled things.

I guess it did, because shortly thereafter I was giving in to the tools of seduction known only to masters of the salon. Icy fingers up and down one's spine are nothing compared to a good scalp massage and intoxicating shampoo scents.

"Hmmmmmmm. Ooooooohhhhh. God, that feels good."

"Just what John was saying the other night."

John was Marc's boyfriend and I liked him a lot. He was a male model and amazingly enough, he wasn't a self-involved screaming queen. Breathtaking as he was to look at, with his dark hair, handsome face, black clothes, and well-muscled torso, the greater shock was meeting him in the flesh and finding out he was a genuinely nice guy. He was also a waiter at a fabulous little Italian restaurant in the Theater District.

Marc really had it made: great sex and great leftovers.

I found myself smiling and relaxing. Hairdressers to the stars do not come cheaply, but the laughter alone was worth the price.

"So what's new with the girls?" I prompted, waiting for the good stuff.

"The girls" were the models who flocked to Marc's salon. Among the Ford and Elite models, it was well known that if Marc Rappaport wasn't doing you, you weren't worth doing.

"I have never seen such a bunch of coked-up sluts in

my life. I swear they give the stuff a bad name. I may have to quit doing blow myself, especially if this inflated market keeps up."

This statement dripped with irony, since there were more coked-up sluts around town than just models, and I doubted Marc was paying for much of his own blow.

"Some of them are smacked out of their gourds too. On this last shoot, it was like trying to get Monroe out of her trailer for *The Misfits*."

"Which one, which one? You gotta tell me."

"That wouldn't be nice."

Snip. Snip. Snip. The slightest sensation of cold metal against my neck.

"Ma-arc," I cajoled, playing the little girl wanting candy.

"The one you like."

I hated most of them. Beautiful women have a strange effect on me. Either I hate their guts or I want to sleep with them, which makes me hate them more. Most of the models fell into category number one. The one I liked was a dark-haired model who'd graced all the major fashion magazines. I didn't read those publications, since I considered them to be pawns of the male patriarchy keeping women in thrall to unreal ideals of beauty, but Jana had them around and I found myself glancing from time to time.

The model's name was Cleo Coltraine. She was dark sexuality defined. Touching the glossy pages with her picture on them was practically an erotic encounter. In the unlikely event that she turned up at my apartment in the mood, I wouldn't have tossed her out of bed.

Except of course that I would, because I was a respectable married woman. Fantasizing about a sultry model was just another pipe dream, like flirting with my cousin Jake, the caterer, who was as sweet as his double-fudge brownies and equally as dense.

I'd seen her in person a few times. Artists and models

often turned up at the same parties. Nobody went to as many parties as Jana Crowley, and I was her shadow. Had Cleo looked messed up at those parties? I asked myself. Not any more than anybody else.

"She's a junkie? Really?"

"That's what I hear. I think she was buying from that gallery that got busted."

I knew all about that gallery, from its extremely annoying receptionist to exactly how the bust might have happened. It was the last thing I wanted to talk about. Luckily, Marc had other topics in mind.

"How about you?"

"I like New York in June. What do you mean, how about me?" I snapped, knowing damn well what he was getting at.

What I lacked in glamour and bread, I was supposed to make up for with my own offering of gossip. I was in a position to glean tidbits from the artsy-fartsy crowd and their pals, the literary stars.

"You just want to know about Jana."

"Well, who doesn't?"

"Not me, pal. I just know what I read in the papers."

That was crock of course. If I just read the papers, all I'd know was a little about what she looked like and how hard it was to adequately describe. Sometimes she was described as sleek, sensuous, glamorous, fabulous, and occasionally dreamy, but usually it was beautiful.

"Beautiful artist Jana Crowley . . ." the item would start, as if "beautiful" and "artist" were handcuffed together.

The funny part was that we were superficially similar in appearance and no one ever called me beautiful. I was designated as cute, smart, and funny, when I was noticed at all. Where I had curls that gave me varying amounts of trouble, depending on the weather, Jana had waves of chestnut brown hair with red highlights.

Describing Jana in terms of lustrous hair, hypnotic

green eyes, or luscious lips was useless because her beauty was almost beside the point. There were other beautiful women in New York that year. What clinched the deal for Jana was the grace and poise drilled into her by her mother, an authentic Southern belle, combined with the all-important Jana Crowley attitude. When Jana walked into a room, every other woman paled into insignificance and every man was vulnerable.

On top of that, she was talented. She was the most famous artist in New York that anyone could still take seriously. She worked in every medium, but her first fame came from her sketches. She'd taken a talent that had first revealed itself in the notebook doodling of a bored teenager and made a small fortune. Books of her sketches were must-haves on the coffee tables of the rich and pretentious.

Her status had been confirmed with a *New York Magazine* cover story entitled "Artist As Exhibition." A reporter and a photographer followed her around for two weeks and produced a story that had lovely pictures of Jana at the Guggenheim, Jana on Broadway, and Jana in Soho. It also had snide insinuations and a lot of sycophantic swill, but no concept of what really made the lady tick. I was described as an "ubiquitous toady." The writer must have had to root around in his Webster's for that one.

"So, are you two like that?" Mark wanted to know.

"I may be a toady, but I'm not ubiquitous."

"Hey, I told you about Cleo."

"Look sweetie, Jana and I are like this." I held my middle and index fingers together, "but we're not like that. I'm a firm believer that anyone at any time is capable of anything, but Jana spreading them for another chick is damn unlikely."

"What about the drugs?"

The article had implied that Jana's glow was attributable to the occasional illegal substance.

"She certainly never did anything in front of those clowns."

"Is she cheating on the Brit?"

All I could do in good conscience was smirk.

Marc backed away and put down the blow-dryer. He looked at me.

"Well . . ." I said, with a note of panic sneaking into my voice.

He put a finger on the dimple in his chin and looked at me some more. His own hair was reddish black that week and moussed into spikes.

"Marc, what have you done to me?" His face opened into a sudden grin. His teeth were almost obscenely white against the tan he'd acquired while working on a fashion shoot in Martinique.

"I like it," he said before stepping away, leaving me to confront the mirror.

"Oh my god," I said slowly, which probably wasn't what the artiste wanted to hear. My eyes were having trouble absorbing what my reflection showed. It had been a long time since I'd seen that much of my face.

I'd had long curly hair as far back as I could remember. When I had to describe myself I always started with "long curly hair." Most of the mass was gone. Mark had left me with hair that barely touched the top of my neck. It fluffed out into a perky halo.

"Oh my god."

"You look adorable."

"I'm too old to look adorable."

"Only if you think you are. How does it feel?"

I shook my head. There was nothing to shake.

"I feel light."

Marc beamed.

"You had the weight of the world on your shoulders and now it's gone."

"I wish I could lose all my problems that easily. I swear, if this keeps up, I'm going to kill her."

"That would give you something to write about."

"Ouch," I said, meaning it.

"Sorry."

He hadn't said it to be cruel, but that was a tender subject.

"I'm going to write a book called *Conversations With My Hairdresser*. It'll be a best-seller by Tisha Ba'av."

"Works for me. I get fifty percent, right?"

I got out of the chair and shook my head again, trying to get used to the hair that wasn't there. Marc went to the front of the salon and brought me my coat.

"What is this?" he said, running a hand over the luxurious fur.

"Sealskin."

"Marti Hirsch, friend of animals, lover of all things cute and furry, how could you?"

"In the immortal words of Mike Hammer, 'It was easy.' It's freezing out. Dogs are dying in the streets. Besides it's not mine. I borrowed it from Jana."

"Should I book your next appointment?"

I closed my eyes against the bleak prospect of coming back in a month and still feeling cold and gloomy and unhappy.

"Go ahead."

"You look like you need a night away from it all."

"In spades, darling."

"John and I going to Danceteria tonight. Want to come along?"

"No such luck. It's the first night of Chanukah and I'm responsible for what, I can assure you, will not be the social event of the year. You and John could come and liven up those festivities."

"I'll pass."

The coat was buttoned, the scarf wrapped, and the gloves put on. There was nothing to do but leave the sanctuary and step back out into the real world. The first slap of frosty air assaulted my furry armor. Frosty tears started forming in my eyes.

Oh well, I thought as my body reacted with a cross between a shrug and a shiver, I can't stand Danceteria anyway.

3

Cold, cold, cold. It was cold in the laundry room. I had to go upstairs where I could get to a phone and call the police. I had to go where it was warm. I had to get away from the body. So why was it so hard to walk away? I didn't want to leave her there all alone. It wasn't as if anything else could happen to her, but she looked so vulnerable on the floor.

"Jana, I gotta go get the cops. I'll be right back."

It wasn't funny but I found myself giggling. I, who considered policemen everywhere to be my sworn enemies, was going to make the call that would bring the boys in blue. It was the kind of giggle that was just a heartbeat away from a sob. That realization got me out of the room. I could feel the effects of the pot wearing off, like taking off clothing one layer at a time. I walked to the elevator and pushed the button. I could hear the elevator groaning its way toward the basement. At the rate it was going I'd be totally straight by the time I got upstairs.

"Come on," I muttered. "It's cold down here."

That cold didn't come close to how cold it was outside, the cruelty of which I'd walked back into when I left Marc's salon that afternoon. My teeth chattered as I thought about the city's fickle affection for its clubs.

Danceteria was in. The Ritz was in. Even the refurbished Peppermint Lounge was hot. Studio 54 definitely was not. Arrests and deaths had tarnished the glitter. People still lined up of course, but now anyone could get in, which was the ultimate sign of outness. The rubes were just kidding themselves. It was all over. Endsville.

In general, grown-ups had moved away from the clubs. By 1981, everyone seemed to be having parties. As Jana's girl Monday, Tuesday, Wednesday, Thursday, and Friday, I'd been to parties at venues ranging from art galleries and restaurants to country clubs and private homes.

The dance clubs were now the province of the kids who dyed their hair green and purple and bought fetish clothing at Trash and Vaudeville in the Village. Their attire didn't faze me; I'd worn tie-dye and headbands with pride, but I hated their attitude that all which had gone before was shit.

The kids had made Danceteria the hardest to get into and therefore the most desirable. Danceteria was five stories of New Wave music, pulsing lights, and food so bad that ordering a cheeseburger was a suicidal act. If you survived the burger, there was dancing on the roof and not much in the way of a railing to stop you from jumping off when a little ditty like "Love Will Tear Us Apart" reminded you how bad life really was.

Chanukah party or lover's leap? It was a tough call, but at least the party would have edible food prepared by my cousin Jake, whose potato pancakes were mm, mm, good.

I pulled the coat more tightly around myself to ward off the cold. I could still feel Marc's disapproval. I didn't want to think about baby seals with long lashes. My fingers were starting to freeze inside my gloves.

The previous winter had been notable for snow.

Record-breaking amounts of snow had fallen on Buffalo, New York with enough left over to bring Manhattan to a standstill several times during the season. I kept hearing how beautiful it had been. People were nostalgic. They missed the snow. Maybe they just missed the excuse not to get to work.

By December, there had been only one light dusting. All anyone could talk about was the cold, and the tone they used to discuss it was not a fond one. It had been down to the forties by the end of October. Thanksgiving came in at twenty-five degrees with a wind that wreaked havoc with the Macy's balloons. Snoopy nearly wound up in the Hudson River. Then things got really nasty.

Single-digit temperatures, freezing rain, and windchill factors that went through down jackets as though they were lace. The papers were full of bag ladies freezing to death, airlines booked and overbooked if they were heading for warmer climes, and warnings about not letting pets out.

I was forced to subject my dachshund to the indignity of a doggie sweater. The usual joviality of the winter holidays was hard to find in a populace obsessed with the temperature. How low could it go? There was no end and no answer in sight.

It was cold and bloody cold as a certain Englishman of my acquaintance was wont to say.

That particular Brit was Thomas Brinkham. He was on everybody's list as one of the richest men in New York when he was in New York, with plenty of prospects for getting richer. He was also Jana Crowley's husband.

I almost wished for the elevator not to come. Going upstairs meant dealing with Thomas Brinkham, and that was never pleasant, even when his wife wasn't dead.

In fact, I had been thinking about Thomas when the cold became unbearable on my way home from the hairdresser, probably because Thomas was a pretty cold customer himself. I had to get indoors. My options were a grocery store and a coffee shop. I went for the grocery. Like most of my choices that year, it was a bad one.

I walked around the store trying to look like I was shopping instead of warming up. I was considering schlepping a six-pack of Pepsi back to 65th Street when I ran into Paul Falzerano, my least favorite brat on the whole East Side of Manhattan. Paul was living proof that two reasonably attractive parents could produce a sniveling pudgeball who had achieved the age of thirteen without acquiring tact, charm, or any other positive attributes. He did have a pronounced facial twitch. The sight of his fat face constantly rising into an involuntary wink had its usual effect on me.

I should have been sympathetic. My earliest memories were of an idyllic time on the road with my showbiz parents. After they settled down in Williamsburg, New York, I'd suffered through a miserable adolescence, having alienated my entire peer group within weeks of meeting them.

Books were my only friends. I was cursed with an unrequited obsession for one of the most popular boys in the whole school. A loving father and a smothering mother were powerless to make me any happier.

I knew enough about Paul to know that he was desperately unhappy and in need of friends. His situation was so pathetic that, at age thirteen, he was turning to adults like my husband, Jerry, for companionship. He took piano lessons from Jerry, and Jerry's innate niceness bowled him over. Jerry urged me to give the kid a break.

I wanted to do it, just to live up to Jerry's faith in me. I empathized with the kid, really I did. So why did the sound of his whiny voice saying, "Hi, Marti," and the first glimpse of his face peeking out of an electric-blue nylon parka make me want to reach out and smack him? Why did he bring out the instincts of a school-yard bully

I WILL SURVIVE

I never knew I had inside me? Maybe because he was so obviously a victim and I had no patience for victims.

I couldn't actually hit the little monster, so I was restricted to verbal venom.

"Marti," he whined, as if I hadn't heard him, when I was in fact ignoring him. On top of everything else, I didn't like his calling me by my first name. I was thirty-two years old and acutely aware of it.

What's wrong with me? I wondered. Once I wanted to tear down the establishment and now I wanted a thirteen-year-old to call me "Ms. Hirsch." Well, this particular thirteen-year-old, anyway.

"Where's Jerry?" he asked expectantly.

"Not here," I replied, happy to crush his hopes.

"He'll be at the party tonight, right?"

"Not if I tell him that you're coming."

Maybe if I was cruel enough, he'd grow some balls and tell me off. So what if he was only thirteen. He was old enough to learn the way the world worked. He was being stupid to boot. The party was a follow-up to the Simone School holiday concert and Jerry was the choir leader. The demon child was actually starting to blubber when Mom came around the corner with a bag of apples and a harried expression.

"What's the matter, dear? Oh, hello, Marti."

She didn't make the connection between my presence and her son's behavior. She must have been used to his crying. Paul was collected against her skirt, a living, breathing argument against procreation, as if I needed one. I despised sonny-boy; I merely pitied his mother.

"Hello, Rhonda."

"Cold, isn't it," she said, miming a shudder for added effect, which caused ripples to form in the thick black mink she was wearing.

Rhonda was classic East Side and classic old money. Her skin was winter pale with pink lips and blue eyes. Having agreed on the fact that it was cold, we had nothing to talk about. What we had were connections. We lived within three blocks of each other. Her husband was my husband's boss. I knew her husband was a philanderer and she could only guess.

"Last-minute shopping?" she asked as if it were important that we make conversation instead of just going on our separate ways. Thomas Brinkham and Jana Crowley were the names on the invitation, but everyone seemed to know who was doing the work.

"Just warming up. My caterer's handling the food."

"Will you be lighting the ... you know ..."

"The menorah." Only a Wasp would have trouble with that one. "Of course."

"I'm looking forward to the party. And so is Paul, aren't you, dear?" She didn't wait for an answer. "It's so wonderful of Jerry to look after the children."

"The children" were the priviliged young ones who attended the Simone School, among them Thomas Brinkham's daughter, Elisa. The adults were to be entertained in the lavish penthouse of the Lancaster where Jana and Thomas resided, and the moppets would be collected in our apartment under Jerry's benevolent supervision.

"Is he being paid?" Rhonda wondered absently.

I looked at her in disbelief. I would have given her a rant about how Jerry loved kids and would be insulted if money were offered, but I didn't want to remind myself of how much I didn't love kids and how much I worried about that becoming an issue in our marriage. It hadn't yet, but you never knew.

Rhonda was just a victim of her own privileges. She'd probably get a nosebleed if she went below 52nd Street.

I was ready to face the cold for the last leg of the journey home, but Rhonda had something on her mind.

"Go get some cereal," she told Paul.

Paul was shrewd enough to know he was being gotten

rid of, but he had to obey. I was left alone in produce with his mother.

"Marti," she started slowly.

"Yeah, what?"

It was a rude way of talking, but I had a feeling I knew what was coming and I didn't want to hear it.

"It's about Jana Crowley."

"Gee, I haven't heard that all day."

Her blue eyes begged me to take her seriously, which was the one thing I couldn't do.

"I'm afraid..."

"Jana doesn't bite."

"Oh yes she does," Rhonda snapped, "and Tony... Tony. I think she likes Tony."

Likes. It was the locution of a high school girl and there was a childlike quality to Rhonda's voice, almost a lilt. It was a more pleasing echo of her son's whine.

"Everybody likes Tony," I said flatly.

It was an undeniable fact, like the cold.

Tony Falzerano, principal of the Simone School for Gifted Children, was six feet, three inches of dark-haired, bedroom-eyed, Italian charm.

Simone was a private school on Fifth Avenue. The gifted children in question were those gifted with rich parents who were willing to plunk down lots of money to make sure their little darlings didn't have to go to schools beginning with the letters *P.S.* Simone was noted for having its alumni accepted into the premier high schools of the city, such as Stuyvesant, Bronx Science, and Performing Arts.

The school had been around since the 1800s, when it catered to the sons of Wasp aristocracy. Now it was mostly the haven of Upper East Side Jews who were one or two generations removed from the Lower East Side and farther than that from the shtetls of Eastern Europe. It was amazing how they managed to ghettoize themselves without realizing or acknowledging it. The student body was at least seventy percent Jewish, with a mixed bag of other ethnicities thrown in for that liberal melting pot feeling.

I didn't know the whole story of Tony Falzerano's rise to his current position. I'd heard that he originally hailed from Flatbush, but there was no hint of Brooklyn in his smooth demeanor and slightly clipped diction. Behind that polish was the energy of a man perpetually on the make.

It must have taken quite a bit of skulduggery and social climbing to charm his way into the world of Rhonda and her family. Their connection to the Simone School predated the Falzerano family's arrival in the United States by several generations.

Tony's approach to his job was to leave the day-to-day academic supervision to his vice-principal, a thoroughly nasty character whose expression, as he roamed the halls looking for students without hall passes, resembled that of an army drill instructor with a terminal case of the piles. Everybody hated the vice-principal. Everybody loved Tony.

Being loved, or at least liked, was Tony's mission in life. I'd seen him in action at school events and I was always impressed, if somewhat revolted. Fathers got the superficial charm, the guy talk about whatever sport was in season, and the sincerely voiced pitch about the superior education offered at the Simone School. Mothers left alone with Tony for even a moment were treated to the longing gaze, the bedroom voice, and the slightest touch of the hand. It was as if putting your offspring in the Simone School bought a promise of further attention. Something was working. Simone had full enrollment and a happy board of trustees.

"I know everybody likes Tony," his wife said crossly. "I just want to know if Jana Crowley likes him."

She quickly brought up a hand to cover her mouth. It

was too late. She'd asked the question that exposed her vulnerability and proved to me that she had something on the ball. She'd been married at least thirteen years, maybe longer. She had to know that Tony's act was just that, an act. He wanted to seduce those women into writing checks, not having extramarital trysts that would prove extremely messy if they were ever exposed. She knew it, but she was still worried about Jana.

The longer I stood there, the more I could sense her panic. She didn't just think her husband was cheating on her. She thought he'd fallen in love. Oh boy.

I'd come in to get warm and now I was much too hot. I was sweating. I had to get out. I took a step backward.

"You must be kidding, Rhonda. Tony would never do that. And Jana is so busy that even if she would, she wouldn't have the time." Did I sound as transparent as I felt, complete with a fake little laugh? "Well, I have to go. Candles to light, potatoes to grate."

I was still walking back. The door was steps away.

"New York Night," she said. Three distinct, deadly syllables that told me I was busted. The situation was so bad I was actually glad to see Paul. He was clutching a box of Cap'n Crunch with Crunchberries. Rhonda had to deal with her son and I was able to escape.

A better person would have eased her pain and told her she had nothing to worry about, certainly not from Jana Crowley, but a better person wouldn't have been in this mess in the first place.

I practically ran home, taking big gulps of frosty air and trying not to slip on ice patches. I was simultaneously shivering from the cold and sweating like a pig.

Damn, damn, damn. No, I thought, rephrasing it, Shit, shit, shit. Just when you thought it couldn't get any worse, Rhonda Falzerano knows all about *New York Night.* Happy Chanukah, Charlie Brown.

There was a slippery spot right in front of 22 East 65th Street and I skidded on it. I managed to avoid the actual fall, but that slippery feeling of disorientation and danger summed up my day, my week, my whole life.

It was hard to believe I was living at an address ritzy enough to have a doorman, not to mention its own name, but there I was, walking into an apartment house called the Lancaster, having the door held open by a man who wore an ornate coat and pissed me off by calling me Mrs. Barlow. I'd been married to Jerry Barlow for nearly a year, but my name was Ms. Marti Hirsch, and the sooner Mr. Doorman figured it out, the better his chances for a decent Christmas tip.

I hated the upper-class sense of privilege represented by having a man to open the door. On the other hand, I appreciated not having to stop and get my keys out of my handbag and then deal with the lock. It was hard to be a former hippie living on the Upper East Side with frozen ideals under a sealskin coat, even if the coat was borrowed.

Home sweet home was apartment 8-F. Two rooms, kitchen, and a moderately attractive view of the building across the street. The best view in the house belonged to the penthouse, seven floors above me. I'd seen plenty of that view because my best friend lived up there. Sometimes I thought about pushing her out a window.

I rode the elevator up to the eighth floor trying to think of anything but Jana Crowley. If I thought about Jana, I'd think about Tony (bleh) and Rhonda (jeez) and Paul (double yuck) and eventually *New York Night*. *Oy vey.* Luckily, the remedy for all gloomy thoughts was waiting for me on the other side of the door.

"Hello honey, sweetie, baby. I missed you so much."

I kneeled down so that Strudel, our adorable dachshund, could lick my nose. She was four years old, but still had a puppy face. Just touching her made me feel better. After a suitable session of puppy love, I went into the bedroom, where I showed remarkable discipline by stopping to take off my boots before collapsing on the bed.

All I wanted to do was lie there with the heat on and the dog next to me. I needed a nap. It was only four o'clock, but the sky was dark and I felt exhausted. A hot bath would have been nice, but I didn't want to mess with the new hairdo right before a party. Of course, if I slept long enough, I might wind up missing the whole thing. Wouldn't that be lovely?

I dozed off still wearing the coat and trying out plausible excuses for such a massive flakeout. How would I explain it to Jana? Ptomaine poisoning from bad chestnuts? Being locked up for attacking a Santa who rang his bells at me too many times?

I had about twenty minutes of divine unconsciousness before I became aware that there was another person in the room. I wasn't ready to open my eyes yet. The situation wasn't serious. Your average New York City apartment thief wouldn't be humming "Jingle Bell Rock" and he probably wouldn't smell so clean with a faint overtone of English Leather.

"Hi honey," he said softly.

It was my husband. I opened my eyes. He was fresh out of the shower and wearing a white terry-cloth robe. I took off Jana's coat and threw it on the floor. I unwrapped my scarf and shook out my hair to show Jerry the cut.

"What do you think?"

"Wow."

"Which means what exactly?"

"It means I like it. I can see your face and it's beautiful."

"How did your rehearsal go?" I asked, blushing from the compliment.

Aside from teaching sixth grade English at the Simone School, Jerry was also the acting head of the music department, which included the task of putting together a choir to do two holiday concerts each year, one for the winter holidays and one in the spring.

"I'll tell you, Marti, we've got some incredibly talented kids. Some of the sopranos are amazing for that age."

"But?"

"But there's one or two who couldn't carry a tune if you gave them a bucket with two handles, and they like to sing loud."

"Can't you just toss them out?"

"I asked Tony about that a few weeks ago."

"What did he say?"

"Their parents pay tuition too," he replied, imitating Tony's overprecise speech.

"Good old Tony," I muttered. Then I remembered the whole mess. "Shit, shit, shit."

"What's the matter?"

"How much time have you got?"

"What did you have in mind?" he asked suggestively.

"Not that. What I really need right now is for you to hold me awhile."

"I always have time for that."

Soon we were cuddled up under the covers, all warm and toasty. We held each other tightly, but I could feel that edge of desperation. We were good at pretending that nothing was wrong. We loved each other, we needed each other, but no matter how close we were, I felt like something was pulling us apart.

"O.K., honey, I'm here and I'm holding you. Now tell me about it."

"It's her." I said, gesturing upward with my head to indicate the penthouse. I didn't hear him sigh, but I could feel it in his body and then I heard the tightness and barely hidden anger that had been there for too many months whenever we talked about Jana.

I WILL SURVIVE

"What is it now?"

"Now . . ." I didn't want to say it, so I said something else, something I'd been thinking a lot recently. "It wasn't supposed to be like this."

4

The elevator finally came. I took a lonely ride back to the land of the living. Funny that an apartment house which went to the trouble of employing an anachronistic doorman had dispensed with the companion status symbol, an elevator operator. I made a mental list of things to do. Number one in bold type was Call the Police. I wanted to do it from the safety of my own apartment, so I went to the eighth floor.

I went to apartment 8-F, where I could hear Jerry inside, singing "The Dreidel Song." I breathed a long sigh of relief. Despite the tension between us, Jerry could calm me down better than any tranquilizer when it came to outside trouble. He'd give me a hug and hold my hand while I made the phone call. He might even dissuade me from saying, "Hey, pigs, come on over. I got a stiff in the cellar for you."

Then I heard the voices of young people singing along and I felt my skin crawl. I couldn't deal with children. I didn't want to see the gifted Simone School students. The sight of Paul Falzerano and his double chin would have been particularly unwelcome.

I changed course and went back to the elevator, which was waiting for me as if it had known what was going to happen. I pushed *P* for penthouse and was taken to the top of the world, or at least the top of 22 East 65th Street.

The door was ajar and I was greeted by the sounds of slightly tipsy laughter, banal chatter, and muted Mozart. Could it really have been less than an hour earlier that I was in the same room, hearing the same sounds?

On that trip, I'd safely hidden Jana's flask, then stopped in the kitchen for a brief chat with Jake. For a while I had stood in a discreet corner of the living room where I observed the goings-on with a deeply divided soul. On one hand I thought it was everything a swank New York party in a beautiful penthouse should be, complete with blue gardenias, pink champagne, and picture windows that gave glittering views of the city, as in "I want to be a part of it, New York, New York."

On the other, I was completely alienated from the people around me. I was in a room full of people my own age and slightly older who had made such different choices, it was hard to believe we were the same race, much less the same generation. They had money, they had children, they had *things* and those things were very important to them.

They were happy to be in the new decade and I wasn't.

The Seventies had been the best years of my life. I'd had Berkeley and activism. I'd worked on a kibbutz. I'd seen England with Jana Crowley. At the end of the era I'd done disco with a vengeance. Now there was nothing.

Ronald Reagan was President. The music on the radio was boring. I'd been to Danceteria and hated myself for missing Studio 54. There were so many people doing drugs and so little geniune joy.

There's nothing worse than being high on weed and still feeling depressed. I tried to count my blessings. I had Jerry. I had Jerry's dog. I lived on the Upper East

Side. I had two psuedo jobs. I had a best friend. Jana Crowley, my best friend in the whole wide world.

I summoned up one of my best Jana memories. It was during the year we spent traveling through the British Isles together. We'd met by chance at the airport in Tel Aviv, two women of the same age with virtually nothing in common. I identified myself as a writer and prided myself on having radical feminist politics. She was an artist, an army brat, and a flirt who had no use for the written word. Somehow we bonded, and while we roamed through Britain, Scotland, Ireland, and Wales, she taught me as much as she could about art and I held a two-woman seminar on Shakespeare.

The memory I kept in my mental pocket like a pill to get through the bad times took place in Cardiff at a pub called the Black Lion. It was the day after Elvis Presley died, which didn't mean much to me. When Elvis broke in 1956, I was six years old and listening to showtunes with my show business parents. It was the Beatles in 1964 who changed my musical world and maybe my life.

I was surprised to find Jana Crowley deeply upset. Maybe it was her Southern roots. She'd grown up all over the world, but started life in Kentucky.

I tried to get her interested in those crazy love-struck kids, Antony and Cleopatra, but she was more interested in getting drunk. We'd been on the road together for three months and it was the first time I ever saw her lose control in any way.

She'd told me that a "lady," meaning a girl pretty enough to attract attention, should never put herself in a position where she can be taken advantage of. (My rule was that if you can't remember, it didn't happen, but Jana disapproved of that.) I was very surprised to watch her down several pints that night. The atmosphere in the Black Lion was extremely lachrymose. You'd have thought Tom Jones had passed on, the way they were all weeping and wailing.

Just before last call, a young man who bore a striking resemblance to the Elvis of 1956 stood up on a table and started singing "Love Me Tender." The whole bar joined him and it became both lament and celebration. Jana hugged me afterward, the first time she had ever done so. Back at the youth hostel, she asked me to read to her. I got out my flashlight and Shakespeare and read a bit from *Antony and Cleopatra* that seemed to apply to the man from Memphis.

> His legs bestrid the ocean; his rear'd arm
> Crested the world; his voice was propertied
> As all the tuned spheres, and that to friends;
> But when he meant to quail and shake the orb,
> He was rattling thunder.

When I finished, I turned out the flashlight, thinking she was asleep. I got into my own bed and heard her say. "Thanks, Marti. I'm glad you were with me tonight."

That was the kind of memory that could carry a friendship through a lot of shit that came after, including the day she told me she was in love with a man with whom I was passionately obsessed. The man in question wound up dead. Jana and I stayed friends.

We'd had some rough times, but things would be better now, as soon as she finished her Juicy Fruit and came back up to be the hostess with the mostess. Except she never came up and her husband flashed me a look across the room that sent me back down the elevator to my grisly discovery.

Now I was back at the party, where nothing had changed, except that I had the knowledge of what was downstairs and the whole glamorous scene looked staged and sinister. I wondered if anyone else in the apartment knew what I knew.

My burden of knowledge saddened me even more than my contempt for the partygoers. From the beginning, this whole event had been a pain in the caboose. It was a job to put it on and an ordeal to get through it. The personification of that ordeal walked toward me wearing a tuxedo that looked too large and a smile that he didn't mean.

"Where's my wife?" he asked with just the slightest hint of urgency. I didn't know if he was expressing concern regarding her whereabouts or irritation that she hadn't appeared at his command.

I took a moment to assess my level of intoxication. About one martini's worth, I guessed. Not that I'd know. Some quirk prevented me from keeping any kind of alcohol in my stomach long enough for it to get to my bloodstream. That was why I still smoked pot when so many of my contemporaries had moved on to liquor. Cowards, I called them, for taking the legal way out. I certainly wasn't giggling anymore, but I couldn't resist an ironic smile as I told him,

"We need to talk."

I was trying to let him know that the situation was serious without spilling the beans. I wanted to be alone with Thomas Brinkham when I told him that his wife was dead.

"Come on, then."

He led me through the penthouse, keeping the smile on his face and nodding at party guests. I wouldn't have minded a stop in the kitchen. I hadn't eaten all day and I knew a culinary genius was at work, but there was no time for a nosh. I didn't want Jana's body to be alone too long. I shuddered at the thought of rats and roaches taking an interest. Not all the vermin were that far below, of course. I was face to face with a real rat, as far as I was concerned.

"What the hell is going on?" he asked me as we entered the bedroom.

He had the right to an answer and I'd had plenty of time to formulate one. I gave myself the luxury of a look around the room, which was dominated by a large four-poster bed covered with a fluffy white comforter. Then I looked back at Thomas.

"I found Jana in the laundry room. She's dead."

"Dead?"

"Deceased."

With the pot still in my system, I could hear a bit of the Dead Parrot sketch, which was most unseemly under the tragic circumstances. Maybe it was just Thomas Brinkham who had that affect on me. He wasn't built for tragedy.

Thomas Brinkham was a man who struck me as smaller than life, from his tinny voice to his spindly frame. He had the finest Savile Row tailoring, but his clothes always seemed too loose. The only sturdy features were the thick silver ring he wore on his pinkie finger and his hair, which was brushed back and sprayed to stay there. It stood up a solid inch high and did not move.

We stood there locked in mortal staring competition as he tried to find the truth in my eyes and I looked for any discernible emotion in his. He wasn't one to raise his voice. The only thing I knew he was capable of showing passion about was Margaret Thatcher. I suspected he'd only married Jana when Mrs. Thatcher proved unavailable. I had just told him his wife was dead. What would he do?

He slowly sat down on the bed and put his head in his hands. He looked so fragile at that moment that I was close to feeling sorry for the guy, which was unusual, because I genuinely disliked him and knew the feeling was mutual. I had an urge to put a comforting hand on his shoulder, but resisted. Thomas was truly untouchable.

He looked up at me with moist lashes.

"Are you sure?" he asked imploringly, not wanting it to be true.

"I'm sure. I'm sorry to have to tell you, but she is definitely gone."

"You've called the authorities?"

"I wanted to tell you first."

He nodded slowly.

"Should we call an ambulance?"

He didn't appear to have absorbed the gravity of the situation.

"Cops and a meat wagon would be more like it," I said bluntly, maybe even cruelly.

"Police, why?"

"Someone strangled her."

"And you waited this long to tell me?" His voice rose at the same time he did. "Are you mad?" He walked over to the phone on the dresser and picked it up with the force of a man used to accomplishing his ends with a well-timed phone call. Then he lost it again. The phone was a touch tone, but Thomas seemed unsure what to punch in. He looked at me again. One hand came up to his mouth and he bit a knuckle in frustration.

"Nine one one," I suggested.

"Yes."

I was surprised. Although he was a British citizen, Thomas Brinkham's money made him the kind of guy that local politicians wanted to know and vice versa. He could rub some powerful elbows when the situation called for it.

If I were incredibly rich, and my spouse had just been killed, and I knew Ed Koch's private number, I might pick this particular moment to use it, but there he was ringing up the cops like a regular Joe.

I WILL SURVIVE

His end of the conversation was predictable. Dead body in the laundry room. My wife. Send someone immediately. If I'd made that call, I would have been screaming hysterically and sounding pretty hostile. I would have told them to get someone over here now! Not Thomas. He sounded calm and civilized as he rattled off the address and told the voice on the other end to send the police to the laundry room. He might have even used the word "promptly." The only sign of turmoil was the clenched fist, the bitten knuckle. I didn't want to keep looking at his face so my eye lit on the big silver pinkie ring that dominated the finger. It gleamed in the weak light of a desk lamp as he put the phone down.

"They're on the way," he told me. "I'll go down there and wait for them."

"*We'll* go down and wait for them."

I waited to see if he was going to object.

"The party . . ." he said weakly, having abandoned the argument before it came out of his mouth.

"The party will take care of itself. It's already done what it was supposed to. I'll tell Jake to send around some more food."

"He's done a splendid job."

It was an incredibly trite thing to say under the circumstances. Trite and true. It reminded me how hungry I was, but there wasn't time to do anything about it.

"Yeah, he has. Hang on a minute." I picked up the phone and rang my own apartment. It took a few rings to get an answer.

"Hello, Jerry Barlow speaking."

"Hi sweetie, how's it going down there?"

"Fine. The kids are having a great time. Some of the little ones have fallen asleep. How is your end going?"

"Don't ask."

"You ran out of latkes?"

"We've got a real problem."

"Is it Jana?"

"Yeah, but not what you think. Are you alone?"

"In the bedroom. A few kids asleep on our bed. They're very cute."

"Jana's dead in the laundry room. Someone strangled her and it ain't cute at all."

"Dead? Oh no. Oh my god! Holy—"

"It's horrible, but I really need you to hold it together, Jerry, because if you lose it, I'm going to lose it, and I don't have time to lose it. The police are on the way. I'm going down to meet them with Thomas. I'm not telling anyone up here and you've got to keep it hush-hush there too. Got it?"

"Of course."

"Oh god, Jerry, it's so . . ." I was starting to shake. I could hear the tears in my voice but I didn't have the time or inclination to shed them.

"Are you sure you don't want me with you?"

"I do, desperately, but it's not going to happen that way."

"I love you, Marti."

"Yeah," I said, hanging up the phone. It wasn't romantic, but Thomas was waiting and my marriage was none of his business, never mind that I probably knew more about his marriage than he did.

We left the bedroom together. I had the brief thought that anyone seeing us leave might jump to a lurid conclusion. It was especially ludicrous given the circumstances and the antipathy I'd had for Thomas Brinkham from the moment I met him.

5

Jana and Marti. Marti and Jana. That's how it was for two years. First in England and then when we came home to the States and roomed together in the Village. David Price changed all that and his murder changed it even more. She went to Europe and when I saw her again she was married to Thomas Brinkham.

Mr. Brinkham and I did wind up making a stop in the kitchen. It was a scene of controlled chaos. Food in various stages of preparation was everywhere. Two food processors were spinning away. Grease was sizzling on the stove and Jake Abelman was making yet another round of potato pancakes.

Jake's Cakes was the official name of his catering company, and he could produce anything from soup to nuts, but when the air was cold and Jews craved comfort food, he was known as the Latke King. Jake smiled at me through a cloud of steam. Most of his business was on Long Island or in the boroughs. This was his first major Manhattan gig and he was grateful.

Jake was a truly good-looking guy who didn't know he was good-looking. That made him even more attractive. It also made trouble. I was happy not to see his wife anywhere around. I got close enough to talk without

35

yelling and nearly passed out from the smell of food. I told Jake there was a problem and the party would be sans hostess and host for a while. He nodded and gave me a thumbs-up sign before returning his attention to the precious pancakes.

Throughout the living room, East Siders in their holiday best were comparing notes on their apartment deals and their children's performances in the Simone School holiday concert. I'd been able to avoid attending that because I had to finish the party preparations. Jerry had been understanding, and possibly relieved. Between my dislike of children and a certain bah-humbug attitude, he knew it was better for all concerned that I not hear young voices piping their way through "Ma'or Tzur" or "The Hallelujah Chorus."

From the comments I overheard, the performance had been a fabulous success and each participant was on his or her way to an exciting career in showbiz. I didn't know which proud parent belonged to a certain twelve-year-old. Jerry had told me this kid was throwing off the whole alto section.

The choir ordeal was a source of frustration for Jerry, but so was the actual work of being a teacher. It wasn't the kids. It was school politics. He'd taught for five years in the public school system in Brooklyn, which was a battleground in its own right, but nothing had prepared him for the Simone School.

Naturally the next obstacle on my way back to the basement was Tony Falzerano. I hadn't seen him at the party earlier. Either he was arriving very late or he'd been downstairs with the children. After what had happened with Rhonda, he was the last person in the world I wanted to see, especially with Thomas Brinkham standing right next to me.

"Thomas, so nice to see you," came out of his mouth thick with dishonesty. Then he did a double take as he actually bothered to look at me. The haircut made me

I WILL SURVIVE

look different, but his reaction was way over the top. His mouth opened wide as his eyes squinted in confusion.

"Hi Tony," I said sarcastically, throwing in a little of my old Brooklyn accent to remind him that I knew where he came from.

"Marti. Good evening." He spoke on automatic pilot, still staring at me as though he'd seen something that worried him as much as an unhappy parent. "Uh... have you..." He was *fumferring* badly.

"Yeah. I got a haircut. Don't worry. It'll grow back. Now, if you'll excuse us."

"Oh. Of course." He stood aside, regaining that suave Falzerano composure. I could see him waving at a few parents who were gesturing at him to come their way, presumably to crow about their talented offspring. Tony was inflating into his usual self, complete with smug awareness of his good looks. "Have you seen Rhonda?"

"Tonight?" I asked, taking care to differentiate a meeting at the party from the confrontation at the grocery store, which he might or might not know about.

"Yes."

"Last time I saw her, she was near the window talking to a woman in a red dress who should be told to avoid ruffles."

I'd been keeping an eye on Rhonda for the specific purpose of avoiding her, but that was before I'd been distracted by the dead body.

"Thanks," he said, going off in search of his wife, or maybe the woman in the red ruffles.

Thomas and I made it to the elevator without further interference. We rode down together in uncomfortable silence, which he broke as we arrived in the basement with a thump.

"You didn't tell him."

"It wasn't my place."

"You suspect him?"

"Of what?" I said, feeling like I was at Wimbledon going against Jimmy Connors. I was at an extreme disadvantage in this game. I knew about Jana and Tony, but I didn't know how much Thomas knew or suspected or cared.

I tried to turn the tables on him as we left the elevator.

"What are you going to tell them?"

"The truth of course."

I suddenly realized it was cold down there and wished that I had Jana's coat. Maybe it was the idea of telling the truth that gave me the chills. There was so much truth and so many people who would be hurt. I didn't know which part of the truth had led to Jana being dead.

"What about you?"

"Huh?"

"What were you thinking of telling the police?"

A few smart-ass responses ran through my mind, but none made it to my lips. I just shook my head.

I let Thomas go down the hall ahead of me, wanting to give him some time alone with what had, after all, been his wife. I heard him say, "Oh, hello there," and thought that he had totally lost his marbles and was having a conversation with the corpse. I followed him into the laundry room and discovered a man bent over the body. He was wearing a down vest over a white flannel shirt and brown corduroys. He had on rubber gloves and was looking at Jana's face.

I'd already seen it and it didn't look any better the second time. Thomas could only stare in shock. Her death face was so grotesque, it started to blot out the image of beauty she had been only an hour or so before. The worst was the eyes, widened by the horror of what had happened to her. Even the swollen tongue and face weren't as bad. I had the feeling that her eyes were begging me to do something, but it was too late. Or was it?

I cleared my throat to get the man's attention.

I WILL SURVIVE 39

He turned around. I immediately wanted to put in a call to central casting and tell them there'd been a mistake. Medical examiners were tough guys like Quincy on television, or Lee Justice, whom I had met in Las Vegas. Lived-in faces and rugged demeanors were absolute requirements for the job. The guy working on Jana Crowley was too young and wholesome-looking for the job. He had a shaggy head of light brown hair, wore large wire-rimmed glasses, and gave me a big friendly smile.

"Hi. I'm Marti Hirsch. I found the body. Are you the medical examiner?"

"One of them. We're having a busy night. That's why I got the call."

"Can you tell me anything?"

"Strangled. I'm not sure with what. See these marks?" He pointed to her neck. "Not rope, not rough enough." I could barely see the marks. I hoped he knew what he was talking about. "We'll do tests and look for fibers."

"That's enough," snapped a decidedly hoarse voice. The police had arrived. I was taken aback by the first one on the scene, who was none of the things I expected cops to be. It was a woman, a short black woman. However, she looked as disgruntled as any other member of the NYPD I had ever met. She looked especially unhappy with my new friend, Mr. Medical Examiner.

"You," she said, addressing him. "What's your name?"

"Dennis Johnson, with the coroner's office."

"You're new?"

"Pretty new."

"Well, I'm Detective Sharon Warner, homicide. From now on you share your opinions with official personnel only, is that clear?"

"Yes, ma'am."

"Good. You do your job and we won't have any trouble."

The room was filling up with enough men in blue to give me the hives, not to mention claustrophobia. They were taking pictures, making notes, and generally acting like worker bees.

Queen Bee was obviously the short lady with the tight afro directing the action. A lit cigarette was now in one hand. It couldn't be helping that throat any.

"You two." She gestured at Thomas and me. "Which one of you called it in?"

"That was me," said Thomas.

"I found the body." I offered, trying to be helpful.

"Uh-huh."

"We're having a party so there's a bunch of people upstairs you'll want to talk to. They don't know yet," I added.

"We'll talk to everybody who might know something, but I'll start with him."

She was telling me to get lost and I didn't like it. I went into the hall to sulk. What was I going to tell her anyway? I thought about it. The truth? What was truth and where did it start? That same old thought kept going through my mind.

It wasn't supposed to be like this.

6

I never thought I'd get married.

I'd had my heart broken by an unrequited high school crush. I'd lived the sexual revolution. I considered myself a hard-core feminist and a free-loving bisexual. I despised the patriarchy, male chauvinism, and all other tools for keeping women subjugated, including the institution of marriage.

Jerry Barlow was different.

We'd both gone to Williamsburg High School, but never really known each other. He stayed in Brooklyn and became a teacher, while I went to Quincy U. and Berkeley, and Israel and England, and finally back to New York. When we met again, there was an instant level of comfort, like finding an old sweater in the closet that you'd forgotten and having it fit perfectly.

Our life together started with "On the Road" romanticism. We traveled together for two years. I could honestly say that I learned to love him rather than tumbling into a passionate heap.

Even then, I didn't see myself with a ring on my finger. I found out the hard way that cheating on him, or even contemplating it, made me feel horribly guilty, but I still feared the ultimate entrapment. The ring was a symbol of giving in to society's rules. I had quite a soapbox lecture ready for anyone who brought up the topic.

Then we went to Las Vegas and I ended up getting married in the Chapel of Love near Las Vegas airport. Lounge singer Donny Brooks crooned "All the Way" as I walked down the aisle.

The five-hour flight from Las Vegas to my beloved New York City had been physically and emotionally turbulent. I was so happy, but so scared of a future as something other than what I'd been before. All I could do was keep looking at Jerry and reminding myself how much I loved this man. Over Chicago, I'd been thinking it would never work and wondering if it wasn't too late to bail out of the plane, the marriage, the whole thing. Then Jerry put his arms around me and I was giddy with delight again.

I was coming home for my father's funeral and I should have been more respectful of that gloomy fact, but it was hard to feel mournful when I was tap dancing down the jetway singing "New York, New York." All you need is love, as some wise men once said. On that day in January, I believed it.

I trembled with happiness, not to mention the fact that it was thirty-one degrees outside. I'd come from Las Vegas and was still dressed for it. The airport terminal was cold enough. I'd be freezing my ass off as soon as we got outside, but I didn't care. I was home.

Jerry headed for baggage claim to retrieve Strudel, who had been confined to the baggage compartment for the duration of the flight. I sequestered myself in a phone booth with some change and a Long Island phone book.

My dear ditzy mom hadn't left much information about the funeral arrangements and I hadn't done a good job of keeping in touch with my relatives. My parents had been living in Miami before Daddy died. I knew some of my mother's family lived in Massapequa (Mat-

I WILL SURVIVE

zoh Pizza as it was known to local wits) and that her maiden name was Abelman. Armed with that information I managed to wake up two people who were not related to me and possibly interrupt one incidence of heavy breathing sex. The breather hung up on me, which made me wonder why he'd picked up the phone in the first place.

By the fourth call, I was getting worried. Maybe I was looking for the wrong people in the wrong place. Maybe the Abelmans I was looking for were in Syosset or Great Neck. Maybe my mom was with Dad's family. I didn't know where the hell they were.

I started formulating Plan B, which was to get my hands on every Long Island newspaper I could find and look for funeral announcements.

Ring ring ring ring.

I was about to give up when a weary male voice answered the phone.

"Hello."

"Hi. I hate to bother you, but my name is Marti Hirsch and I'm looking—"

"Marti Hirsch! Is that really you? Where are you?"

Paydirt. Now if I could get a word in edgewise.

"I'm at JFK."

"Wait. Stay there. Your mother . . . you know about the funeral, right?"

"No, I schlepped three thousand miles so I could see the Rockettes."

"Same old Marti," he said, with a barely suppressed yawn.

"Who is this anyway?"

"Don't you remember me?"

"Should I?"

"I'm your cousin Jake."

"Jake? Cousin Jacob. Oh my god! I went to your bar mitzvah."

"And my sister's wedding."

The bar mitzvah was a vague memory of boredom and honey cake. The wedding was a disaster of legendary proportions where my misdeeds were only a small fragment of the nightmare. Of course, telling the bride not to sell herself into marital slavery might have been uncalled for.

"Is she still married?"

"It didn't last six months. Look, let me come and pick you up. I'll tell you everything."

"We could take a cab."

"I need to get out for a while. Your mom is . . ."

I could tell he didn't want to say anything unkind about the grieving widow. I decided to be equally gracious.

"I'm sure it's been tough on her."

"On all of us."

"Right. Well, I'll deal with her now. Uh . . . look . . . I'm going to baggage claim to meet Jerry. We'll be down there."

"Jerry?"

"My husband."

"You got married?"

The disbelief was obvious in his voice, with equal emphasis on the words "you" and "married."

"Yeah. Yesterday as a matter of fact."

"You?"

"Jake, honey, it happens all the time."

"But to you?"

Did I hear disillusionment?

"I must have been pretty dogmatic at that wedding."

"Unforgettable."

That's what you are . . . immediately came into my mind. It would take a while to get Las Vegas completely out of my system.

"When you meet Jerry, you'll understand. By the way, do you remember what I look like?"

"I'm pretty sure I do."

I WILL SURVIVE

"I'm wearing a white sundress. I'll be with a tall guy and a dachshund. Is that O.K.?"

"I like dogs but you'll probably be too cold in the sundress. Do you have a coat?"

"It was a lot warmer in Vegas. Could you bring me a sweater or something?"

"Sure." Another yawn.

"I'm sorry I woke you up."

"Don't worry. I was up anyway." Suddenly he switched gears. "Oh, hey, gotta go. I'll be right there." A click followed as the phone went dead. I assumed someone had interrupted him and he didn't want that person to know whom he was talking to.

I hung up the phone and left the phone booth. I hadn't turned into Superwoman, which was unfortunate considering what I had to face. It had been years since I'd flown into JFK and I had somehow forgotten the sheer enormity of the place. McCarren Airport of Las Vegas, Nevada, was a trim tidy complex where one could go from plane to baggage to the heart of the strip in under half an hour. It took that much time just to get from the arrival gates at Kennedy to baggage claim itself, and once there I had to fight off an impulse to turn around and leave.

I finally arrived at the escalator that would take me to baggage claim, and found myself contemplating a circle of hell that Dante was fortunate enough never to imagine. There were thousands of people moving around in a dance of chaos centering on the massive luggage carousels. The gleaming, slow moving metal contraptions stood out against the badly lit cavernous space and the dark grays and browns of the human forms bundled into their dark winter coats. Sounds of confusion, alarm, and despair were punctuated by announcements on a loudspeaker summoning unwary souls to variously hued phones and offices, no doubt for the final judgment.

Maybe I wasn't cut out for New York City anymore.

I'd never find Jerry in this madhouse. My cousin would never find me. I was doomed to spend the rest of my life in this snakepit of lost souls and lost luggage.

Wait a minute. I could see Jerry. He was standing up and waving his arms at me. He looked silly, but I could see him. It was a good thing he was tall. Not as tall as a basketball player, but tall enough for me to see him in the sea of humanity. Tall and blond and solid. I was as shocked to be married as Jake had been to hear about it, but with Jerry it all made sense.

Everything was going to be fine. The crowd would part before me like the Red Sea and the mass of bodies would turn into extras for my "Welcome Home Marti" production number, complete with dancing suitcases. It wasn't exactly like that, but I did get to Jerry. Bring on New York, I thought, I'm ready.

Jerry had our meager luggage and our darling doggie all set up against a wall in the back of the cavernous baggage claim area. We were spared the added torture of clearing customs. Las Vegas was another world, but at least it wasn't another country.

I got a big hug from Jerry, but a hurt look from Strudel, and there's nothing like a hurt look from a dachshund to get you right in the *kishkes*.

"I'm sorry. I'll never do that to you again. I promise," I said, apologizing for her five-hour ordeal in the baggage compartment of the airplane. "Next time you can ride on my lap all the way."

She went back to her water bowl. She'd forgive me eventually, but in the meantime, I'd be made to suffer the kind of guilt usually dispensed by Jewish mothers and Catholic priests.

"Did you find your mother?" Jerry asked.

"I found my cousin Jake. He's coming to get us."

Jerry looked around. More people were flooding in.

"Do you know what he looks like?"

I shook my head. The last clear memory I had was

from the bar mitzvah and one could hardly hope to recognize a grown man based on the thirteen-year-old he had been. His sister Rayna's wedding was a blur, which was probably just as well.

"He says he remembers me."

"What's he like?"

I shrugged my shoulders. How was I supposed to know? All I cared about was that he was going to rescue us from the current hellhole.

My pocketbook had a notebook in it. I had already started the first chapter of a book about our Las Vegas adventure. I'd solved a murder there and it was going to make a great novel. I was still playing around with the wording for the first line when I was struck by a bolt of weirdness.

Jerry and I had both grown up in the Williamsburg section of Brooklyn, New York and even gone to the same high school, but we hadn't gotten to know each other until ten years later, and that was only because of the David Price murder. In Las Vegas, Dorothea Jones had been killed in the casino where Jerry was working as a piano player. How many times does a noncop, non–private dick, nonreporter get to solve one murder, much less two?

The second one had been incredibly lucky for me, although certainly not for Dorothea. Jackie Vogel, my literary agent, had gotten Mortimer and Sweeney interested in publishing *Broken Heroes,* the book I had been emotionally compelled to write about the Price case, but they wanted two books. I could have just made something up, but a real-life murder made it ever so much easier. I took the liberty of changing names and details. In the books I was much prettier, which I told myself didn't matter to me. It was just for the marketplace.

I was glad M&S didn't want three books. I wouldn't want people getting killed just so I could write about them. Besides, solving the damn things was hard work, although not as hard as writing about them. Solving a murder required balls, brains, and luck. Writing was an emotional roller coaster pitting the heights of my ego against the depths of my insecurity.

After the Las Vegas book, I'd write something else. By then I'd be so famous I could sell a real literary novel, maybe a love story, maybe even one with a happy ending. I'd never written one of those, but now I was ready to. Instead of working on that first sentence I drew a heart in my notebook that said, "M.H. Loves J.B."

I was so engrossed in my doodling, I lost track of my surroundings. It took a nudge from Jerry before I looked up and saw a man staring at me through tortoiseshell-framed glasses. The glasses indicated that he might come from the same bloodline that had produced my faulty vision. The eyes themselves were a nice warm brown. He had full lips and brown hair in a modified shag that needed brushing, and he could have used a shave. I didn't care. Hello good-looking. I was related to that? I couldn't believe it. Oh speak, bright angel.

"I see a guy, a dog, and a head of Hirsch hair."

He had a slight case of the famous Lawn Guyland accent. I got the idea that he must have thrown on clothes in a hurry. Big black coat over maroon sweater and green pants. I went back to the lips. Just yummy, especially the lower one. The kind of kissing I had in mind wasn't cousinly either. Wait a minute, wasn't I the happy newlywed? Forsaking all others, especially blood relations?

"Cousin Jake?"

"In the flesh."

The word "flesh" took on more significance than he could have intended. The handsome stranger handed me a black cashmere sweater while I hauled out my best imitation of composure and made introductions. The men shook hands and Strudel responded favorably to a pat on the head. Jerry and Jake each took a bag and I carried the dog. We trooped from the gloom of baggage claim into the immense expanse of short-term parking. It was cold out there, despite the friendly beam of the morning sun. The cashmere sweater didn't seem to help much. I had tons of questions, but I couldn't ask them because my teeth were chattering.

After the long march, we arrived at a white Buick station wagon with red lettering on the side that said "Jake's Cakes."

"J-J-Jake's C-C-Cakes?" I asked, trying to sound sardonic, which was difficult because I could barely get the words out. He got the message though.

"It's a living," he said with a shrug. "Bar mitzvahs, graduations, weddings."

He didn't give that last word any special emphasis, but I formed an instant hypothesis about what had led Jacob Abelman into life as a caterer.

My appearance at Rayna's wedding in jeans, tie-dyed shirt, and army surplus jacket had been a minor incident compared with the caterer getting lost and the food turning up an hour late. It was a warm day and something had managed to go particularly bad. One of the bridesmaids didn't make it to the bathroom in time. And that was all before my mother twisted her ankle doing the hora.

Jake opened the car door for me. If possible it was even colder on the inside. I wondered if my lips were turning blue. Then I wondered if Jake liked blue lips. Luggage went in the back. I sat in the front seat. Jerry squeezed in next to me and Strudel sat on his lap. She was a traveling dog, used to adjusting to new surroundings. She seemed to have forgiven us for the airplane ordeal, but now she was starting to tremble from the cold and I was worried about her.

Jake got in the driver's seat and turned on the ignition. As the engine came to life, so did the heat. I felt the pleasure of primitive man warming himself by the fire.

The radio also came on. WPLJ. Cousin Jake was a rock fan. Bruce Springsteen was starting to sing "The River" when Jake turned it off.

As he drove out of the parking lot, Jake started talking a mile a minute with an intensity that reminded me of my mother.

"Everyone's been dying to know if you were going to show up. Barb's been frantic. She said she left you a message at some trailer park. You weren't really living in a trailer park were you?"

I had been, but I didn't get the chance to answer. Jake kept going full speed ahead, although his driving remained steady.

"Then she realized you only had her Florida number and she really went crazy. Crazier than she was already, just from Maury going like that on New Year's Eve and her having to get the body sent up here and everything."

I gave him a look of disbelief.

"Why didn't she just leave another message telling me where the funeral was? It would have saved me a lot of work."

Jake shrugged.

"It was hairy, and by the time anyone thought to call you again, you were gone."

"Right."

"Usually the funeral would have to be right away, you know, but she insisted that we wait so a lot of his friends could get here and of course you. We all knew you were smart. We just had to hope you were smart enough to find us and that you wanted to."

"Like I wouldn't want to come to my own father's funeral? That's a nice thing for my own family to think about me."

"Well you know, Marti, after that wedding..."

"Can we drop the wedding, already?"

"O.K. I just meant that you were always such a rebel.

I WILL SURVIVE 51

And I know you had some rough patches with your dad."

"I can't believe that I'm only one in the whole damn family who thought that the war should be stopped and was willing to go out there and do something about it besides sit at home and shake my head—" I realized I was shouting and I stopped myself. I was having a ten-year-old fight and I was having it with the wrong person. "I'm sorry, Jake. I loved my father, do you understand? I loved my father."

On one side of me, Jerry was holding my hand. On the other, my leg was touching Jake's very slightly.

"What now?" I asked, hoping to change the topic.

"We go to the house. Your mom's staying with us. I'll get you guys some breakfast. She came in while I was talking to you. I didn't want her to know yet. I'm gonna spring you on her."

There was a certain glee in his voice.

"I'm here for a funeral, you know," I said to remind him of the solemnity of the occasion.

"I know. I always liked your dad too. And I think Barb's a hoot. She's been upset, but who could blame her? I actually think she's taking it pretty well, considering. I'm not saying that this isn't a sad time, but your dad lived a good life and he wouldn't want it to be too sad. I just can't wait to see the look on her face when you come in. And tomorrow at the funeral. Hoo boy. It'll be like the Prodigal Son."

"Do we have to kill the fatted calf? I'm trying to cut down on my red meat."

"I've got some great vegetarian recipes I can do for you," he replied enthusiastically. I looked for any indication that he had gotten the joke. There was none. I glanced at Jerry and we shared a smirk.

We were now driving through the prettiest, most affluent stretch of Massapequa, Long Island. Big houses with lawns in front, pools in the back, and gray flannel families inside. The lawns were invisible under shrouds of white. The sky was clear but the snow on the ground was of recent vintage, unspoiled by the murky grime that would have occurred almost instantly in Manhattan.

A few inevitable bumps and bounces occurred along the way, causing additional leg contact between my left leg and Cousin Jake's right. I was hyper-aware of this, but he didn't seem to notice. The attraction seemed to be all one-sided, which was just as well.

We arrived in the driveway of a small house on a typical Massapequa corner. There was no such thing as a local grocery store or even fast food in walking distance. Getting milk would mean either a car ride or a long hike. In the spring there would be leafy trees. Now there were only tall sticks with snow on them.

As soon as the car door opened, Strudel jumped out and started running into the front yard, where she left a signature of some tiny footprints and a little yellow snow.

We were led inside to a living room that screamed middle-class respectability. Beige carpets, tan couches, and a TV set in a central position of authority. Be nice, Marti, I told myself. Perhaps I was just translating the fierce look that Jerry gave me as the door shut behind us. He knew me well enough to know I was the same girl who had refused to wear a dress to my cousin Rayna's wedding.

Before my behavior could become an issue, there was a shriek that could mean only one thing.

"Oh god! It's my baby!"

"Hi Mom."

Barbara Hirsch came bounding down the staircase and across the living room. This was her big moment. All I could do was stand there and wait for her embrace. She wasn't a big woman, but she had a hug that could squeeze the life out of you.

While Mom was doing her boa constrictor routine, I

looked over her shoulder at another woman coming down the stairs. I did a quick rundown. Brown hair with streaks and perfectly manicured nails. I figured at least two hours a week at Elizabeth Arden.

Jake made the introductions.

"Marti, this is my wife, Annette. Annette, honey, this is my cousin, Marti Hirsch."

I stared at her over my mother's shoulder. She stared back.

"Marti. I've heard so much about you."

I could imagine exactly what she might have heard.

Now that I knew she was Jake's wife, I took a more critical look. The nose had enough of a bump to be the original model and she was about to pass it on to the next generation. Mrs. Abelman was enormously pregnant. Well, I thought, this is going to be interesting.

I imagined myself telling all this to Detective Warner. She'd probably haul me off to Riker's Island on a charge of boring a police officer. As they were slamming my cell shut, she would ask me in an aggrieved tone of voice:

"What the hell does your fucked-up family have to do with my murder investigation, anyway?" And the worst part was that I wouldn't be able to answer the question without continuing the story.

Well, I could skip some of it. She didn't need to know about the funeral. I showed up in proper black attire, ready for my feature appearance as the surprise guest. My plan was to let them gawk, while maintaining my cool detachment throughout. I was a tough broad. I could say good-bye to my father without an emotional display.

One minute I was standing there thinking how great it was that there were all those people who loved my dad. The next thing I knew I was overwhelmed by some deep-seated grief erupting out of me like Mount St. Helens. Within seconds I was crying hysterically and I couldn't stop. I sobbed through the service, the ride to the cemetery, and the burial. Jerry must have gotten a cramp from spending the entire day with his arm around my shoulder. He kept handing me Kleenex and discreetly disposing of the used ones.

If I created a stir, it certainly wasn't the kind I or Cousin Jake had in mind. Mom was in her glory. She was the loving, concerned mother, and looked like a model of composure by comparison.

We went back to the Abelman house afterward. Friends and family sat around the living room telling stories. Jake had a bunch of boiled eggs ready for the traditional post-funeral meal. The mirrors in the house were covered. Shivah had commenced for a man whose most religious attendance in life had been lunch at the Carnegie Deli every day when he lived in New York. Maury and Barb retired to Florida after the first heart attack, but the condo life and daily swimming couldn't save him from twenty years of pastrami on rye.

I couldn't face hardboiled eggs, so Jake made me a bowl of soup. Jerry wanted to take care of me, but he also had to go out and be the dutiful son-in-law. That left me with my cousin, who had no idea what to say to me, except remind me of family stories about how I always hid out in a room reading whenever the family got together. At least he didn't bring up the wedding.

Every time I thought I'd managed to cry myself out, there was more. I could in no way deal with the *gantze mishpocha*. There was no need to. Barb was holding court. I was left to deal with my personal sorrow and wonder when I was going to get a better grip on my emotions.

For years, I'd been bouncing up and down the emotional spectrum like a Duncan yo-yo. Some days I'd be happy, elated, downright ecstatic, but then Ms. Cool and Groovy would take a header into the Valley of the

I WILL SURVIVE

Shadow of Death, or someplace equally gloomy. I'd dabbled in therapy and rooted out deep dark secrets, but the catharsis never quite kicked the depression out of my life. This particular outburst had me embarrassed and terrified by its intensity.

Jake offered me a glass of wine. I waved him off. He went back to something he was doing at the stove. It was a *House and Garden* kitchen and it was funny to see a man in an apron running it. Alcohol would just make me sick, but I started to muse on the possibility of getting something stronger. I excused myself to go to the upstairs bathroom, the one in the master bedroom. The medicine chest there proved disappointing.

I didn't find any painkillers or tranquilizers, and what was worse I had to face an uncovered mirror. The face that looked back at me was old and tired. Crying all day had left me with a red nose, swollen cheeks, and ruined eye makeup.

There had been months and sometimes years when I didn't talk to Daddy. The entire first Nixon administration comes to mind. My politics and radicalism had driven a wedge between us, but that didn't take away the fact that I loved him. Everything about me that was smart and hip and funny and streetwise came from him.

What am I going to do? I asked myself, wishing I had a friend to talk to. Jerry was the love of my life, but a gal needs a best friend that she's not sleeping with. I added the pain of missing my best friend to the loss of my father.

Jana Crowley had left the United States in 1978, shortly after the murder of her fiancé, David Price, the handsomest session piano player you never heard of until he got shot. At that time, she was a presence on the New York art scene, but hardly a superstar. Her biggest claim to fame was having one of her sketches appear on the cover of a disco album.

She'd taken her exhibition overseas. Jana had her talent and her looks and the luck to go abroad just when the international art scene was starving for somthing new. Within months she was popular in Europe, successful in Australia, and even big in Japan. Wherever she went, the art critics and collectors couldn't get enough of her or her work. The last postcard I had received was sent from Tokyo and said she was on her way to Hong Kong.

I assumed that Jana was flitting around the Pacific with her artwork while I was looking for drugs in a strange bathroom and avoiding my own relatives. The pathos of it all made me start crying again. I was getting annoyed with myself, but the annoyance didn't make it any easier to stop. I tried to remember the breathing exercises a shrink had once taught me, but I was interrupted by a knock on the door and the voice of Annette Abelman, Jake's wife, asking if I was all right.

The question was so stupid that I didn't waste the energy a snide answer would have taken. Then I remembered she was pregnant and probably just wanted me out of her personal bathroom. I relinquished the facility to her.

I went out in the hall and stood by the top of the stairs. I could hear laughter in the living room. That's what Daddy would have wanted: stories, jokes, and laughter. If he saw me crying like this he would have cued Mommy into a few choruses of "Get Happy" or told me a joke with a Yiddish punch line that would make sense only to a Jew, even one as unreligious as himself.

I went downstairs to eat an egg and make Maury Hirsch proud of me. On the inside, I still wanted my best friend there to do it with me.

That's what I would tell the police. Jana Crowley came back to the United States in April because I needed her so much, and if she hadn't come back, she wouldn't have gotten killed.

* * *

I WILL SURVIVE 57

By this time, the laundry room was a madhouse. Policemen were swarming around doing a hundred little tasks that would no doubt make interesting reading in a police report. Picture-taking cops, note-writing cops, cops dusting for fingerprints, all of them eager to find some piece of information that would bring a smile to Sharon Warner's serious face.

I had to stand there a few feet away from the action, shifting uncomfortably on my high heels and feeling the scratchy lace from the bodice of my dress. I could hear the muted British voice of Thomas Brinkham and the hoarse bark of Detective Warner, but I didn't know exactly what she was asking or how he was responding.

I had a spot between the elevator and the laundry room. New York's finest kept coming down in droves, but as far as I could tell, no one was going up. I didn't think anyone had made a formal announcement or was questioning party guests. It was getting late. If I were all those Upper East Side swells, and the swanky host and hostess had disappeared, I'd be grabbing my little moppets and going bye-bye.

Even if there was a flatfoot in the penthouse taking statements, what good would it do? The police had no concept of the games Jana played. Sharon, for all her moxie, probably didn't even know who Jana Crowley was. She didn't know which party guests had nothing to do with Jana and which ones had so much to do with her that they wanted her dead.

Thomas Brinkham had wrapped up his version of the truth. He was still in the doorway of the laundry room watching as medical types made preparations for the removal of what had been his spouse.

I was leaning against a cold wall, wondering exactly how the news would play all over town. Some people loved her; others hated her guts. Often the feelings occurred simultaneously, a phenomenon with which I was personally familiar.

Detective Warner finished conferring with one of the camera cops and motioned for me to come over to her.

I'd been listening to her voice. That had to be one doozy of a sore throat, unless she sounded like that all the time. I would have recommended that she quit smoking, except that she wasn't there to ask me for health tips.

"O.K., miss," she started, flipping over a page in her small spiral notebook. "You're the one who found the body?"

I nodded.

"And your name is?"

I didn't answer right away, which made me look either dumb or devious. I needed a minute to decide on how much honesty to use. Sharon Warner was a black woman. That was good. My knee-jerk liberal reaction was to trust her. She was also a cop. I hated cops and the feeling tended to be mutual.

I never used my given first name or my married last name, but faced with a police officer, I had a sudden impulse to introduce myself as Martha Barlow. I shook off the urge to lie.

"I'm Marti Hirsch. What did Thomas tell you?"

She looked up from her note taking.

"I'll be asking the questions here, Miss Hirsch."

She was all cop. I'd have to be careful. I compared our heights. I had two-inch heels on and we were about equal. That made her five-six, which wasn't very tall for a New York cop, but still gave her two inches on me. Detective Warner was not about to take any guff.

"What brought you down here in the first place?" she continued.

"I came to bring her back to the party. I'm her best friend," I said meaningfully, ready to launch into the whole story.

Knowing how long it was likely to take, I was about to ask if the interview could be conducted in a more

I WILL SURVIVE

comfortable setting, such as my apartment. I was prepared to tell all, but I really needed something to eat and a place to sit down.

At that moment, I heard the elevator come to a landing. The door opened and a heavy-booted pair of feet made the trip to the laundry room.

"Hey, Shar, what do we got here?"

The voice was pure Bronx and vaguely familiar. A few seconds later, the speaker appeared, brushing past Thomas Brinkham and poking his head into the crime scene. I recognized him instantly.

Just when I'd been thinking that things couldn't possibly get worse, Detective Johnny Rostelli swaggered in wearing tight jeans, motorcycle boots, and a leather jacket. He didn't notice me right away as he was concentrating on being briefed by his partner.

"We got a dead body named Jana Crowley, medical examiner says she was strangled, but not sure what the weapon was. There's a bunch of society fish up in the penthouse. They've been having a party and the deceased was the hostess. I put Peterson on the door and told him not to let anybody out. We still have to interview those folks and I don't how much longer they'll hold. I've got a statement from the husband." She jabbed her thumb at Thomas Brinkham. "And I was just about to get one from the woman who found the body." She nodded in my direction and referred to her notebook. "This is Marti Hirsch. She says she was best friends with the victim."

I'm not sure which Johnny recognized first, the name or the face, but I doubt he heard anything his partner had to say once he had me firmly in his sights. I watched his face shift into a mask of fury. It was the same look of blistering hatred that had focused on me three years earlier.

I met his gaze and tried to act like I wasn't scared to death. Not much had changed. I remembered his deep blue eyes and neatly clipped mustache and goatee. The hair was slightly longer, mushrooming around his head in a white man's afro.

The last time I'd seen him, he'd been mad enough to want to kill me. As he stared at me now, with his nostrils flared and lips pressed tightly together, I wouldn't have been surprised if he had pulled out his weapon and dispatched me then and there. The effort it cost him not to do it caused a slight tremor. I was shaking in my shoes, but determined to hold my ground.

"Hi, Johnny," I said softly, maybe even seductively.

He turned away from me abruptly and wouldn't look back. He started barking orders.

"Get the husband up to the party. Have him make the announcement, then everybody can go home. Make sure we have names and addresses. We'll cover them all, but I don't want to step on any big toes. No calls from City Hall, asking what the hell we're doing. Make it all by the book, nicey-nice. Get me a forensics report as soon as these guys can get it, and don't take no garbage about how they're understaffed for the holidays. I don't wanna hear it."

He started to stomp off.

"And what are you gonna be doing?"

Under stress, Sharon had a bit more of an accent and sounded even raspier.

"I got some people to talk to and a record to pull."

He still wouldn't look at me but I could guess whose record he had in mind and it wasn't the White Album. The other cops, including Sharon, were left in stunned silence. It was a good thing the elevator was still there. Who knows what would have happened if he'd had to wait?

I took a survey. My best friend was dead. I was cold, hungry, and tired. My feet hurt. The lead cop on the case hated my guts and would love to pin the murder on me. There was only one thing left to do.

I WILL SURVIVE

I passed out.

O.K., it wasn't exactly passing out, but it was a good enough imitation of a swoon to prevent me from having to deal with any further unpleasantness for the rest of the evening. Evening, of course, had already given way to night, and there was precious little of that left. It wasn't much of a respite, but it was worth it, even though I had resorted to extremely unfeminist behavior by pretending to faint.

I was escorted to my apartment by the medical examiner with the wheaty hair and wire-rimmed glasses. He handed me over to Jerry, who put me to bed, and even helped me out of those miserable high heels.

Whatever happened in the penthouse happened without me. Jerry kept an eye on all the small fry in our living room until their shocked parents came down to collect them. When the last brat was gone, he locked up the apartment and joined me under the covers. I'd already shed the dress.

Take care of it.

I could barely take care of myself. If I let myself think too hard, I'd lose it. The crying and hysteria at my father's funeral would be nothing compared to what would be unleashed by the reality of losing Jana.

After the funeral, I'd vowed never to be that way again, and I would do anything to keep the emotion from getting the best of me. I took a double usual dose of Xanax and let it send me into a numbed-out approximation of rest.

I let myself smile as I drifted off. I could still see Jana's dead body. I couldn't even begin to absorb the horror, but at least I didn't have to talk to Sharon Warner until the next day. I was still hungry, but I could deal with that in the morning.

In the meantime, there would be a nice long sleep.

7

The phone rang at 6 A.M. I reached out to grab it by instinct.

"Yeah, Jana, what is it?" I murmured as I had so many other times at so many other hours of the day and night.

It wasn't Jana on the phone. Whoever it was got a bit flustered.

"Uh . . . O.K. . . . This is Larry Ramsey with the *Post*. Would you like to comment on the Jana Crowley killing?"

"What? Huh? Oh shit!"

I hung up on the *Post*. I wondered if they would use my pithy quote on the front page. Reality came back with a cold dark thud in my chest. I wouldn't be talking to Jana on the phone anymore. All my conflicted feelings came back. It was too much to absorb. I was starting to hyperventilate, but I was interrupted by another phone call.

This time it was WPIX, followed closely by WOR and WABC and the *New York Daily News*. The *New York Times* was not heard from. Apparently Jana Crowley was big enough for the popular press and local television, but too common for the *Times*.

I WILL SURVIVE

Further sleep seemed an unlikely proposition. I decided to let the answering machine deal with the media for a while. Time to take care of business, starting with my tummy and the dog.

"You awake there, Jerry?"

"Ever since the first call."

"Let's blow this Popsicle stand and get some yummies."

Strudel gave a bark at the sound of the word "yummies."

"We should take her out too," said Jerry, ever the dutiful dad.

"I was thinking that."

"Are you O.K.?" he said. I heard concern and caution in his voice.

"As long as I don't have to think about it before breakfast."

We both dressed for another cold day. Layers and more layers. Tee-shirts, sweatshirts, and sweaters. Even the multicolored toe socks Mom had sent as a birthday present. I'd laughed at the time. Now I was grateful. I looked like a fat pile of laundry, but I topped it off with Jana's sealskin coat, so I wouldn't be deported from the East Side. Jerry had an equally dapper assortment topped with a heavy gray coat that I called his Cossack Coat. It's amazing how little one cares about fashion when the thermometer is below zero. Unless of course, one is, or was, Jana Crowley.

The phone was ringing again. I decided to pick it up. Maybe the gray lady of journalism had finally twigged to the story of the day.

"Yeah," I said, ready to hang up quickly.

"Your rich-bitch friend is dead."

"I heard that too, Harvey."

It was easier to act tough than to deal with the situation, and my boss at *New York Night* was the perfect costar for the script.

"What are you going to do now?"

"I'm going to eat. I'll call you later."

"Wait'll you see the *Post*."

"I can hardly wait."

I put down the receiver and Jerry picked up the dog's leash.

When we got downstairs, I had a sudden urge to ask the doorman some questions about the previous night. Had he seen anything unusual? Did anyone suspicious come in, saying they were going to the party? How about somebody running out of the elevator looking conspicuously guilty? I managed to restrain myself. For one thing, it wasn't the same doorman. Besides which, I wasn't investigating this murder. Or was I?

A gust of wind tried to push us back into the building. Jerry and I burrowed into our respective coats like urban turtles. Strudel barked and put her head down. The wind made her ears flap, but she was a brave dachshund and really needed to go out.

From the spate of phone calls that had begun the day, I would have expected a small contingent of journalists determined to get the story or at least a picture of the building. The street was empty. Making a phone call from the warmth of the office was as far as they were willing to go. I'd always thought reporters were made of sterner stuff. Another illusion frozen to icicles.

Sunday morning on the Upper East Side of Manhattan. Cold and gray. Quiet and gloomy. The East Side always felt quieter than the West, but this morning it was absolutely ghostly. I could see carefully arranged patterns of Christmas lights blinking on and off, but it was all muted into dim pastels by the frost and fog.

Jerry was humming a tune he was working on. His breath made smoke in the frigid air before blending into the fog. We were approaching Central Park in the shadow of the gray monoliths of Fifth Avenue. I briefly wondered if I could disappear in Central Park. Then I wondered why I wanted to. Sink or swim, Marti, I told myself.

We didn't have to go very far into the park before Strudel found a friendly bush in which to do her business. Some of her friends frequented the area, but not at that hour. We let her run around a little, even though I had the feeling she was trying to cheer me up with her scampering rather than get any exercise for herself.

I was feeling woozy and this time it was absolutely for real. I rubbed my tummy and Jerry got the message. It was time for breakfast. I wouldn't have minded eggs Benedict at the Stanhope but that would have been a long fifteen blocks and there were no cabs in sight. We settled for a place on 77th Street, the kind of coffee shop that spells it "shoppe." Copious amounts of coffee were necessary before I could even think about taking the coat off.

The waitress was going to say something to us about how we couldn't bring a dog in, but one look into those big brown eyes and she was bringing leftover cold cuts along with our menus. Considering how many people loved to feed her, it was amazing that Strudel hadn't developed the unseemly potbelly that affected so many of her breed. She'd been the runt of her litter. Even at four years old, she was undersized.

Jerry waited until he knew I was sufficiently warmed and fed before asking the big question.

"Who do you think did it?"

Instead of answering, I pulled a paper napkin out of the dispenser, jotted down the names of some possible suspects, and handed it to Jerry. He looked it over and nearly did a spit-take when he saw his name there.

"Why me?" he asked, looking genuinely hurt.

"You know why. And if you'll notice, my name is a lot higher on that list than yours is. The only person who heard you bitch about Jana is me. On the other hand, I can think of at least five people right off the top of my head who've heard me say that Jana's driving me crazy, that I hate her, that I want to push her out a window, that kind of thing. I don't think I ever actually threatened to strangle her, but you get the idea."

"O.K. then, did you do it?"

"Did you?" I shot back.

We looked at each other through coffee steam. There was an unwelcome moment of distance and suspicion where we were out of synch, not knowing if the other one was joking or not. Then Jerry shrugged and smiled.

"I've got at least fifteen kids who can give me an alibi for the whole night."

"Gee, I knew I should have cozied up to those brats."

"Seriously Marti, do you really think the cops are going after you?"

"This is the NYPD. Anything is possible."

"How about the rest of the list?"

"Number one with a bullet is Thomas Brinkham. That marriage was on the rocks, big time. Tony Falzerano, the smooth-talking slimeball and your boss. Tony and Jana had an affair, if you can call it that. The parting was not amicable. Maybe that hot Italian blood kicked in. That leads us to number three, Rhonda, the wife who knew too much and too little at the same time."

"You never told me any of this."

The fact that I'd been holding out on tawdry gossip offended him more than my placing him on the suspect list. It was symptomatic of how Jana had taken over the number one attention spot in my life and kicked him into second place.

"Jana never got killed before. Moving from lust to professional problems, we have Max Washburne. New York City hath no fury like an art critic who's been carved up for public consumption like the turkey he is."

The last name on my list was Charlotte LaFayette, who had the bad fortune to be a female artist in New York at the same time as Jana Crowley. Charlotte had been championed by a small clique of avant-garde vultures, but couldn't come close to Jana in looks, charm, and connections.

Jerry pointed to something I had put at the bottom of the napkin.

"What's that?"

"It's a question mark."

"What does it mean?"

"What do question marks usually mean?" I snapped.

He nodded as if that made sense.

"Who are you going to question first?"

"This isn't my case. It's the cops' . . . Oh god! I can't believe I'm saying this. Let's get out of here and find out what the *Post* has to say for itself."

Back into the coats and out into the cold.

Cold. That was how I felt inside and out. Somewhere in the distance there was an emotional reaction to Jana's death. It was waiting to hit me like a wrecking ball. I intended to avoid it for as long as possible.

One way to do that would be to throw myself, body and soul, into nailing the scumbag who'd strangled my best friend. I already knew more about Jana Crowley than the fuzz ever would. Sharon Warner wouldn't like it one bit, of course. Cops hate it when you get in their way, but Johnny already hated me and I needed to take care of myself. Who should I question first?

Who was I kidding? I was paralyzed by the same fear and depression that had been shadowing me for months. It was so bad, I was actually considering a visit to my mother in Florida. At least I'd be able to get away from the cold, if not myself.

I might have frozen to death in that very spot if Jerry hadn't gently but firmly steered me down the street, toward a newsstand. I shook myself out of my frosty reverie and realized I was keeping my baby out in the cold for too long. Jerry was shivering too.

Jana hadn't made the front page. The big story was

yet another record-setting cold temperature: how people were dying on the street, or as the *Post* put it, ICY DEATHS CHILL HOLIDAY SPIRITS.

ART GODDESS FOUND STRANGLED was on page three and would have to wait till we got home.

"Goddess?" Jerry asked in disbelief.

Jerry had never been a believer in the Jana Crowley mystique.

I shrugged and walked faster. Jerry matched my stride and Strudel ran along on her short legs. We all needed the exercise and arrived at our front door panting and almost warm. It was a good feeling. Maybe those joggers weren't so crazy after all, although those women in aerobics classes definitely were.

I took the *Post* up to the penthouse. There was someone there I wanted to see. It wasn't Thomas Brinkham, but he was the first one I ran into. He looked absolutely forlorn. The tan he had brought in from Hong Kong had faded a bit and even his usually erect crown of hair seemed to be drooping. For a man who prized dignity above all else, this was quite a show of despair. In spite of everything I knew or suspected about him, I felt guilty for putting him at the top of my suspect list.

His daughter, Elisa, was right next to him. She exuded shock and pain, but of the most theatrical nature. She was only twelve, but tall for her age and she comported herself like a miniature Sarah Bernhardt. My understanding of the family arrangement was that she considered Jana a wicked stepmother, so it was unlikely she'd spent the night shedding tears over Jana's demise.

I nodded at both of them with appropriate gravity and ignored the disapproving glances that said I should return the key now that Jana wasn't going to be summoning me anymore.

My destination was Jana's studio, a small room on the east side of the apartment, which was blessed with morning light through a small window. When the sun wasn't shining, it felt like a cell. I suspected it housed a maid back in the good old, bad old days.

I took a deep breath. The room smelled of turpentine and oil paints as well as an expensive French perfume that I couldn't pronounce very well. Jana and I had spent hours in that room together. She would paint or sketch while I wrote in my notebook. I was probably stoned on the fumes, which would explain the claustrophobic, dizzy quality of the stories I came up with. I called them "Dreams of Decadence" and had dreams of a published collection. The dream was impossible. Short story collections were rare and certainly out of the question for an unknown author.

"Hi there," I said to the face on the canvas.

Jana's type of man hadn't changed much in the years I had known her. He had blond hair and the inevitable bright blue eyes. There was glow to the portrait that I believed was a reflection of the artist's love.

This was Mr. Question Mark. I didn't know much about him, except that he'd become very important to Jana very quickly and now she was very dead. That's how he made my list of suspects.

I thought if I stared at his picture long enough, he would start to talk and tell me what the hell was going on. It was like staring at the *Mona Lisa*.

"Is it only 'cause you're lonely . . ."

Singing wouldn't help either.

I sat down on the small sofa and felt a piece of paper under my butt. It was an envelope from an accountant to whom I'd referred Jana. I stuck it in the pocket of my coat to look at later and opened the *New York Post* to page three. The by-line was Larry Ramsey, the same clod who had disturbed my slumber. The *Sunday Post* had to hit the streets earlier than the weekday editions, so Mr. Ramsey probably had his story written before he ever placed that call. The article he had put together was interesting for two things, what it said and what it didn't.

ARTIST ON HER WAY TO THE TOP MEETS HER END IN BASEMENT

Touching.

They knew she was dead and that the cause was strangulation. The weapon itself was still unidentified. The background information on Jana came straight from her press kit, which meant it highlighted her military forbears, degree in art history from the University of Texas, and extensive popularity overseas. It also noted that she was married to Thomas Brinkham, "British business mogul," which sounded so much nicer than "filthy rich robber baron."

Completely omitted was any mention of her previous fiancé, David Price. He was three and a half years dead and might just as well have never existed.

One interesting quote found at the end of the story:

"While no arrests have been made, sources in the police department have indicated that the investigation is centering on a suspect among Miss Crowley's closest associates."

It was either amorphous gobbledy-gook or it was Detective Johnny Rostelli using his press contacts to point the finger directly at me.

I stood up and looked at Mr. Question Mark. He was wearing a light blue Izod polo shirt, almost the same shade as his eyes. I was going to ask him if he thought I was being paranoid. Before he could tell me that asking a painting for reassurance didn't speak well for my mental health, I was interrupted by Detective Sharon Warner. She was carrying her own copy of the *Post*.

"Who the hell are you and what did you do to my partner?"

She threw the paper down on the sofa to show me she meant business. I threw mine on top of it as if I had a winning poker hand.

"What's he trying to do me?" I shot back. "Close associate? I am the close associate, dammit! I think it would be nice if I were read my rights before they try to crucify me in the press."

"I'll agree he's out of line, but he must know something. You *do* have a record."

"Ancient history."

"Four arrests for disturbing the peace."

"I wasn't disturbing the peace; I was disturbing the war."

I hadn't had the chance to trot that one out since 1974.

"You're making jokes and Johnny's getting a warrant to search your place."

"At least I had it cleaned for the party."

"I can't help you if you don't start leveling with me."

"I don't think you can help me anyway."

I glanced out the window at the rooftop terrace. During the long hot summer that had preceded the cold miserable winter we'd sat on the roof with cool drinks in tall glasses and surveyed the majesty of the East Side and the park. Now it was just an empty space.

I turned back to Sharon and did an assessment. In the morning light she wasn't very intimidating. I wondered if the hoarseness wasn't the result of yelling "freeze" at fleeing perps who weren't inclined to take her seriously. I assumed she had a gun on her person.

"How much do you know about your partner?" I asked as a opening move.

I could sense her rising irritation as I again usurped her right to be the questioner. I held up my hands in a plea for forbearance.

"We've been working together about six months, ever since I transferred to homicide. He's never given me any shit about being a woman or being black, which is more than I can say for some of those guys. Johnny's a hell of a cop. When it comes to going down a dark alley, or going in on a bust, I'd follow him anywhere."

"Out of morbid curiosity, no doubt."

Her mouth tightened and she made an exaggerated motion toward her watch.

"Johnny hates me because I used to fuck his partner."

"So? Why should he care about that?"

"'Cause I also fucked him over pretty bad. Him and the whole department. You ever heard of David Price?" She nodded. "Well, Jana Crowley was engaged to David Price, I was close to both of them, and I'm the one who wound up solving the case."

"You expect me to believe that?" She was shouting as loudly as the hoarseness would permit.

"Sit down and think about it."

She wound up on the sofa in a beam of light. Aside from skepticism and confusion, I noticed freckles on her face, barely visible against the brown skin.

"Shee-it," she finally announced. "I was working vice in Queens when that stuff went down. It was a big hush-hush thing. I didn't know Johnny had anything to do with it."

"It was a fluke that I happened to be having an affair with his partner. Johnny was working narcotics then and there was a drug angle. A lot of really ugly stuff came out. He wound up walking a beat for a while."

"And how come I never heard of you, if you're the big crime-stopper?"

"Can you say cover-up? It's a long story. I wrote a book about it and got blacklisted for my trouble. Is Tommy Morrison still running homicide?"

"He had a stroke. Retired to Ocean City."

"If he can still talk and you feel like calling him, he'll let out a string of profanity and then he'll back up my story, but you know I'm telling the truth because your partner went bonkers the minute he saw me. He wants me to rot in hell."

"He don't care if you rot in hell, honey, he just wants you to rot."

I thought that would be a nice note on which to end

the conversation. Detective Warner had other ideas. she had her notebook out and a cigarette lit up.

"Tell me about Miss Crowley."

"She was my best friend in the whole wide world," I responded automatically.

"What was she doing in the laundry room?"

Sharon probably knew that Jana wasn't down there separating her whites and colors.

"It was kind of like a clubhouse for us. We were down there talking and then I came back up here. She was supposed to come up, but she never showed. I went looking and found her body."

"Uh-huh. Why did you need a 'clubhouse'?"

"Privacy."

I saw her look around at the obviously private studio, and by extension the whole penthouse with its many rooms.

"And why did she stay down there after your little meeting had broken up?"

Sharon Warner had clearly regained control of the interaction. She was tiptoeing back into territory where I didn't want to go. I didn't care who knew about my pot smoking. Let 'em put that on any front page they wanted, but I was still taking care of things for Jana. That included protecting her posthumous image. The cops didn't need to know about Jana's hip flask full of Chivas Regal and the Juicy Fruit. If Thomas hadn't told them he disapproved of his wife drinking anything but the occasional festive glass of champagne, who was I to mention it?

I picked up tube of paint from the easel. It was a green that Jana had been using to create a leafy background for the portrait. I put it down. I didn't want to draw Detective Warner's attention to Mr. Question Mark.

I didn't want to answer her questions. I had no problem lying to the cops, but Sharon was already in a bad position, and telling some whoppers to her face would only make things worse for all of us. If I were in custody with Sharon and Johnny playing good cop/bad cop, she was more likely to be playing good. I should put aside my own bullheaded loathing of cops and cooperate.

I was starting to form an answer that might or might not have been the truth when I was saved by the bell. The phone rang somewhere in the apartment and was followed by footsteps. It was Thomas Brinkham with the news that Detective Warner had a call from headquarters.

He led her to a phone and I took the opportunity to run like hell. I didn't say good-bye and I wasn't about to wait around for an elevator either. I ran down seven flights of stairs.

Jerry had a pile of messages for me. They could all wait. I needed a hot bath. With enough steam and bubbles, I could avoid the police indefinitely.

Once I was comfortably submerged, I tried to focus. In life, Jana had been the center of her own small universe. Which part of the universe was responsible for her killing? I wanted to approach it in a rational, linear pattern, but the images kept blending and blurring. Thomas. Tony. Question Mark. Green leaves. Blue eyes. The horrible purple of Jana's swollen face.

I felt a great sense of urgency to do something, but no idea what I could or should do.

I would have stayed in my watery cocoon until I shriveled away to nothing, but I was interrupted by Jerry in a bathrobe.

"Marti."

"Hold my calls," I grumbled as I resurfaced.

"You can't avoid the cops forever."

"Just watch me. Is she out there?"

"No. She said she was going downtown to see some reports, but she'd be coming back."

"That sounds ominous."

"Her voice sounds awful. She should stop smoking."

"I noticed that too."

"Have you got a game plan yet?"

"I was thinking of lying around, watching football, and burning incriminating documents before the Cossacks show up with a search warrant."

Jerry untied the bathrobe sash.

"Maybe it's time to talk to a lawyer."

"Yeah, I'll call up William Kuntsler and see what he's doing this week."

The bathrobe dropped to the floor. He had more on this mind than legal problems or ablutions.

Hot, wet, steamy sex with my sweetie would once have been a treat, but I was too distracted by the current situation to indulge. Of course I'd been too distracted for a long time. The last time we'd had any sex had been some time before the cold front settled in.

Maybe without Jana's all-consuming demands in the picture, our sex life could make a comeback, but not yet, not now. Jerry took the rebuff without making me feel any guiltier than necessary.

I knew I had to deal with this situation, but I was afraid of the emotions. I was afraid to find out that my marriage might really be over, afraid that I might be alone again, afraid of how afraid I was. What had Jerry said about calling a lawyer?

I did need a lawyer.

As soon as I was rinsed off and wrapped up in a big towel, I jumped back into bed and grabbed the phone. I dialed Jake's number from memory and hoped that Annette wouldn't answer.

"Hello."

"Oh. Hi, Annette, it's Marti. Is Jake there?"

The air on the line was as frosty as the wind off the East River.

"Hold on."

I wondered how a sweet, if vaguely dim, guy like Jake had ended up with such a tight-assed bitch.

"Hi, Marti. Some party, huh?"

"Some party. Your latkes were the high point."

"I've already gotten calls. This is a big step for the business. Thanks again for the gig."

"Yeah, yeah, yeah. Jake, honey, I need to talk to a lawyer. I know we've got one in our family. Who is it?"

"Marti, that's my father."

"You're kidding! You think he'd talk to me?"

"You'd probably have to pay. But you're family. I'm sure you could work something out. Is this about your friend?"

"Yeah."

"She was really murdered?"

"It looks that way."

"That never happened at a party I catered before."

"Welcome to the big time. Where can I find your father?"

"My folks live in Manhasset."

"Very ritzy. Could you call him for me? I'd like to do this today, if possible."

"I don't know."

"You know you owe me one."

"No. I mean calling is no problem. It's just that he doesn't do murders. No criminal stuff. His practice is all family law."

"Divorces?"

"Mostly."

"Close enough. Make the call."

"You're gonna come all the way out to the Island?" He lowered his voice conspiratorially. "Pretty serious, huh?"

"Well you know, dead body and all that."

"I'll call you right back."

Calling me "right back" took long enough for me to grab my clipboard and listen to all the remaining messages on my answering machine. I also sifted through the messages that Jerry had taken down.

There were fifteen calls from the media. I toyed with the idea of calling them all back and promising the lowdown on Jana Crowley in return for publicizing me, my brilliant writing, and my shabby treatment at the hands of the publishing industry.

Six attendees from the party thanked me for Jana and Thomas's hospitality. Two wanted the name of my caterer. None mentioned the murder.

The sniveling voice of Paul Falzerano asked the machine if I was there and then hung up abruptly. Child rearing was hardly my area of expertise, but Tony and Rhonda had to be doing something severely wrong. The least they could do was keep the little brat off the phone.

I was transferring my suspect list from the napkin to a clean sheet of lined paper when the phone rang with Jake advising me that his father, Simon Abelman, would see me that very afternoon. Jake also wanted me to come by his house afterward. He was testing a new cookie recipe. I said I'd be there.

I wasn't about to turn down an invitation to nibble on Jake's cookies.

8

If Jana Crowley had to make the trip from Manhattan to Manhasset, it would be time to call a limo company, usually Vincent Limousines, which provided bars and patient drivers. Since I no longer had vicarious access to the deep, well-tailored pockets of Mr. Brinkham, I was only willing to indulge myself in a cab ride to Penn Station, followed by a trip on the Long Island Rail Road.

Before leaving, I put together an outfit that would be suitably mournful without rendering me completely dowdy. I wound up in a black sheath skirt, pumps, and the cashmere sweater that I'd never returned to Cousin Jake. It retained a trace of Annette's perfume.

The hair looked even shorter than it had when I saw it in the salon mirror the day before. How could I have been so spineless? He was supposed to be working for me and here I was stuck looking like . . . Go head, Marti, say it . . . You look like a grown-up. Yeah, that was it. I'd turned thirty-two in October and now I looked it, which I never had before. Marc, I'm going to get you for this, I thought.

Even with Jana's coat, I knew I'd be cold, but I wasn't planning on being outside for very long. The few minutes it took for the cab to show up was enough time for me to start shivering.

To make it worse, a small pack of media wolves had deigned to leave their dens. They were clustered near the door of the apartment sniffing for scraps of news. I thought they were going to swarm around me, only to find to my relief and chagrin that they had no idea who I was.

It reminded me of all the times I'd stood next to Jana at parties and been rendered invisible by her very presence. Some of those reporters might have actually seen me before, but they never saw me.

I'd been planning to use the cab ride to examine the contents of the envelope I'd picked up in Jana's studio, but it was too cold. I shivered through the ride to Penn Station. The taxi had a broken window to which the cab driver seemed oblivious. I suspected a conspiracy to turn me into a Popsicle.

Speaking of sinister conspiracies, what if the NYPD had a tail on me? I had to scrape frost off the inside of the back window to get a clear view. All I saw was traffic. I probably wouldn't recognize a tail if it rear-ended the cab, which several cars appeared likely to do anyway.

I arrived at the station shaking with cold and paranoia. At least the mass of humanity inside provided warmth. It also added fuel to my fire of anxiety. Anyone could have been following me.

I told myself that this particular throng was more interested in Christmas shopping than in finding out what I was up to.

I bought a *Daily News* and went to the platform. The train was already there. I settled down to read the paper. The LIRR pulled out of the station without my noticing. The story in the *News* regarding the Jana Crowley murder was virtually identical to the one in the *Post*, with a slightly less tacky headline and without the incriminating paragraph about the "close associate." Conclusion: Johnny Rostelli's contacts didn't extend to the *Daily News*.

I looked through the rest of the paper. There was no news. There were ads for Christmas sales. There was cold. There was Ronald Reagan, Ed Koch, end-of-year lists. More cold on the way. For this I left Las Vegas?

A glance out the window showed that the city was gone and the rural outcroppings of Queens were passing by. Back to the Island. I hadn't been there since the spring. It took a murder to get me back.

Just under my anti-establishment radicalism lurked the worst kind of petit bourgeois longing for luxury. I'd been impressed by the middle-class opulence of Jake and Annette's home in Massapequa, which was a ramshackle hut compared with the house I encountered when I finally got to Manhasset and followed the directions to Chez Abelman. Stage-managing divorces was more lucrative than catering weddings.

It was a long walk from the sidewalk to the front door of a mansion built on human suffering. I rang the bell. As I waited, I felt the tips of my ears turning to ice. There were footsteps and a pause. Someone on the other side of the door had to check me out through the peephole. Then there were locks to be undone.

When the door finally opened, I rushed inside, ignoring the woman who had let me in from the cold. Once I stopped shaking, I was able to admire the taste of her decorator.

"Hello, Marti," said the woman, trying to get my attention and perhaps chide me for my lousy manners.

She was tall. Her skin had the look of a woman who had spent every summer getting a deep tan. This year's had faded, leaving a fine network of wrinkles that showed her age. I caught her eyes. They were big and brown. In fact, she was a beautiful woman. I suddenly knew where my cousin Jake got his good looks.

"Mrs. Abelman, how nice to meet you."

"I was at the funeral," she said gently. She must have been at the wedding too, but had the grace not to mention it. "You were under a lot of stress that day."

Jake's mother had a talent for understatement.

"Would you like something hot to drink? Tea or coffee?"

It was nice to know that it was still pronounced "cawfee," even in a mansion, but I didn't want any.

"No, thank you."

"At least let me take your coat."

"O.K."

When I gave it to her, she ran a hand over the fur and nodded approvingly. Didn't she care that I was running around in the skins of cute little seal puppies that had been clubbed to death? I looked around again. She probably had a chinchilla in the bedroom closet.

"Simon's waiting for you in his office. It's upstairs and to the right."

I followed her directions. The door was closed. I didn't bother to knock and walked into a puff of cigarette smoke. I paused for a second until I could see the man sitting behind the desk.

"You clean up real nice," he said.

"Gee thanks."

"Sit down."

I found myself facing a man in his sixties. His hair was almost gone, leaving him with a monk's tonsure. He had a pronounced paunch. He could afford suits tailored to hide it, but ruined the effect by constantly unbuttoning and rebuttoning the jacket. His earlobes were prominent in their detachment. He looked like a Jewish Buddha.

"I appreciate your seeing me. I'll be honest; I have no idea how I'm going to pay you."

"I do. What seems to be the problem?"

"My friend Jana Crowley was murdered last night."

"I heard. My condolences. It's sad that such a young woman should die, but how does this bring you to a lawyer's office?"

"It's a long story."

"It's a good thing I already saw the Jets beat the Packers or this would be a problem."

"I really appreciate—"

"You said that already."

"All right. Here's the thing. She's dead and I didn't do it, but there's this psycho cop who might want to frame me for it."

He nodded his head as though this was a perfectly reasonable statement and picked up a yellow legal pad. At least he didn't tell me I was nuts.

"Let's hear it from the top."

"When I first met Jana?" I asked dubiously.

"Not that much top."

"When I got back here in January?"

He looked at his watch.

"All right. Jana came back to the United States in April. It was the first day of April, 1981. I was still living here on the Island."

"Good. Roll 'em."

So I closed my eyes and played the movie of Marti and Jana part two and showed it to Simon Abelman.

Jana had showed up just in time. I couldn't have stood living on the Island one more minute.

Jake was a total peach. He would have let us hang around indefinitely, but Annette and I just never got along. First she was pregnant and making the most out of it by having Jake wait on her hand and foot. Then she had Ashley and you would have thought no one ever had a baby before. Babies in general, I'm not that crazy about, and Ashley was no exception. All in all, Annette thought I was a witch or something that rhymed with it.

I WILL SURVIVE

Simon knew all that.

"The plan was for me to get my book published and then find a great place to live in the city. None of that happened."

"What book?"

"I wrote a book called *Broken Heroes*. It's about the David Price case from a few years back. All the names were changed, so it's just like any regular murder mystery except the hero is a woman who sleeps with a cop and solves the case, thereby embarrassing the whole department. I had a contract with Mortimer and Sweeney. It was all ready to go and I was working on my second one about this other murder that happened in Las Vegas, when one day I get a call from Jackie Vogel, that's my agent."

"I've heard of her."

"Good, so you know I'm not a complete fruit loop. I go into the city and I know I'm in trouble because she wants to take me out to lunch. Turns out Mortimer and Sweeney is canceling the book and they don't want the other one either. And you know why this is happening? Because someone in the upper echelons of the city government doesn't like it. It makes the department look bad. Never mind that I had a contract. Never mind the fucking First Amendment."

Simon gave me a disapproving look.

"Sorry. I couldn't sue because they paid me off. Jackie couldn't sell the damn thing anywhere else because all the insiders knew about it. I was too hot to handle. Blacklisted in 1981. Just for writing a book. Sheesh."

I still couldn't believe it.

I remembered the absolute horror of knowing I wasn't going to be published combined with the hassle of looking for an apartment.

We were living in Jake and Annette's guest room till the baby came but after that she didn't want us there and I couldn't deal with the screaming baby moppet monster.

"Jerry and I got a room at the Days Inn Ronkonkoma," I continued. "We had money in the bank from Mortimer and Sweeney and a few other goodies, but if we stayed in a hotel in the city, we'd have been wiped out in three months. This way we were close to Jake." Simon raised his eyebrows. "And Annette," I added hastily. "They felt like they were responsible for us till we were set up."

That was all Jake. I assumed his father knew that.

"Cozy," was his only comment.

"I'm sure you know what it's like looking for an apartment in New York City. Well, I'd forgotten that all the ads in the paper are written by compulsive liars and the only way to get a place is to check the obits and even that's no good because everyone with a good rent control deal leaves it to his nephew or his Pekinese or something."

"But now you're on the East Side?"

And then I had to tell him about the big brouhaha. I knew he wasn't going to like it.

I'd been planning to skip that part and go right to the arrival of Jana. Of course, the arrival wasn't as dramatic without the setup. On the other hand, it wasn't the coolest thing to tell Jake's father either.

Part of the problem was that I never stopped flirting with Jake. Flirting outrageously in front of his wife who was out to there with her impending motherhood. I told myself it was O.K. Jake was my cousin, I was a respectable married woman, and dear adorable Jake never seemed to realize exactly how flirtatious I was being, even if his wife did.

I didn't mention what I told Jana when she asked me about the relationship. I told her I hadn't and I wouldn't but if it I did . . . "Two taboos for the price of one."

"So what happened."

I WILL SURVIVE

"Well you gotta understand." I was losing my grammar and reverting to my Brooklyn accent, now tainted by the months spent on Long Island. "Jackie Vogel felt so bad about the whole thing with the book that she gave me some space in her office with a typewriter so that I could work on a new one. She thought I could use a pseudonym or something. She promised me she'd try and sell whatever I came up with. Unfortunately what I came up with was writer's block. Nothing. Nada. Zilch.

"I was nutting out and she knew it. While that was happening she was also trying to sell some of the songs that my husband, Jerry, wrote. And damn if she didn't do it. I can't write and she sells one of his songs."

"You sound bitter."

"No, not bitter." I replied, realizing how bitter I really sounded, not to mention whiny. I struggled to modulate. "It just freaked me out. It's a pretty song called 'Better Left Alone.' Big power ballad. It's on an album by Vicky Dell. Jerry had to go out to Los Angeles to meet the producer and the arranger and all that jazz. So I was all alone for a week with the dog. Don't get me wrong. I love that dog, but I was still lonely. It got really bad one Sunday night in April. Jerry and I had this little ritual of watching the news on channel five, because Martin Abend and Sidney Offet just crack me up. Then we'd watch Jimmy Swaggart, the preacher. Have you ever watched him?"

"Why would I?"

"Because he's a hoot. He sings, he cries, he dances in the spirit. Sometimes he speaks in tongues. It's incredible. It's especially amusing if you're high."

There, it was out. I could see the disapproval on his face, so I hit him with the real whammy.

It was Sunday night and Jerry was gone. I was all alone in that lousy Days Inn. I didn't want to be alone. I got Jake to come and get me. Then I told him to take me into the city so we could do some weed.

I remembered the sheer recklessless of making that call. I couldn't wipe the smile off my face.

"You turned my son on to drugs?" Simon's voiced was raised in fury and disbelief.

"I didn't turn him on to anything, pal. He did go to Brown, you know. He didn't want to go at first. Said he hadn't done it since college, and Annette was home with the baby, but I think he liked the idea of doing something different. He didn't know where to get it on the Island so we had to go Manhattan. Even then, we almost couldn't find any. All my old pickup sites weren't happening. I was almost ready to give it up as a bad idea. I told him to make one more pass down St. Nicholas Avenue really slow. He hadn't been creeping enough to let them come up to the car. I made the buy and we were out of there. We came back to the house and got high in the driveway, so that Annette wouldn't smell it in the house."

This particular monologue was not what I had come to Manhasset to talk about. I'd never been ashamed of using drugs, but telling it to Simon Abelman made me feel like a small, stupid child about to be reprimanded for putting beans up her nose.

"We went into the living room and I put on Jimmy Swaggart. He was going at it hard and heavy, talking about Jerry Lee Lewis, who's his cousin and how Jerry wanted to be saved but couldn't be or something like that. Anyways, Jimmy was crying up a storm and Jake and I were cracking up because it was so funny. We weren't doing anything naughty, just sitting on the couch laughing our asses off and watching Jimmy Swaggart. We might have been close together 'cause we were sharing some cookies. And we must have laughed pretty loud because Annette came down the stairs carrying the baby and shouting, 'What's going on here?' Well if that wasn't bad enough, Jerry was coming back from L.A. that night and he didn't find me at the Days Inn, so he came to Jake's house and walked in on the whole thing. Annette told him what she thought she saw. It was a big mess."

"I can imagine."

No, he couldn't. It was unbelievably awful. Jake hadn't had any pot in years and we must have gotten some good stuff, so he couldn't get his shit together at all. I was trying to chill everyone out. Annette was doing her woman wronged shtick. Jerry was just looking hurt and disappointed. He knew there was nothing was going on with Jake, but he thought I'd be at the motel waiting for him and he doesn't like my smoking dope either. To top the whole thing off the baby started crying.

I shuddered from the memory of the sound.

Simon made a note on his pad. I hoped it wasn't something like "Ms. Hirsch is a raving lunatic, get her out of here as soon as possible."

"Then what happened?"

I closed my eyes to remember the whole wretched thing.

"Jake giggling, baby crying, Annette whining, Jerry glaring. Then there came this voice from the doorway saying, 'I hope I'm not interrupting anything.' I looked over and there was Jana Crowley in this fabulous gray Halston suit. I practically leveled Jake to get to her. I had to hug her and make sure she was really there. I'd been missing her for so long. She didn't have any way of knowing how bad things were. She just showed up when I needed her most. And she got me off, you should pardon the expression, this miserable fucking island."

"Right away?"

"That night. She had just come in from Europe if you can believe that. She had Jake's address because I had given it to the manager of the trailer park where we lived back in Las Vegas. She came in a limousine. She took us back to the Days Inn for our stuff and the next thing I knew we were in Manhattan staying at the Milford

Plaza. Two weeks after that we moved into our apartment at the Lancaster, an apartment that just happened to have a piano in it. She got Jerry hired at the Simone School. Everything was hunky-dory, right until it wasn't.''

"Wait a minute. Why would she do all that for you, and furthermore how could she do it?"

"She *could* do it because she'd married Thomas Brinkham. You know him? One of England's 'New Millionaires,' as they say in *Time* magazine. Importer, exporter, buyer, seller, and art collector. Collecting Jana Crowley originals has become very fashionable in certain circles, so the fashionable Mr. Brinkham decided to buy the original Jana Crowley. That's my take anyway."

"What was her excuse?"

"He had swept her off her feet when they first met in Hong Kong. He's big in Hong Kong and she was there with her exhibition. He glommed onto her and they did the whirlwind romance thing."

"Romance, as in love?"

That was a toughie. Jana never actually said she was in love with the guy. I never liked the idea of Jana marrying Thomas just because of his bankbook, although it was hard to imagine any other explanation. Blond hair and blue eyes he did not have. Biggo buckos and a whole apartment house on the Upper East Side, he did.

Thomas Brinkham had picked up the Lancaster when the poor bastard whose family had it since the Twenties got himself in over his head with coke and had to liquidate in a hurry.

He and Jana were moving into the penthouse, but he was doing his big deals somewhere and wanted her to set up everything. I thought that was asking a lot. Then he sent his daughter, Elisa, over and told Jana to get her into the best school, which was of course Simone.

I looked at Simon.

"He wanted her to do all this stuff and keep her career

going. That's *why* she did it. She needed me. I'm the smartest person she ever knew."

"Did she say that?"

"She didn't have to. She was beautiful, but I was smart. That's the whole thing. Don't you see?"

"I'm afraid not."

I was getting tired of sitting and looking at the top of Simon Abelman's head as he bent over his legal pad. I stood up and stretched. I caught him looking at me. I folded my arms accusingly and he looked away with a shake of his head. He rebuttoned his jacket.

"I'm telling you this because I'm afraid of the cops. It's kind of lurid after this."

"Marti, I'm a divorce lawyer. I specialize in lurid. Go ahead."

"Fasten your seat belt; it's been a bumpy couple of months." I reached into my pocketbook and pulled out the list to hand to him. "You can't tell the suspects without a scorecard."

He looked it over and his broad, smooth forehead wrinkled in confusion.

"As I said, things were hunky-dory. Jana and I were together every day. I got things taken care of. I wrote letters. I made phone calls. I didn't take 'no' for an answer."

"You were a girl Friday."

"I was more than that. I was her best friend. She told me everything. We went to lunches and dinners and parties. She got invited to everything. Broadway, gallery shows, football games."

"I don't get it." Simon said, shaking his head. "New York is full of good artists. Why would your friend be Queen of the May all of a sudden?"

"Because she was beautiful. Plus she had talent so that people could think they were admiring her for more than beauty. You could set your watch by how fast it took a man to fall for her. Beauty and talent. Maybe New York needed her as much as I did."

"Were you jealous?"

"Why should I be?" I bristled, knowing several excellent reasons. "The whole thing was like a dream come true. I forgot that every time a dream comes true, a nightmare starts. All I had to do was be available twenty-four hours a day and follow Jana around with a clipboard."

"Why were you at the parties? Why not her husband?"

"He wasn't there a lot and when he was there, that's when it stopped being hunky-dory."

I took a deep breath. I focused on the beautiful wood paneling of the office and the volumes of law books in shelves along the walls. It was a technique to relax myself. I needed to be relaxed because the topic of Thomas Brinkham could drive me into a mouth-frothing, man-hating frenzy, which I didn't want to display to my lawyer, much less a member of my own family.

"Men are scum," I'd told Simon's daughter, Rayna, at her ill-fated wedding. Meeting Thomas Brinkham ten years later, when I was married and presumably more mellow, nearly convinced me that I was right the first time. He was a classic male chauvinist. I took another breath and let it out slowly. When I spoke, I concentrated on sounding calm.

"Thomas came to America about three weeks after Jana rescued me from Long Island. He'd been here before, of course. He had business interests all over the place. What he wanted was to live in his new property on the East Side, at least enough of the year to duck Inland Revenue back in jolly old England."

"Tax exile?"

"Don't say that to his face. I did it during the first dinner, and right away I knew this was not going to be the beginning of a beautiful friendship. He kept going on about Mrs. Thatcher and Ronald Reagan and lowering taxes and doing in the labor unions. I thought I was either going to throw up or wring his neck. I kept looking at Jerry to see if he was as revolted as I was. I could tell he didn't want to get into a fight with our benefactor. Then I looked at Jana. She looked numb. This beautiful, talented, vivacious woman and she was just shutting herself down.

"As soon as I could get her alone, I said 'What's up with Mr. Mousse? I haven't seen hair not move like that since Jack Lord stood in the wind on "Hawaii 5-0".' Then I got real serious and I said, 'How the hell could you?' She just shrugged her shoulders like I was supposed to understand."

"Did you?"

"Not then, but I've had a lot of time to think about it. You want to know what I think?"

The expression on his face said that he didn't, but I continued anyway.

"I've been a feminist since before I could vote. I've said, 'I don't need men' enough times in my life, but there was always some kind of anger or desperation involved. With her it was just a fact. She always knew there would be another man, so any particular one wasn't much to get excited about."

"Sounds like a first-class ball buster to me."

"You'd think so. If I did the exact same thing, I'd never get away with it. She was able to handle men like a lion tamer, her husband for instance. Every single time I was around Thomas, we'd get into it. He didn't think women should work, if they did work, he didn't think they should get the same wages as men. He thought women should change their names if they got married. Maybe his great admiration for Mrs. Thatcher had as much to do with using her husband's name as proving that she could be as much of a right-wing prick as any man.

"At the same time, he had married a woman who had a career and a name and who flirted with every man, woman and child she ever met, because that was how she related to people. I think she managed to get away with it because she played the game so well. She'd give him the sweet talk and the big eyes. She never argued with him or did anything to threaten his ego. 'Never threaten the male ego,' she told me. I never learned how to play that game. She was the grand champion."

"Marti."

The Buddha was losing his patience with my monologue.

It just drove me crazy that she got trapped, as surely as any housewife with bad skin in Schenectady. She had the career, the glamour, lunches at Elaine's, dinners at the Rainbow Room, nights on Broadway, the savvy to take care of herself anytime, anywhere, and she was still trapped by his power and money.

I imagined what she must have thought when she went down the aisle. Skinny Thomas with his fake tan and big hair would be the ultimate worshipping fan. Instead she had to put up with his condescending remarks in that tinny little voice.

I went on with the story.

"He'd bounce into town on the Concorde for a few days to make a deal or raise someone's rent or maybe for a roll in the hay. They'd go out to the opera or a party. He'd sign some checks. Then he'd disappear again, leaving her alone with that brat of his.

"It got so bad, she couldn't even do her art. She'd stare at a sketch pad or a canvas and it just wasn't happening. Once I made a crack that maybe she should try some different music. I didn't think 'God didn't make little green apples,' was all that inspirational. You should have seen the look on her face. It was a mixture of anger and terror. Then she sent me out on a coke run, and I don't mean cola. You know, when I first met her, she

I WILL SURVIVE

got uptight if I smoked a joint. She must have picked up the habit in Europe. Not a major habit, like losing your life savings or needing a new nose. Just a little sniff to get through long nights."

I had to smile. I think I enjoyed some of those parties more than Jana did and she was supposed to be the belle of the ball.

All those people, with all that money, throwing all those parties. Jana doing her flirting thing and me with my clipboard. Sometimes she had me dress like her so that we could pull a switcheroonie if she was so charming that some lame-brain wouldn't leave her alone. We'd do two parties in one night, or a gallery show and a party, or a party and a Broadway opening, and on and on and on.

I'd been boring Simon to catatonia, but suddenly he was very interested.

"And how did you stay awake for all of this partying? Cocaine?"

"No," I said firmly, not mentioning the speed. "Her husband got really pissed off about the coke, though. Mr. New Millionaire turn out to be Mr. Old-Fashioned Prig. He'd make these prissy little comments, which were usually aimed at me, because apparently I was forcing her to do the blow and drink the Chivas Regal. He didn't want to admit that she was doing it because he managed to make her feel like shit when he was there and like worse shit when he wasn't there. That's the only reason she got involved with Tony."

"Tony?"

"Anthony Falzerano. This is where it gets really good or really bad, depending on how you look at it. You know the Simone School?"

"Of course."

"He's the principal. Elisa, Thomas's daughter, got jumped over a large waiting list due to a nice infusion of her daddy's money. He said he loved her, wanted the best for her, you know the drill. Then he left her in New York with Jana, who mostly left her with a nanny or whoever takes care of a fifteen-year-old. I would have felt sorry for Elisa, but . . ."

"But what?"

"But I didn't. So there was Tony the principal and Jana who was kind of taking care of the kid."

"So Tony and Jana . . ." Simon wanted me to get to the lurid part and it was coming along right on time.

"She must have seen him several times before, but nothing happened. Then there was a Halloween party at the school and naturally Thomas was out of town. I think he was buying pre-Columbian art in the Cayman Islands and working on his tan. So picture it: me and Jana in our almost matching outfits watching a whole room full of teenagers in overpriced costumes, presumably being kept safe from apples with razor blades and candy with drugs.

"Jana had a smile on her face because I was comparing the party to a vision of hell, when Tony came striding over to make his usual charming, harmless overtures. He's a slime, but he's no fool. Actually boffing a Simone mom would screw up his deal, right?"

"I guess."

"Anyone at any time is capable of anything. One of my little rules. On that particular night, his charm ran into her charisma and *fwoomph*." I snapped my fingers to indicating a match being struck and igniting. "I was surprised they didn't wind up going at it on top of the table with the candy apples."

"Did they have an affair?"

"They tried. The first time was a few days after the Halloween party. Thomas was still gone so they met at the penthouse. I went up there and actually saw him on the way out. He was straightening his tie. He gave me a 'just got laid' smirk. He stood by the elevator whistling. I drew the obvious conclusions. I went inside to get the postgame scoop, but she wasn't talking. All she said was that he had good hands. They had two other dates. One at the Sherry Netherland and one time they went to a cheap hotel downtown thinking that if luxury didn't work, tackiness might.

"After that she came up to my place and said it was over with Tony. I asked why. She told me he was all talk and no action. I wanted details and she gave me the whole thing. The Latin lover could barely get it up. When he got it up, it wasn't very far and he couldn't get it in. He was all heavy breathing and hot talk. The most he could ever do was come on her tits. She was actually offended. She was a down-home girl, and a teeny-tiny, limp weenie was like saying she wasn't hot enough. Nothing like that had ever happened to her before. It was worse than not being able to draw. I tried to cheer her up with my Darth Vader imitation."

"Huh?"

"You have failed me for the last time?" I said à la the heavy-breathing *Star Wars* villain. "That made her laugh, but she was worried. I think she said something devastating to him."

"She was afraid he would hurt her?"

"She was mad at herself for breaking her own rule about hurting a man's ego. She said that made him dangerous. Her mama wouldn't have approved at all."

"Is that what this is all about? Tony coming in and strangling her over . . . over impotence?"

It seemed difficult for him to say. Maybe it was hard for any man.

"Maybe him, maybe his wife, maybe Thomas, if he knew."

"When in doubt, bet on the husband," he said, sharing what sounded like hard-won wisdom.

"Did they teach you that in law school?"

"In the Long Island district attorney's office. I worked there for five years. It cured me of any interest in criminal law, which this conversation has not reignited, by the way."

He glanced at my list.

"Well, I've got him right up there, but when I saw him this morning he looked awful. I actually felt bad for him," I said. "I really loathe the guy, but ... strangling his own wife ... ?

"Tell me about the rest of this, and try to move it along. I'll tell you, Marti, you don't know how lucky you are."

I thought over the past two days and the past two months. In neither case did the word "lucky" come springing to mind.

"How am I lucky?"

"I'm not charging you by the hour."

I had to smile at that.

"Jana went on a real tear after Tony Falzerano let her down. She was alienating people right and left. I couldn't figure out how much was deliberate and how much was just not caring. She was stomping on egos like they were grapes. If you're looking for emotional cripples to trip, the art world is your happy hunting ground. Charlotte LaFayette, for instance."

"Never heard of her."

"Her stuff isn't bad, if you don't mind self-indulgent symbolism. She's got the personality of a sponge. I don't know why Jana would even bother sharpening her nails on Charlotte, but like I said, she was on a tear. She'd get right in Charlotte's face at parties and just rub it in that Charlotte wasn't as pretty or famous or successful as Jana was. It might have been the nose candy talking, or maybe just fear. Charlotte was putting out new stuff and Jana wasn't. The shelf life of any New York celebrity is limited.

"Some critics were starting to snipe at Jana. She was

too classical, too neo-classical, too post-neo classical, too traditional, too feminine.''

I couldn't believe people got paid to write that crap.

"A few of them were touting Charlotte as the new kid in town. Max Washburne wrote this piece in *Art Weekly* basically saying that Jana was washed up, that she was worthless to begin with. He implied that she had slept her way to the top and was now losing not only her following but her looks. It made a big splash among the people who read that kind of thing. Young, rich, pompous assholes, who think art is about money and don't want anyone to know they think that.''

Simon nodded.

"I've seen some of them come through my office. When they get divorced, they fight harder over those paintings than they do over their children.''

"Exactly. There was a lot of whispering when this piece of *dreck* came out, so Jana told me to take care of it. I couldn't have the guy strung up by his gonads in the middle of Times Square, so I did the next best thing. I wrote a letter to the editor, where I called him a desiccated hack, accused him of taking bribes, made slanderous allegations about his sex life, and demonstrated conclusively that the emperor had no clothes. I think the highlight was 'pudgy, preening angel of banality.' ''

I noticed Simon struggling to repress a smirk.

"Naturally the letter was signed by Jana Crowley, who delivered it to the offices of *Art Weekly* in a wave of mink and perfume. The new issue came out Monday and by that night we'd heard from Mr. Washburne and Mr. Washburne's lawyer. They were both in a bit of a tizzy. I doubt that the old coot actually has it in him to do physical violence, except for what his pathetic prose does to the English language, but I can't rule him out.''

"You've been a busy girl, haven't you.''

"Busy woman," I corrected, "and you don't know a tenth of it."

"I don't want to, but you'd better tell me why you put yourself and Jerry on this list."

I told him how Jana Crowley was sucking the life out of me. I got trapped too. I liked the parties and the glamour, all that establishment crap that I used to rail against. I was a big sell-out and I hated myself for it. And she wouldn't leave me alone. She called me all the time. When Thomas was gone we'd hang out in her studio or her bedroom. When he was in town, we went to the laundry room. She wanted someone to talk to, to be with, to bitch at. I would have done anything for her at first, until it turned ugly. She made me feel like a servant instead of a friend and still expected me to be there for her. I'd rant and rave and tell people she was a bitch and she was driving me crazy and I wanted to kill her. Then I'd go do whatever it was that she wanted."

I could feel myself getting hysterical.

"Marti, calm down."

"I know, I know, I'm O.K. I kept going back because I thought it was going to be like it was before, but it never was, until that last night."

"What about Jerry?"

"Jerry and Jana never got along. He was one of the few men on the planet who was immune to her charms and I think she resented it. Plus when she walked into the living room that first night, she walked right up and said, 'You must be Jerry, it would take someone special to get a ring on her,' and gave him a big hug. Unfortunately she was giving it to Jake."

"I see."

"I wanted things to be perfect with me and Jerry and it drove me crazy that they weren't. I know it's my fault, but I blamed it on her." I was being more honest with my lawyer than I usually was my husband, or for that matter, myself. "I was never there for him. He had the Simone School, which turned out to be a snakepit with dollar signs. He was used to toughing it out in the public schools. He said that Simone was a beautiful facade with maggots crawling behind it. He needed me to listen to him and I wasn't there because I was up in the penthouse listening to Jana. Even on Sunday nights." I said sadly.

"Tell me about the night of the murder. Wait a minute, what's this?" He was pointing to the question mark.

Now I had to explain how I had a suspect, but didn't know who he was.

"Thomas came back to New York around Thanksgiving and stayed put. It was either the tax thing or some perverse desire to be with his wife and child. I was off social duty, but she'd still call me around three in the morning and I'd have to go up. I remember being in the studio and wondering when she was going to start bitching at me again. Then I noticed a picture on her easel.

"It was this gorgeous man with blond hair and blue eyes and a smile to die for. At first, I thought she was going back to her past and painting David Price, her former fiancé, but it wasn't David. David was beautiful, but he was all angles. This one was younger and softer. He had such a sweet smile. Jana had the same smile when she caught me looking at it. I knew she was in love.

"She wouldn't tell me anything about it. All she did was give me an errand list. I had to arrange the party because it was time for her to throw a party for the Simone parents. She couldn't be bothered with the actual work of doing it.

"I was so angry with her."

Simon nodded.

"Why should I do the gophering if I wasn't getting the closeness that made it worthwhile. I couldn't take it anymore. Jerry couldn't take it anymore. I was going to wait till after the party and then just tell her off. Say good-bye baby and amen. It wasn't a very good plan because I hadn't told Jerry about it and I had no idea where we would go or even if we could go, but I had to get out."

"What happened?" Simon asked.

"So come party night, everything's all set and ready to go. It was after the concert. Everybody came over from the school. The kids went to our apartment and the parents to the penthouse. Jana took forever getting ready. We were both wearing the same black, lacy number and she couldn't get her bow right or something. I was waiting and waiting and waiting and finally she came out of her dressing room with her hip flask and said, 'Come on' and took me down to the laundry room. I thought, Fine, this is it, Jana Crowley. I'm going to tell you exactly what I really think of you."

This was it, the climax of my story. I didn't think I could do it justice, but I knew I'd never forget it.

That small elevator. Jana and I in identical black, sparkly dress which made her look like a star and me like a stand-in. A ride down that was cold and not just because of the ambient temperature.

I spent the time in the elevator carefully crafting my complaint. I knew I'd have the advantage in words. I followed her to the laundry room and prepared to assault her with my grievances. She beat me to the punch with a swig from her flask, and her most imperious manner, which had gotten a lot worse since she married Thomas.

"I don't like your attitude."

I could almost hear an echo of her husband's accent.

"I don't need you moping around here. I need you to be helpful and supportive. You're supposed to be taking care of things around here. And if you don't like it, you can by all means lump it."

I was taken aback, first by the idea that she should

I WILL SURVIVE

chew me out when I was so obviously in the right and secondly by the ridiculous phrasing. I forgot all about propriety and pretty words. I let her have it right back.

"You know what Jana, you're nothing but a spoiled, selfish bitch and you shouldn't take it out on me just because you sold out your body and talent like some whore."

She blinked and stared at me. I wasn't sure what was shocking her more. The revolt of the oppressed or hitting below the belt. Either way, she was giving me the Martian Look. She heard me but I wasn't sure she understood me. The frustration boiled up into a full-scale rage.

"What happened to the way things used to be with us? Jana and Marti. Marti and Jana. Tel Aviv. England. New York. What about when we read *Macbeth* near that castle in Scotland? I know you're miserable in your marriage, but that's not my fault. I'll find you a good feminist lawyer who can get you out of it, if you like. And don't think that I don't know about the pretty boy you're in love with either. That's what you won't talk about. That's what's killing our friendship!" I ended up screaming.

She was staring at me with her mouth open.

"Well, go ahead. Say something. Tell me I'm fired. Tell me to get out. Tell me you don't need me. Find someone else to carry the clipboard."

Then she said the last thing I expected to hear from her.

"I'm sorry."

"What?"

"Sorry. You're my best friend. No matter what I do sometimes. It's just been, I don't know where to start."

I knew a thing or two about emotional manipulation. I had a Jewish mother. I was determined to hang tough.

"Tell me about the guy in the picture."

Her whole body broke out in a glowing smile.

"Oh Marti, I love him so much."

It was the same glow of her early days with David Price. This was for real.

"He looks really young in the picture," I said.

"Twenty-three." There was an extra glint in her eyes. Twenty-three made him half Thomas Brinkham's age and close to ten years younger than Jana. "He's wonderful and sweet and handsome. You'll like him."

"I'll bet."

"I can't tell you too much."

"Why not?"

"For your own good."

And then she clammed up again.

Simon had been listening to this so intently that he hadn't buttoned or unbuttoned his jacket during the narrative.

"Did you believe her?" he asked, seriously.

I nodded.

"She needed to get herself together and chew some gum to get the booze off her breath before she faced her husband and the guests. I went upstairs, did my surrogate hostess act for a while, went down to get her... and you know the rest."

I finished with a recap of my encounters with Detectives Warner and Rostelli, including my tangled relationship with the latter and the fact that I was actively ducking an interview with the former.

"And that's it?"

"That's it."

He got up slowly. It had been a long time. Nearly two hours. He put his face in his hands, rubbed the inner corners of his eyes, and took off his glasses. He shook his head in disbelief.

"Well?" I implored, asking for help, reassurance, direction, something.

I could see him formulating what he was going to say. He stood up and started what I thought was his courtroom stride. He did a well-choreographed pivot to face me.

"O.K., Marti, first the legal advice, which you're not going to like: find the lady cop and tell her everything."

I opened my mouth to start protesting.

"I know, I know. You hate cops. And the fact is they might make trouble for you on the narcotics stuff, but they'll probably be so happy to get cooperation that they'll pretend they never heard that. If you don't talk and this Johnny guy is as loco as you say he is, he's going to dig up some of this and then find a prosecutor to get you on an obstruction charge.

"Now for the legal advice you might take: tell the police the bare minimum and get a good criminal lawyer. You'll need one unless you can personally deliver the killer and credible evidence. If you can actually nail somebody, you'll get yourself off the hook. Of course you can't do it, which is why I still think you should go with full disclosure."

Mr. Simon Abelman, attorney at law, had just casually dismissed my ability to catch the killer. Obviously he didn't know who he was dealing with. The Great Detective was going to take care of this. I could already see myself striding down Park Avenue to solve the murder. I'd need a hat and a trench coat.

I stood up ready to shake hands with Simon and make the 3:10 to Yuma, or whatever train would get me back to grime and crime in the canyons of steel.

"Thanks for your time, Simon. I appreciate you sitting here and listening to me. Maybe that's what I needed more than anything else."

"Sit down, Marti."

He didn't actually push me down, but his tone of voice left little alternative.

"We haven't talked about my fee yet."

I winced.

"Yeah. Right. Your fee. I'm sure we could do an

installment-plan thing. I can wash dishes in your kitchen. I'd offer my firstborn, but I'm not planning on having any."

"I already said I'm not charging by the hour. I don't need your money and I've got enough children."

"What then?"

"A favor, Marti. You are going to do me a very large favor."

"Sure. Anything." There was a silence. "What kind of favor, exactly?"

He'd been leaning against his own desk. Now he stood up and stepped forward, looming over me, as I squirmed in the chair.

"Stay away from my son."

"What?" I exclaimed. "I already told you, there's nothing going on."

"And I believe you, but Annette doesn't."

"I should give up a friendship with my own cousin because some Long Island Jap is a hormone-driven, paranoid nut-case?"

"In a word, yes."

"I don't believe I'm hearing this."

"Believe it. Look Marti, I know Annette isn't the brightest light on the chandelier, but she's not as stupid as you think. She's got woman's intuition. She's also got a wedding ring, a baby, and half the house in her name. I don't want to be in court representing my own son. Annette's a good daughter-in-law. She confides in me. Let's just say she finds you threatening. She also thinks you're a bad influence. On that count, I'm inclined to agree. Do we have a deal?"

I couldn't answer. I felt overcome by a tornado of resentment and embarrassment. Simon was so close I could smell the cigarettes on his breath.

"Maybe Rayna's marriage was doomed, maybe not. Either way, I'm not taking any chances with Jake. Do we have a deal?"

"O.K., O.K."

"Good," he said, backing off. "I know you think I'm being a real prick, but I know what I'm doing. In fact, it's really a favor to you too, and that nice fellow your married to. Now I'm going to give you some advice."

"Didn't we do the advice already?"

"That was professional; this is personal. Cousin to cousin. Maybe even the kind of advice your dad would give you if he were still here."

I thought of important advice Maury Hirsch had given me over the years: Don't take no for an answer. Gambling is for suckers. Don't get killed.

The last had come after he realized that no amount of nagging would keep me from going to anti-war demonstrations. He had never lectured me on morals.

"Lay it on me, cuz."

"Grow up."

"What?" This time I stretched it into two syllables full of Brooklyn indignation, with extra emphasis on the letter *T*.

"Look at yourself. When you came in here, I said to myself, She finally looks like an adult, but now that I've been listening to this crap for over an hour, I can see that you're still acting like a child and a particularly irresponsible one at that. If you want to take drugs, that's your business. Self-destructive and illegal, but your own business. However, giving them to a man with a wife and child is practically criminal.

"You need to take a good, hard look at your life. Clean up your act. Being a flunky isn't exactly a stellar listing on your resume. Get a real job, or better yet, stay home and have some kids. And for heaven sakes, give Annette back her sweater. She's been *kvetching* about the sweater for a year."

I couldn't believe I was having to sit still for such a line of establishment bullshit or that it could bug me so much. If I hadn't made a deal, I would have gone straight to Massapequa and tried to *shtup* Jake on his living room floor, preferably with his wife watching. As it was, I had to satisfy myself by getting out of the chair with a much dignity as I could muster.

"You're wrong Simon," I said, forcing calm into my voice. "I don't think you're a prick."

"That's nice."

"You're an asshole!"

He shrugged. Maybe he was used to clients telling him that.

"Here's the phone number."

He handed me a business card.

"You know the magic words?"

"I want to see my lawyer," I enunciated slowly. The words that cops hate to hear during an interrogation.

"I'll drive you back to the station," Simon offered.

"No thanks. I'll walk."

9

It was a very long walk back to the train station, too long to be walking on high heels and too cold, even with the coat. I could barely feel the envelope still resting in my pocket. I wondered if I should have mentioned the accountant to my lawyer. The cold blotted out all rational thoughts except the survival instinct to keep moving. I reached the station with aching calves, frozen fingers, and a hefty dose of self-pity. I wasn't sure which was more irksome, the injunction to stay away from Jake or the self-righteous lecture.

Grow up, my ass, I thought, stamping my feet on the concrete to keep warm. I wanted to think about getting back to the city and planning my next move, but my mind felt as frozen as the rest of my body. The wind sliced through the sealskin and the cashmere. Like fun, would I give Annette her damn sweater back. I closed my eyes, trying to shut out the chill.

When I opened them, there was still no train, but there was a figure on the platform. It wore a brown bomber jacket, ski cap, and scarf. He or she walked toward me with mittened hands extended, possibly trying to tell me something.

I was frightened by this faceless apparition but I was

too cold to move. The walk had a masculine quality. I also noticed a button fly on the jeans and decided I was dealing with a male. Who was this masked man and what was he going to do me at the Manhasset station of the Long Island Rail Road?

He was tall enough for me to have to look up to see his eyes, the only part of his face left exposed. They were the blue of June skies and baby clothes. I was locked into them, fully expecting to be throttled where I stood, when I heard the blessed music of a train coming into the station. I was so happy to see it that I would have done a snappy song and dance, were I not nearly frozen stiff. It was all I could do to get onto the train, taking note that my new friend was following me.

I found a seat in an empty car. The stuffy heat surrounded me and started to dispel the cold that had blown into my bones from Long Island Sound. The bomber jacket man came down the aisle and hovered near me. His eyes silently asked for permission to sit down. I shrugged my shoulders, wanting to cover my curiosity and anxiety with a gesture of nonchalance.

He took the seat opposite me. I stared as he unmasked himself. First the woolen cap came off, revealing fine blond hair, cut short in back, with bangs falling against his forehead. I instantly wanted to reach out and brush the hair to one side, so it couldn't obscure the dazzling eyes.

The scarf came off, slowly unwrapping from the face, prolonging the curiosity as to what was underneath. Would it be the Elephant Man? The Invisible Man? Just another boring Wasp?

The unveiling concluded and I found myself gasping and dizzy with shock.

"I should have known," I managed to get out, before losing my ability to form sentences.

Even Jana's love-struck skills hadn't done him justice. Mr. Question Mark was sitting there being more handsome, more blond, and more blue-eyed than any real person had a right to be.

Jana had told me he was twenty-three, but he looked younger. It was a good thing he did, because if he hadn't been too young and too pretty, I would have wanted him. Except, and this was part of the shock, I found that I wanted him anyway.

He'd been Jana's lover, which made him relevant to her murder and extremely desirable to me. I'd always felt that Jana owed me one for all the men who'd gone for her when I never had a chance.

Question Mark had come all the way out to Long Island to talk to me and I couldn't get a coherent word out of my mouth. Instead I babbled.

"You. How? Why? Jana . . ."

I slammed my mouth shut before I could do any further damage to my intellectual self-esteem. He seemed slightly uncomfortable, but my going ga-ga didn't really faze him. It must have happened to him all the time.

"Hi, I'm Glenn Doyle."

He took off a mitten so that we could shake hands. His skin was soft and warm. I let go quickly.

"I need your help," he said, taking off his other mitten and unzipping the jacket.

"You can't have her. She only comes in twice a week and the place is a mess as it is."

He frowned in confusion and then smiled. He tried again.

"I think I'm in trouble."

"You don't look pregnant."

I did that just to see the smile again. He looked out the window. Bleak afternoon was blending into dark evening. He faced me again.

"It's serious. She's dead."

"I know. I'm sorry. I loved her." I said solemnly, adding the word, "Too?" as both an afterthought and a question.

He nodded.

"Yes. I did. You know who I am, right?"

He was wearing a checked flannel shirt over a long-sleeved polo. Effective layering against the weather, but it made it difficult to scope out what kind of build he had.

"You're the extremely attractive young man who lit up Jana Crowley's life, in spite of the prominent ring on her left hand."

"That's right."

"And you want to talk to me about it, instead of, perhaps, New York's finest."

"Yeah."

"I'm in the phone book, you know?"

This time the smile came with dimples.

"Jana told me about you. She said you could be like this."

"Sometimes. I'm really sorry Glenn. I feel like I've been talking all day. Why don't I shut up for a while and you tell me what's on your mind?"

"O.K., but you can't tell anybody."

"I can do what I want, cutie, but talking to pigs isn't my style."

"Even if I was there last night?"

The polished softness of his voice almost drained the significance from the words.

"Where?"

"There," he said emphatically "At the Lancaster, in the basement. In the laundry room."

The polish was gone, replaced by an almost strangled whisper. He was scared.

"Did you . . . ?" I started the obvious question.

He shook his head violently. The bangs swung from side to side.

"Do you know who?"

Slower shaking.

"But you suspect?"

He held out his hands in a gesture of helplessness.

I leaned back and crossed my legs to show I was prepared to listen. I also showed a little leg, just for the hell of it. He let me know he saw it with the slightest flicker of his eyes.

"I loved her," he started dramatically.

I pulled the skirt down over my knee.

"I just got blown away the minute I saw her. Plus she was an artist so we had that in common. I'm an actor."

I assumed "actor" was a euphemism for "waiter."

"You should be a model," I said instinctively.

"I don't want to be a piece of meat," he shot back.

"Very feminist of you."

"Thanks. I've had some TV walk-ons and chorus work. I was an understudy for *Pippin*."

Through the shy boyishness, I was starting to see some of the toughness necessary to face the New York theater jungle.

"Jana could have done you a lot of good."

"She wanted to, but she couldn't. It was all sneaking around. We didn't even see each other that much. She was scared of her husband."

It made me mad that he could have that kind of power over Jana.

"That creep," I muttered.

"That rich creep," he reminded me.

Wasn't that the truth. Jana had once outlined for me exactly how little money an artist made, even a well-known one. She wasn't a gold digger, but I knew she liked rich a lot better than poor or getting by.

"Mostly we talked on the phone, wrote letters."

"Letters? Jana Crowley wrote letters? It was all I could do to get a postcard out of her when I hadn't seen her in two years."

I'd known instinctively how serious this thing was.

"Was she going to leave him?"

"I'd already asked her to marry me."

I gave him what must have been a skeptical look.

"I know it sounds crazy."

"Not really. I've seen this before."

"But it was different for us."

"Let's say it was. When was she going to tell him?"

"After the party."

Oh really, I thought. She hadn't mentioned that to me amid all the hugging and tears.

"How do you know this?" I demanded.

"I went to talk to her."

"I didn't see you on the guest list."

"I wasn't invited to the party," he said sadly. "She said she'd be in the laundry room. She knew it was dangerous."

"But that was part of the fun?"

"Maybe. If she was willing to take the risk to be with me, I was willing to do anything to be with her."

"Very romantic," I said snidely.

He was so sincere that I felt compelled to inject some venom into the dialogue.

"How did you get into the building?"

"I wore a suit. I told them I was a guest. Jana gave me a name."

"That was sneaky. Way to go Jana."

"I went downstairs. I must have just missed bumping into you. Jana told me that you knew, but that she could trust you. She was up, but scared. I thought it was just nerves. She couldn't stand it anymore. Really jumpy."

"Maybe she was coked up," I suggested.

"Then she got kind of weepy and mushy."

"That was the Chivas Regal."

"She wanted me to make love to her."

"Right there?"

"Yeah. She started taking off her panties."

I felt the train hit a bump in the track that shouldn't have been there.

"Was she wearing stockings or pantyhose?" I asked in the voice of a prosecutor.

"Stockings."

He had just increased his credibility without even knowing it. Jana was strictly a stockings kind of woman. Glenn also got points for knowing the difference. Most straight men don't.

"Did you do it?"

"Someone came."

"I would think so."

"I mean we got interrupted. We heard the elevator and then footsteps. Jana thought it was you. She called your name, but there was no answer. Then she figured it was Thomas. I wanted to stay and confront. I was very brave."

Irony doesn't sit well on a twenty-three-year-old face.

"She told me to hide."

"Hide where? In the dryer?"

"The hallway past the laundry room. It's dark and nasty in there and it leads to this big room where they have the meters and stuff. There's a staircase up to the second floor. I could hear her talking for a second. She said, 'You're pathetic' and that was all I heard. I wanted to go down and see what was going on, but I didn't want to screw things up for her, so I left."

"Up the stairs, second floor, back down the elevator, out the front?"

He bit his lower lip. I thought he was going to cry. There wasn't much I could do for him. This guy had bought himself a shitload of guilt.

"This is all fascinating, but I'm still not sure why you're giving this performance for me."

"I had to tell someone."

"Why not the cops?"

"I wasn't supposed to have been there."

"To say the least, but Thomas Brinkham can't divorce a corpse so—"

"You don't understand."

I looked him over again.

"Your parents?"

He shook his head.

"I have a friend that I stay with." His speech had become halting. I realized that he'd prepared what he wanted to say about Jana. We were up to the unprepared part, the stuff he didn't want to talk about. "And my friend doesn't know."

It was completely dark outside, but the light was dawning on the LIRR.

"You're being kept by some rich old queen, aren't you?"

"It's not what you think. I don't—"

"You don't have to. You and Jana had a lot in common. Did she know?"

"Not everything. She thought it was a rich ... duchess."

"Uh-huh. Let's see if I have the whole picture. You think her hubby did her in. You want to make sure he gets busted for it, but you don't want to screw up things with your sugar daddy, especially now that Jana's out of the picture, so you can't tell the cops what you know. Am I missing anything?"

We were rolling into Pennsylvania Station.

"What am I doing to do?" he asked desperately.

The train came to a stop.

"Well, we have to get off this train unless you fancy a trip back to Manhasset. What was the point of following me all day anyhow?"

"I wanted to see what you were doing. If you went to the police, I knew I couldn't talk to you." There was a pause. "I'm glad I was wrong."

Was I reading more into that than he meant?

We walked off the train together. I should have felt better because I was back in the city, but instead I felt like Alice on the way down the rabbit hole. Glenn had a certain bunnyish quality, including a cute tail. Where was he leading me? I wondered.

"Let's see the letters."

"Right now?"

"Yeah. You've got them, right?"

"Not here, at my place."

"Fine. Your place it is."

There was a cross-armed staring contest that I won. Since he'd already told me he was withholding evidence, I wanted to see just how incriminating it was. Besides, I wanted to see what a love letter from Jana Crowley looked like.

We had to cross the main terminal with its never quite believable crowd of humanity. Hands were joined just to make sure we didn't lose each other. He took me down to the subway level where we picked up the A train. I figured we were going to the Upper West Side, a likely spot for the rich, sophisticated type who might like to keep a promising young fellow in Izods till the big break came. Ten years earlier, it would have been the East Village, but the city was going downhill and the Village was going downhill faster than any other neighborhood with the exception of Times Square.

It should have been some refurbished brownstone in the 70s or 80s but the train rolled right through those numbers and we were into the 100s with no indication that we were getting off the train. Harlem and Spanish Harlem, 125th, 145th.

"Where the hell are we going? It's a little late for a trip to the Cloisters."

"Here."

The filthy walls of the station said 179th Street.

"Washington Heights? I lived here when I was on unemployment for crying out loud."

Glenn looked embarrassed. I decided to tone it down.

"It's not that bad. I hear you can still get terrific deals here. Maybe your friend likes the ambiance."

"No."

"No what?"

"My friend lives on West 73rd, about a block and a half from the Dakota. We're going to New Jersey."

"Excuse me?"

I'd never been to New Jersey in my life.

"My mom's house," Glenn explained. "She thinks I'm taking acting classes at NYU and sharing a place with three guys from school. I go home every couple of weeks for a hot meal."

"Because Mom doesn't realize you're dining out every night. Is that it? She thinks the old mac and cheese with frankfurters is a big hit."

"Tuna casserole. I'm kind of staying with her this week because of Christmas. She likes me around for the holidays. Frank understands that."

"But he wouldn't understand a little laundry room tête-à-tête with your lady friend. He's the jealous type, isn't he?"

"He's a nice guy." Glenn protested. I was not convinced.

We were now walking through the long tunnel from the subway station to the George Washington Bridge–Fort Washington Avenue bus station. It stunk of urine. I wrinkled my nose as we passed a sleeping beggar.

"I've got to go to New Jersey to see this stuff?" My voice no doubt betrayed the anti-Jersey bias that every New Yorker, even a Brooklynite, is born with.

"Jersey's O.K.," he said softly. "It wasn't a bad place to grow up, it's just a good place to get away from."

I felt like I was in some bizarre game where the object was to see how many different means of transport one could use in a twenty-four-hour period. Car, train, subway, and now bus. Could the horse and buggy be far away?

A horse and buggy might have been faster. We had

to wait an awfully long time for that bus. We huddled with a band of other wretched refuse watching a monitor with a grainy view of an empty platform. To take up time, I got Glenn to tell me about himself.

I wanted to know how one twenty-three-year-old had gotten so sweet and so conniving at the same time. Listening to his autobiography, I could see my father, the publicity maven, shaking his head at the sheer mundanity of it and imagining how he would punch it up for public consumption.

Glenn Doyle grew up in stultifying suburbia, went to Catholic grammar school, and had gotten bitten by the acting bug during his first year in public high school. Mom and Dad split up at some point, but Glenn didn't seem to think this was terribly traumatic. It did result in Mom pulling him out of St. Dominic's after a unpleasant meeting with the monsignor. Mr. Doyle seems to have been the big practicing Catholic of the family (although not so practicing as to stay put after he fell in love with his secretary.) Mom was a good-natured Presbyterian from Terre Haute who managed to cream the old man in the genes and give Glenn her fair features.

He'd gone to Fairleigh Dickinson University to pursue his dream by majoring in theater. In his senior year, he starred in *Stop the World, I Want to Get Off*.

"You sing too?" I interrupted.

"Sing, dance, act. I'm the whole package," he said with self-confidence that skirted the edge of arrogance.

Whether it was the package or the wrapping, Mr. Frank Polaris was impressed when he saw the show. Soon after graduating, Glenn had a cushy spot to come home to after a long day of cattle calls. He didn't like lying to his mother, but he didn't think she would understand.

He was running this line past me when the bus finally showed up on the monitor. An impatient crowd went pushing and shoving into a small staircase to get to it.

At the top of the stairs, I was greeted by a blast of cold Hudson River air and a twinkly night view of the George Washington Bridge.

The bus started its journey to New Jersey. It was as dark as it had been when my day started with that first phone call. Only when I leaned against the window and closed my eyes did I realize how tired I was.

I was starting to doze off when I became aware that Glenn was getting awfully close, even for the cramped confines of a bus seat. His hand had crept from the space between us to the top of my leg and was working its way around to the inside of my thigh.

What the hell is going on here? was the first thought to jump into my brain. Several others followed in quick succession. *That feels really good. His hand is so warm. I can't do this. Why the hell not? This guy's currently running more scams than I've even thought of. He's trying to con me. Keep going. Please don't stop.*

"What do you think your doing?" I whispered.

He didn't bother to answer. I could put the whole thing to a stop any time I wanted to so I decided to see exactly what this handsome fellow had in mind.

I let my fingers do their own walking toward the buttons on his Levi's. There was certainly heat there and as far as I could tell the beast was waking up, if not yet raging.

The situation felt completely unreal, like the time I went to Elaine's on mescaline, which I would not recommend to anyone. I was caught up in a slow-motion, monochrome fantasy. I turned to face him, meaning to express my shock and outrage at his behavior. The bus was dark. I could barely see Glenn, but somehow his eyes grabbed mine and the next thing I knew we were locked in a tight embrace and kissing.

I pressed my hands against his leather jacket, wanting to push them into his very soul. I treasured the feeling of soft, sweet lips and a teasing tongue. Best of all was

I WILL SURVIVE

the knowledge that I absolutely shouldn't be doing this. The more I thought about all the reasons I shouldn't, such as my husband, the more exciting it got and the harder I found myself kissing back. When we came up for air, my lips felt tender and I half expected a round of applause from the other passengers.

The complete lack of reaction sparked a little common sense.

"O.K., pal, why are we playing this game?"

"Couldn't I just want you?"

He sounded hurt that I could doubt his sincerity.

"You could, but you don't. For one thing you've been getting it on with Jana..."

"No, I haven't. I wanted to, but she wouldn't."

"Come on, she was lit up like the Rockefeller Center tree. You expect me to believe that was just love?"

"She wouldn't do it. She said she was afraid."

"Of getting caught?"

"I don't think so. She'd get sad and far away, so I stopped asking. That's why I couldn't believe it when she started last night."

"She was afraid of getting disappointed again."

"I don't get it."

"Does the name Tony Falzerano mean anything to you?"

"Nope."

"Let's keep it that way. I still find it hard to believe you're all that hard up. I'm sure Frank would love to lend a helping hand and you probably don't lack for female admirers."

He smiled.

"So this sudden interest is flattering, but not convincing."

He took my hand and put it back on the bulge in his pants.

"O.K., that's somewhat convincing, but you have to level with me."

He looked out the window. We had left the bridge and were going down a highway.

"I just want you to nail that . . . that bastard."

"Thomas Brinkham?"

"Yeah." he said, sounding even younger than twenty-three, although he kissed like a guy who knew more about women than most twenty-three-year-olds. Of course, I'd never kissed a twenty-three-year-old, not even when I was twenty-three myself.

"You're sure he did it?"

"I'm sure."

He said it with such conviction that I could practically see the sense memory exercises.

"Why?"

He looked shocked that I would even ask.

"Because!"

"And the motive was jealousy?" I asked reasonably.

"Of course."

"Than why couldn't it have been your boyfriend?"

"He's not my—"

"Whatever he is. He was being deceived as surely as Thomas. He may be more attached than you think he is. Maybe Frank found out what was going on."

"How could he? Nobody knew."

"I have a few simple rules in life. Some people dig the Ten Commandments. Well, my rules are more applicable to the world we live in. One of those rules is that there's no such thing as a dumb blond, so please stop acting like one. If Thomas could know, Frank could know. Maybe he has woman's intuition, if you know what I mean."

"He wouldn't."

"Another rule: anyone at any time is capable of anything. Think about it. Tell me something else, are you bi or are you just jerking this guy around for the money?"

"That's a dirty crack."

"It's a dirty world," I said, believing it to my soul.

That shut down the conversation and any further hanky-panky until he indicated it was time to get off the bus. I hesitated at the door. I had no idea where we were. New Jersey was a foreign country to me. Nobody back in the real world knew where I was.

I was walking into the unknown with a man I hardly knew. Why? Just because he was pretty and Jana had painted his picture? He'd already told me he was there the night of the murder. What if there was no interruption? Maybe he'd strangled Jana. Maybe I was going to end up by the side of a road in this godforsaken place. Was I insane? Get right back on that bus and go home. Call the cops and tell them everything. That would be the day.

The bus driver was getting impatient. Glenn was gesturing for me to come with him. I told myself I had to do it to solve the case and stepped off the bus.

Talking was impossible. We'd bundled ourselves back into our individual cocoons against the cold. He led me away from the highway and into the darkness. I shivered with a mixture of fear, anticipation, and cold.

I saw the first house and actually thought, Merry Christmas. It was a street full of small homes and every single one of them was decorated with a display of multicolored bulbs. Some had blossomed into full house outlines complete with Santa and reindeer. It was the warmest, most welcoming thing I'd ever seen in my life. Menorahs just didn't have the same effect.

It was another long walk, but I distracted myself with a critical analysis of the lights and tried to figure out who had the money and who was just pretending. I only saw one actual crèche, so I was able to enjoy the secular holiday spectacle without too much fear of rampant suburban anti-Semitism. I wondered if a peek at any of the interiors would produce the sight of chestnuts roasting on an open fire.

We stopped in front of a small white house. The lights were used to outline the windows and the front door. It was a puny showing compared to the others on the same block. The house itself could have done with a new coat of paint. Glenn held up a warning hand and then his index finger. I nodded my head to show that I understood.

He walked up to the front door and opened it. I didn't see him use a key. I tried to imagine growing up in a neighborhood that safe. It made me shiver again. I waited until he appeared at the door with his scarf off.

"All clear," he called, and I went inside.

There was a tree in the living room with a hardy covering of tinsel. Cards were taped up around the inside of the window. No open fire. No chestnuts.

We went upstairs to Glenn's room. If the Museum of Natural History was going to have an exhibit of adolescent male in his natural habitat, it would look just like this. The obligatory posters were on the wall, the albums were on the floor, and the dresser drawer had a globe on top of it. I took another look around. Make that adolescent Catholic male. There was a crucifix in a prominent position on the wall over the bed. Probably an old one that had never been taken down after it ceased to be meaningful to the room's occasional inhabitant.

"Mom's not here. I think she's working tonight."

"What does she do?"

"She's a nurse. She works at Valley Hospital in Ridgewood."

I nodded my head as if that meant something to me. Then I relaxed enough to show my own ignorance.

"Where are we, anyway?"

"Teaneck."

"Oh."

"John Travolta's from Englewood. That's pretty close to here."

"And Bruce Springsteen's from New Jersey." I

I WILL SURVIVE

added, attempting to prove I wasn't completely ignorant about the Garden State.

"Yeah, but that's South Jersey," he said scathingly.

"Fine," I snapped, "Why don't you just show me those letters so I can get out of here."

"O.K." He seemed to be getting testy with me too. Then he caught himself and went back to his better angels. "Why don't you sit down?"

There was no place to do that except the bed. It was small and firm. The well-worn quilt was red and white. The bed was made so neatly that I suspected Mom the nurse had access to the room for cleaning purposes. In fact the exhibit might have to be canceled due to a lack of authentic dirty laundry strewn about. Of course, he wasn't really living here. His laundry was probably done by Frank's valet.

The love letters were secreted in a volume of Shakespeare.

The sight of the book opened up a door to the pain I was trying to avoid. I wondered if Jana had told her paramour about our thrilling days of hitchhiking through the British Isles when I taught her to appreciate Sweet Will. Maybe they hadn't gotten to the talking yet. Infatuation is about all the things that aren't verbal. It can't really be love until you've heard each other's stories. It's marriage when you've heard those stories so many times you can tell them to other people. I'd been infatuated many times, usually unrequited, but only with Jerry Barlow had I made it to the talking phase.

"*Romeo and Juliet*?" I asked, as he opened the book to the right place.

"*Antony and Cleopatra.*"

I felt the warmth of my Wales memory.

He handed me the letters and sat down next to me as I looked them over.

There were three pieces of paper. The first one was a postcard with a picture of the New York skyline, the kind you can buy at any schlock shop in town. It was postmarked December fourth and the mailing address was a P.O. box.

I held the card up to Glenn and pointed at the address. I raised my eyebrows questioningly.

"For my professional mail."

"Uh-huh."

The text was simple. She'd written, "*You light up my life*" in red pen and sketched a burning candle.

Letter number two was a page from her sketchpad, which had been folded up into tiny squares, presumably to fit into a legal-sized envelope. I was sure it was a preliminary sketch for the painting on Jana's easel. I always saw a touch of the high school notebook in Jana's sketches. Here it was more than a touch. She was thirty-one years old and Glenn Doyle, age twenty-three, had turned her back into a teen.

The only text on the page was "*Can't wait to see you again.*"

There was only one more. This one was a real letter, on Jana's monogrammed stationery. I myself had written hundreds of thank-you notes on that same stationery and forged Jana's signature for her. This was no forgery. I'd know her swooping capitals anywhere.

The letter was in a matching envelope and postmarked December 14th.

Dear Glenn,

I want to be with you more than anything. This is driving me mad. I hate lying to everyone. How can they look at me and not know how much I love you. Thomas is acting like the lord of the manor and I hate him for it.

Hate was underlined three times.

> *Come to the house on Saturday night. Tell the doorman your name is Reed Hadley and that you have an invitation. Meet me in the laundry room. I'll never get through this miserable party without seeing you.*

She had ended the letter with signed flourish and a lipstick kiss. I could feel the giddy haze she must have been in as well as the dark anger toward her husband.

I had a clear idea of what Jana was thinking and feeling, but I still didn't know who had killed her or why Glenn was quite so quick to accuse her husband. We could all agree that Thomas was a scumbag, but New York was full of those and they hadn't all disposed of their wives.

I put the documents on top of the book and laid it on the floor.

That lock of hair was falling across his forehead again. I tried to think of a good question.

"By the way, where'd you meet her?"

"Well, it wasn't at the candy store," he said. "Actually, you were there."

"Excuse me, pal. You know you're a looker, right?"

He nodded modestly.

"I think I'd remember seeing you before."

"Not when you were keeping your eye on that dachshund. I would too. She's beautiful."

"You know about Strudel? How could you? Ohhhh ... Son of a—wow."

I thought back to several times when Jana had accompanied to me the park when I walked Strudel. She'd bring her pad and sketch while I tended to the dog. One day in late November stood out, because the cold had already settled in for its brutal siege and I was taking my baby out later than usual. Jana and I were already dressed for a night of festivities, which meant that I was attempting to walk my dog while dressed for an opening.

My high heels were scraping on the paved walkways and the wind was attacking my knees. That was the day I came back to Jana's bench and found her distracted. She told me to go home, saying she'd meet me there before the limo showed up.

I looked where her gaze was and saw a Great Dane, a Rottweiller, and a Doberman, all attached by leash to one hand. I disapproved of professionals. I was adamant that dogs should be walked by their owners. I had barely looked at the face of the dog walker, but I remembered that he was a blond.

"You walk dogs?" I said numbly. "Couldn't you just wait tables like every other aspiring actor?"

"I like dogs better. I started out with Judy, that's Frank's Rottweiler. Frank recommended me to his friends. There's lots of busy people with dogs on the West Side. See, I'm not as kept as you think I am."

"Five bucks says you're not paying rent."

He looked down.

"I'd seen you in the park before, but that was the first time I'd seen you all dressed up. You looked great, like now," he said meaningfully.

"And you wound up with Jana?"

"Well she had that . . . you know?"

"I know." I sighed.

"But I thought you had better legs."

He put a hand on my knee. I'd never known that particular spot to be such a big erogenous zone, but something about that hand on that knee got me feeling weak and dizzy.

My loving husband at home didn't matter. The sheer fact that I shouldn't be doing it made doing it almost mandatory. Simon wanted me to stay away from Jake? Well, Glenn Doyle was younger, hotter, and didn't have a c-word of a wife riding roughshod over him.

I looked at the exhibit again. A KISS poster, a lobby card from *Apocalypse Now*, the cross over the bed. I

I WILL SURVIVE

thought about all the guys I hadn't had when I was that age because I wasn't one of the pretty girls who got those guys. I thought about Jana telling me to "take care of it." Maybe this was one of the things I needed to take care of.

I reached out to brush the hair off his forehead and we fell into each other's arms again, picking up the kiss from exactly the moment we had stopped on the bus. This time there was no reason to stop. I closed my eyes and let myself get swept away with it.

I took stock of the situation. I was lying on the bed with Glenn on top of me. We were still fully dressed and my skirt was hiked up. We were pressed together like teenagers in a backseat somewhere. The teenager in a backseat I had never been. My glasses were still on which must have been painful for the other party.

Before I took them off, I looked at his face. In lust, it looked less youthful, more like a man on the make. I remembered that he was conning his mom, his keeper and even his dead lover. He was an actor who still had to walk dogs. He had tracked me and lured me into his lair like a very cunning animal.

His goal was getting me to prove his accusation that Thomas Brinkham was the murderer.

I pushed him away so I could sit up. I took my glasses off and placed them on top of Shakespeare. It was the deep insecurity of Williamsburg High and unrequited crushes, rather than logic, that spoke.

"I'll get Thomas. You don't have to do this to convince me."

He stood up and walked to the door.

"I want to," he said, flipping off the light switch.

He went to the stereo and hit a button there. A scratch and a crackle, then the rich, bombastic music of Queen came on. The KISS poster glowed in the dark.

When Glenn came back to the bed, I didn't waste any more time on logic, guilt, or fear. It was pure sensation.

Glenn's velvety skin, his warm body. Clothes flying in various directions. Kisses that never seemed to stop or end. The heat between us driving everything else into oblivion. If he was conning me, he was doing a hell of a job.

I got on top and took him in slowly, sinking down to make sure I felt every inch, the kiss imitating the action below, both going on forever and ever or at least a whole side of a tape. I heard the line "rolling around in ecstasy." Oh yeah. I pushed myself against him harder. It was a good thing our mouths were locked or my propensity for screaming would have alerted the locals.

The end itself seemed endless. Since I couldn't scream, it seemed to expand through my whole body. Every cell was part of the explosion. It was a climax that ripped me apart and put me back together feeling younger and weaker and wiser.

It was so good that as soon as I got my breath back I broke into tears.

I cried for my lost friend Jana. I cried for all the shit I'd put up with from her and how much I loved her. I cried for all the things I would never be able to say to her. I cried with the knowledge that I would have to catch her killer and the fear that I wasn't good enough to do it.

It was the cry I needed to have as much as I needed the sex. All the feelings I'd been keeping in check with force of will and drugs since my father's funeral were coming out. Glenn held me through the whole thing. When I was all cried out and ready to fall asleep in his arms like a child or a kitten, he kissed me gently on the head.

Suddenly I was overwhelmed with guilt. I didn't feel bad for having betrayed Jerry sexually. I was in New Jersey, and one my rules was: out of town doesn't count. It was the crying on a strange shoulder. That should have been my husband and no rule would compensate for that betrayal.

I WILL SURVIVE

I reached for my glasses. Putting them on was my way of saying the party's over, back to the real world.

Before I could look for my pantyhose, there was a knock on the door. Glenn and I froze.

"Glenn, are you in there?"

The knob twisted and the door opened a crack.

Mom was home.

"Uh, yeah Mom. I'm just getting dressed. I was taking a nap. We had a late rehearsal. How was work?"

I gave him the "What are you, nuts?" look and he made a helpless gesture, like "Whaddaya want me to do."

"Oh, the usual. Have you eaten yet?"

"Uh, no."

"I was going to whip up a tuna casserole."

"That sounds great. I'll be down in just a minute, O.K.?"

"O.K. Is everything all right? You sound funny."

"I'm fine, Ma."

Footsteps walked away. Why hadn't we heard them coming? Never mind that.

"You didn't lock the door?" I hissed.

"I didn't think of it. Let's get you out of here."

"How?"

"I'll deal with it."

Dressing was as hurried as undressing had been, although for less pleasant reasons. I found myself giggling. Glenn glared at me.

"Oh, it's the vicar," I whispered, imitating a British accent.

The actor had to smile at my allusion to stereotypical farce.

I was happy to note that the shorter hair was easier to repair than the old mop. I still looked unkempt, but not so bad that I couldn't blame it on wind rather than seriously hot sex.

Glenn made a few repairs too. He did something with

hairspray and a brush. The hair that had been flopping over his forehead now stood up in a blond salute.

Heels, gloves, coat. Ready to go. I looked at Glenn.

"Now what?"

He was wrapping his scarf, but not going for the full mummy look.

He led me out of his room to the top of the stairs. He went down and stood by the front door.

"Mom . . . I'm going out for a few minutes. I'm going over to Mike's house. He wants to borrow one of my albums for his party. I'll be right back."

It sounded pretty lame to me, but maybe Glenn's mother was used to believing improbable things.

"O.K. The tuna will be done in about fifteen minutes."

"Make sure you save some for me."

He gestured for me come down the stairs. I ran at top speed, nearly twisting my ankle in the process, and barreled out the front door. There was an ugly yellow Duster in the driveway.

"Get in. I'll drive you home."

I would have protested my independence, but I couldn't face any more public transportation.

Once we were in the car, the giggles caught up with me again. The emotional ups and downs of the day were now replaced with relief and Glenn started catching it too. I hoped that my chauffeur was obeying the rules of the road, because if any cops had a mind to stop us, they would have busted us for some kind of intoxication, even though I was stone-cold sober.

After we crossed the bridge, I realized the evening was going to end when he dropped me off and I wasn't ready for that.

"Hey, take me downtown. I'll buy you dinner."

"I should treat," he offered.

"You already have," I smirked, "and besides, you're driving."

Mom's tuna salad was apparently forgotten.

We went to Theater District where God smiled on our endeavor by providing a parking place only six blocks from where I wanted to eat.

"Hello beautiful, beautiful, beautiful city," I exulted. Nothing like a day on Long Island and a night in New Jersey to make me remember how much I loved the Big Apple. Broadway. The theaters, the Christmas windows. It was just the thin-blooded Upper East Side that had been making me crazy. "My little town blues..."

Glenn picked up the lyric so he wouldn't have to listen to my lousy singing. He did a fairly credible Sinatra, including that long hold of "a-a-a-nd" that led into "if I can make it there..."

"You're very talented."

"I know."

"Humility is such a charming quality." I commented as we reached Serenissima, the hopping, happening Italian restaurant on West 44th and Sixth Avenue, where John Stewart, the cuddly male model and boyfriend of my hairdresser, presided over towering plates of pasta that were inevitably served to pencil-thin models who wouldn't eat them. It was the kind of paradox that made for a New York success story.

I'd be lucky to get in without a reservation, but I thought I was having a lucky day and it would be worth a try. I was starving and had it in my head that it would be better to go home smelling like fettuccine Alfredo than smelling like sex with a stranger in New Jersey.

There was the usual hubbub by the door, but John spotted me and waved me inside. It was like being on the list at Studio 54 in the old days, which were only three years ago. I'd plugged the restaurant in *New York Night* and I was a good client of Marc's although I was reconsidering that given the recent butcher job.

I did the kiss-kiss number with John.

"Hi, sweetie. Where have you been. I haven't seen

you in ages. So sad about Jana. She was a witch, but she was magic. What happened to your hair?"

"Your sweet babboo happened to my hair."

"Well then it looks great. And who is the blond? He is simply divine."

"And taken. Does the name Frank Polaris mean anything to you?

"Money. West-side import/export, antiques."

"Anything shady?"

"Not that I've heard, but he's not glam enough to really warrant any dish. However that kid . . . ooh la la."

"Mais oui, pal. Give me a table for two and something with lots of garlic."

On the way to our seat, we ran smack-dab into Cleo Coltraine, the model.

Seeing her in person was always a shock. She was so alive on the glossy pages, it seemed impossible she could live and breathe in the real world. Yet there she was looking like a magnificent animal barely able to contain herself from pouncing. Actually that was all *Vogue* hype. She did look gorgeous, but she also seemed edgy and distracted. It was impossible not to notice the slightly emaciated look endemic to the trade.

Marc had told me she was a junkie. Heroin not being in my particular drug repertoire, I wasn't sure exactly how to tell. She had long sleeves on, so track marks weren't showing. The major indicator that something might be wrong with her was the fact that she was grasping her companion's arm as though she were afraid of falling over, but maybe that was just the stiletto heels.

The companion was shorter than she was. His name should have been Svengali, but it was Gustave Klausman. He had a German name, vampiric features, and a generically European accent. He was either an artist who dabbled in fashion photography or vice versa depending on whom you listened to.

His artistic pictures were shown in galleries and his

fashion work was in every major magazine. Everybody (meaning everybody in the art and fashion scenes who liked to gossip, which meant everybody in the art and fashion scenes) knew that he had discovered Cleo with a different name and ten more pounds, waiting tables in Allentown, Pennsylvania, although nobody ever explained what he was doing in Allentown in the first place.

He'd taken her to New York, put her on a diet, and the first time he pointed a camera at her, a star was born. The initial set of photos to hit the streets were notorious for their kinky symbolism and Cleo was tagged "The New Bettie Page."

I vaguely remembered her dark divinity hovering in the background that night at the Whitney when Jana had reduced Charlotte LaFayette to tears. In fact, we'd been at a lot of the same parties, but we'd never really talked beyond the most idle party chitchat. She probably thought I was just Jana's flunky, if she thought anything about me at all.

That was before the murder. Now she pulled herself away from Gustave and grabbed me in a full-frontal embrace as though I were her long lost sister. I found myself overwhelmed by the closeness of her lithe body as well as her perfume, something dark and poignant with a heavy note of citrus.

"Oh my god. It's so horrible about Jana."

It was of course, but I didn't know that Cleo and Jana were all that close either. She seemed genuinely distraught. She could barely construct coherent sentences. She had a broad Pennsylvania accent. God came out sounding more like "guard."

"Do they know anything? The cops, I mean? Like, who did it?"

I took a step backward. I needed to get away from her scent and her intense demeanor. I didn't want to drown in her.

"Don't you read the *Post*?"

"Just Page Six."

She wasn't a blond, so I didn't have to give her the benefit of the doubt on the brains. Maybe she really was as stupid as she acted. I decided to be playful.

"Well, I hear the cops think it was someone close to her."

"Wow, that's awful. Having someone turn on you like that."

Even as I was congratulating myself on my superior intellect, I found myself drawn into the blackness of her eyes. They were breathtakingly deep, but also sad. Up close, I could tell that she was wearing quite a bit of makeup under her eyes, the kind used to cover up dark circles.

I felt a nudge and remembered that Glenn was standing next to me. I made introductions. Gustave shook hands and uttered continental pleasantries without ever taking his eyes off Cleo. The vibe between them was just too creepy. There's nothing wrong with making the color black a hallmark of your wardrobe, but as a couple, they looked like a Charles Addams cartoon.

It was time to stir up some shit.

"Cleo, if you're not busy tomorrow, let's do Elaine's."

"Yeah. I want to. Because, you know, if I can help or anything, I want to."

Gustave must have had smoke coming out of his ears that only Cleo could smell because she looked at him and got scared by what she saw there. She quickly resumed her grip on his arm.

"You know what? I just remembered. Tomorrow. I've got a photo shoot for *Cosmo*. I might get the cover."

"No problem."

"Thanks."

The conversation had clearly run its course and then

some, but we were still stuck there, like actors waiting for a cue.

John saved us by noting loudly, "Your table's waiting." No wonder he made as much in tips as he did modeling.

We had a good table, which meant that the couple sitting next to us were only halfway in our laps. I could see Gustave making a call from the phone at the bar. I looked for Cleo. She was missing in action until she came back into view from the direction of the bathroom. I couldn't tell if she was stumbling, or if I just thought she was, thanks to the power of hairdresser gossip. They departed arm in arm.

I turned my attention to the large plate of food that had arrived at the table while I was making my observations. Unfortunately, Mrs. Bridge and Tunnel next to us insisted on going on so fulsomely about "A Chorus Line," that I lost my appetite.

Glenn had a strange, faraway look in his eyes and wasn't making much of a dent in his dinner either. Maybe he was thinking about tuna casserole and the fact that his mom had had plenty of time to call Mike and find out that he wasn't at Mike's house and never had been.

"Let's get out of here," I said. "You don't have to drive me home. I can get a cab."

"It won't take that much longer. I want to make sure you get home safely."

I let him have his delusions of chivalry, but I made sure that I settled the bill.

We had to get back to the car. It was a silent walk. I was too drained to come up with any more witty banter. One day can take a lot out of you, I thought. One hell of a day.

The car was parked in an alley off Ninth Avenue. It was far enough from the theaters that the crowds were sparse and the lights belonged to the peep shows and dirty bookstores that couldn't get prime real estate in Times Square. One of them had a small Christmas tree in the front window that was festooned with traditional lights and garlands as well as dildos and handcuffs. There was an angel on top who seemed unaware of triple-X-rated goings-on around her. From across the street I could see the sign in the window: ERNIE'S EM-PORN-IUM.

Glenn broke his silence.

"What about us?" he asked plaintively.

I was so taken aback by this ludicrous question right out of a daytime drama that I stayed in place even though the light had turned to green. I couldn't keep myself from responding like a character out of the same bad script.

"There is no us. My name is not Mrs. Jones and we do not have a thing going on." I resisted the temptation to say, "We'll always have Teaneck." Instead I tried to soothe him.

"Look, you've got your career and your mother and Frank Polaris to deal with. I've got this murder. We'll need to stay in touch. I'll meet you in the park . . ."

As I said "park," I stepped off the curb, completely caught up in role. I was vaguely aware of the light turning, but assumed I could make it. I heard squealing tires, but thought that was just typical, bad New York driving. Glenn and I were halfway across the street and I was still talking when Glenn screamed,

"Watch out!" and threw his arm back to push me out of the way.

He was strong. I wound up getting shoved back to the curb and hitting the ground hard. He looked back to make sure I was safe. He didn't have enough time to get himself completely out of the way of the car that was careening toward him. I could only scream as I saw what was happening, but there was nothing I could do about it.

The car caught him with its front corner and the impact sent him flying into the window of Ernie's.

"Noooooooo," I hollered, as if I could stop the shattering of the glass by making enough noise. I thought it was going to work. For a split second he seemed to be suspended in midair and nothing happened. Then the window exploded into a million pieces and Glenn went through it, landing right on the tree. I heard a noise like bugs being zapped by the light at a barbecue.

The electricity in Ernie's display wasn't meant to accommodate a large male flying into his tree. First it shorted, then it exploded with a loud *pop!* and the next thing I knew the store window was illuminated by flames instead of bulbs and I was still screaming.

"Help!!!! Help!!!! Help!!!!!"

I was lying on the ground. I'd hit the back of my head so hard I couldn't see straight. Then I realized it was because I had lost my glasses in the fall. I didn't care.

"Help!!!! Call the ambulance. Call the cops. Do something!!!!"

I couldn't scream any louder. I was losing my voice and consciousness along with it. I knew I was about to pass out, but I fought to hold on. I had to get out of there.

"Fuck, fuck, fuck," I tried to yell. Nobody heard me, although it was certainly appropriate to the crowd that was forming.

First were the patrons of Ernie's escaping the fire. Some of them were still zipping up their pants. They were followed by the Ninth street hookers who had been plying their trade in the dark. I heard various sirens, so I knew that help was coming. *Please let them be in time. Please don't let him die.*

The crowd was thickening with the addition of gawkers from the Theater District. With all the talk of blasé New Yorkers, it was nice to know that you could still get a nice audience together for a fire and a shattered plate-glass window and one burning young actor.

I couldn't see, I couldn't think, and I had a major attack of pain and guilt coming. I wanted to lie down and die right there.

Take care of it.

"Not now Jana. I've had a beast of a day and—"

I stopped when I realized that she couldn't hear me. I started crawling backward like a crab. That way I was able to get through the crowd that was surging forward all around me. I must have gone two blocks like that. My hands were raw from scraping the sidewalk and had gotten bits of pebble and glass embedded in them. My skirt was torn. I kept going till I was free of the crowd. I laid there looking like a drunk or a corpse, till I could get myself off the ground. It took more than one try.

I stood there, still feeling wobbly, and assessed the situation. Being dizzy and not having my glasses was a particularly bad combination. At least my shoes were still on.

I should have been grateful just to be alive, but then I would have had to thank Glenn for taking the time to save me, the time which might have cost him his life. That was too painful, so I concentrated on movement.

Clicking my heels three times would have been the preferred method of transport or maybe having Scotty beam me to 65th Street, but I had to settle for the means at hand. Blurry instinct got me to 52nd Street and Broadway, where I made out the lovely mottled yellow that indicated a subway station.

I ran down the stairs, risking my own life and limb, not to mention those of anyone who got in my way. I had tokens, somewhere in my bag, but didn't want to futz around looking for them. I jumped the turnstile, showing more athleticism than one would have expected from a slightly battered broad in a tattered tight skirt.

Another flight of stairs took me to the platform just

I WILL SURVIVE

as a train was coming. I ran onto it without thinking. As the doors closed, I was gripped by a simultaneous feeling of delicious relief and horrible guilt. The hideous set of noises, the squealing, the shattering, and worst of all that disgusting noise as the lights sputtered and shorted out. Glenn must have been electrocuted right there.

Why had this happened? I wondered. A bunch of answers came to my mind and I didn't like any of them.

I found myself huddled over in anguish, not really crying, but making noises rooted in pain and remorse. Any self-respecting New Yorker would have had the sense to stay far away from me, but I could sense someone approaching, probably a tourist. I sat up, prepared to give her my best "I'm a New York psycho and you don't want to fuck with me" look. Before I could freeze her blood, I looked out the window of the train and saw something that froze mine.

The station we were coming into was 42nd. I didn't want to see 42nd Street. The numbers were going the wrong way. I was headed downtown.

"Godammit!" I exploded in anger, successfully driving off the would-be good Samaritan. I could have gotten out and just picked up a train going in the other direction, but I had another idea. When you're on a downtown train, sometimes there's nothing you can do but go all the way down.

I rode the A train all the way down by Varick Street. I was going to see my other "boss," Harvey Kleinberg, editor in chief, not to mention publisher, of that illustrious beacon of journalism, *New York Night*.

Walking in that area at night represented a self-destructive drive, second only to a midnight stroll through Central Park. The barely lit streets had ghosts of the pickle factories and pushcarts that had once been part of a community. Now there were empty warehouses and apartments so scuzzy you could hardly foist one off on a poor immigrant. It was a neighborhood of rats, dope fiends, and squatters living below the radar of polite society, which made it perfect for Harvey.

He had a basement apartment in the middle of a dark alley. I pushed the secret code on the buzzer, which was the rhythm of " 'Scuze me while I kiss the sky." "Shave and a haircut" would have been inappropriate. Harvey hadn't seen either one since before the Tet offensive.

The woman who lived with Harvey let me in. I had never been completely clear as to her function. She acted as secretary, housekeeper, and errand runner. I knew they shared a mattress on the floor, but I'd never picked up any sexual heat between them. Maybe it would have interfered with planning the revolution.

"Hi Minnie," I said as I walked inside.

Minnie wasn't her name. I called her that because on the rare occasions when she spoke, it came out in mousy squeaks. She always appeared to be scurrying somewhere, and her single dark braid reminded me of a tail.

"He's driving tonight," she squeaked before disappearing into the room that wasn't the kitchen and didn't have the mattress on the floor. That room was the "pressroom." I could hear the machinery running. Another issue of *New York Night* was getting ready to hit the stands.

I sat down on a particularly lumpy couch and called out to Minnie.

"Can you get in touch with him? It's an emergency."

"I'll try the dispatcher."

"Wait a minute, let me use the phone first." There was a beat-up pink Princess phone on the floor near the mattress. I heard a dial tone although I doubted that Harvey was paying any kind of legitimate phone bill.

I had to call and find out if Glenn was alive. Call who? I wondered as I helplessly stared at the phone. Call the fire department and ask if the body flying through the window in the porn fire had survived? Call every hospital in town and ask if they had a very handsome young man who'd been electrocuted on a Christmas tree decorated with condoms? Call the police department and explain why I hadn't stuck around to answer questions?

While I dithered, the dial tone changed to a harsh buzzing. Minnie was watching me patiently, her eyes obscured by thick lenses, thicker than the ones that had hit the street when I did. I wondered if they'd been picked up and used as evidence to link me to the event.

I handed Minnie the phone and listened halfheartedly as she called the dispatcher for the unlicensed taxi service that Harvey drove for.

Driving a New York City gypsy cab was the perfect job for Harvey Kleinberg, the perfect underground man. From the couch, I could look into the soulful, doomed eyes of Harvey's hero, Che Guevara. Huey Newton was on the other wall. The room smelled of old pot, moldy books, and printer's ink.

My professional association with Harvey had started in the spring, when I was stuck in a corner of Jackie Vogel's office, trying to write a book. We were still living, if you could call it that, on the Island, and Jerry was spending his days trying to find an apartment for us. The weather was lovely, but I couldn't write. I started taking long walks. I told myself I was looking for inspiration. What I found was one of my oldest loves, the movies.

I went to a lot of matinees. The lights, the sounds, the colors. It was all preferable to dealing with the tyranny of the blank page. I had nothing to say, so why should I bore anybody with it? I think Jackie and her staff were happy to have me out from under their feet.

That particular day I was at a scratch theater in Times square that was wedged between two XXX theaters seeing a double feature of *Knightriders* and *Dawn of the Dead*.

Knightriders was an interesting little movie in which

a group of outsiders have formed a family where they travel the country having "jousts" on motorcycle. They live by a chivalrous code and take care of each other. It reminded me of my best days in the anti-war movement. The most disturbing part came when the group was invaded by the outside world.

The leader of the group was a Christ figure, which I considered unnecessary, but the intensity of the actor's performance got to me regardless. I was between movies in an empty theater, writing down my thoughts in a notebook, when I was interrupted by a raspy voice.

"What did you think?"

I looked up and saw a face that was mostly beard. For a second, I thought I was being visited by the ghost of Karl Marx. He was wearing denim overalls over a tie-dyed tee-shirt and carrying a knapsack.

He looked disreputable in the extreme and I wasn't thrilled about being approached.

On the other hand, I've never been shy about sharing my opinions.

"The symbolism was over the top, but the acting redeemed it. The guy who played the King should have a great future."

Then I walked out, giving up my chance to see *Dawn of the Dead*, which was too much a description of how I felt those days to be a good choice for entertainment.

The guy followed me out of the theater. I stood outside blinking in the sunlight and contemplating the horror of going back to Jackie's office.

"I don't go that much. It's a waste of time, but I know some of the people who made this one. Romero's a friend of a friend."

"That's nice," I said, walking away.

"Don't I know you from somewhere?"

I spun around, ready to let him have it, but was taken aback by the shock of recognition.

"Oh my god, I think you do."

We stared at each other and I figured it out first.

"Your name is . . . Harvey, isn't it? You know Les Hutchins, right?"

"Yeah. You're his friend . . . the one he was going to movies with when he should have been at meetings."

Les had been one of my buddies at UC Berkeley, when I was majoring in pot and politics. Les's political affiliation was with the Black Panthers and he was big on leafleting and propaganda. He also had a thing for movies and had been known to miss a demonstration if there was a sufficiently compelling show at the University Theater.

"Last time I talked to Les, he was in Chicago doing something for Jesse Jackson."

"Yeah." Harvey snorted derisively.

I'd met Harvey at some anti-war demonstrations during the early Seventies. I didn't see a lot of him because he was at Columbia while I was enjoying the mellower climate of Berkeley, California. I remembered the big rally in Sacramento, for which he had flown out just to show his loathing for Governor Reagan. He made an impression on me then by telling me he had quit SDS because it wasn't radical enough.

If that was his opinion of SDS, you can imagine how he felt about me, a mere left-wing liberal who thought that everything would be O.K. if we could just get George McGovern elected in 1972. He seemed to think I hadn't paid sufficient dues because I wasn't in Chicago getting tear-gassed during the 1968 Democratic National Convention.

It wasn't my fault that I was in the hospital with pneumonia at the time.

I got hit on the head with a billy club during the Sacramento demonstration and spent the night in jail. It's a wonder I ever got to a class at all, considering how much time I was putting in on the McGovern campaign and the anti-war stuff. I thought I was doing enough. Harvey Kleinberg's sneer had told me I wasn't.

He was right of course. McGovern lost, the war went on, and I cracked up. My answer had been to run away from the country for a while. Harvey had gone right on fighting.

Standing there on the street, I wanted to run away from him. I didn't want to remember the past. I missed Berkeley. I missed my dreams. Jerry Falwell and his ilk were taking over and there wasn't anything I could do about it. Harvey, looking like a refugee from a commune, was a walking rebuke.

On the other hand, I didn't want to go back to the office and the typewriter either. It was one of the first warm spring days of the year, a nice day to sit in the park, eat a hot dog, and reminisce. At its height, the movement was massive, but incestuous. From our respective coasts, we had known a lot of the same people. A lot of them weren't with us anymore, either in spirit or body. Too many had been lost to guns, prison, drugs, and the lure of Republican respectability.

I assured Harvey that while I had learned to function in polite society, I had never been tempted to change my party affiliation.

He hit me with "Whoever you vote for, government wins," which I thought was a low blow in the sloganeering department.

I told him about my adventures in crime solving. That interested him, because I'd thwarted the cops in both cases. I described the heartbreak associated with my writing about the murders and broken dreams of publication.

"You write?"

"Yeah. One book. Various short stories. Of course, nothing's seen the light of day, thanks to the combined treacheries of the police and the publishers. Talk about

I WILL SURVIVE 145

a gruesome twosome. Mostly I go to the movies and write scathing reviews in my journal."

"Here. Look at this."

He delved into his knapsack and came up with a small newspaper, which he handed to me. As I perused it, I noticed how small it really was, just four pages of newsprint. The banner said *New York Night*.

If I expected a tabloid devoted to the beautiful people, I didn't get it. Of course that wasn't to be expected from a Harvey Kleinberg. The "news" stories were complete propaganda, devoted to the following principles: the Republicans were scum, the Democrats were pathetic, El Salvador was the new Vietnam, and Ronald Reagan was evil incarnate. I was willing to go along with most of that. I still considered myself a Democrat, but had sat out the last few elections being wrapped up in my own angst.

The other purpose for *New York Night* could be found in the crudely drawn ads on the sides of the pages. By peppering his creation with plugs for all manner of local restaurants and clubs, Harvey kept himself fed with as little exchange of capital as possible.

His only two "real" jobs were driving an unlicensed cab and occasionally working shifts with the sanitation department. It amused him to infiltrate such a symbolic part of the city infrastructure, and the work provided excellent scrounging opportunities.

Other than that he lived by his wits and worked the welfare system for every penny he could get, happily accepting checks from the government he wanted to bring down. He was deeply offended by Reagan's proposals to cut off "freeloaders" such as himself. Scrounge, scam, and sneak was the name of his game, as well as sounding a lot like a law firm.

"This is so groovy," I said, handing it back to him. "I wish I was still doing stuff like this."

"You could be," he said enthusiastically, which is

how I became the entertainment editor of *New York Night*.

I started out with movie reviews. I had a backlog of vitriol just waiting to hit the presses. So what if I didn't get paid? Seeing the words in print was its own reward. I even helped with "distribution," which meant leaving piles of the paper in various bars and coffee shops as well as making drops near newsstands selling more respectable publications.

The paper was free. Charging for it would have compromised Harvey's principles. Besides, who would pay for the damn thing?

I also fulfilled a long-standing ambition to become a rock critic. With the demise of the big discos, there was a resurgence of small, scuzzy clubs, many of which advertised in *New York Night*. I attended and reported on shows by such up and comers as Detox and D.T.s, whose level of punk volume was tough on my ears, and I'd been to the Fillmore West when the music mattered.

I liked them though. I understood the anger and I knew in my heart why the party of the seventies was over, even though I could have danced through another ten years.

After Jana's return allowed me to infiltrate the East Side, I expanded my journalistic duties. I started writing a gossip column about the big names I was coming into contact with. It was one outlet for my simmering resentment.

If my movie reviews were bitchy, then my gossip was pure venom. To avoid lawsuits or violence, I used blind items for the really hardcore stuff such as calling a local news hen a "hosebeast" who was "sucking her way to the top." I didn't really expect any of my subjects to see such a low-ticket item, but I was taking a risk. Just to make things interesting, I increased the risk that it might happen. *New York Night* came to the Upper East Side.

I WILL SURVIVE

I started leaving piles near some of the classier news shops, the ones that specialized in newspapers from around the world. You never knew who might come in to buy the *Times of London* or *Izvestia* and pick up a copy of *New York Night* near the door, especially when it had the timeless allure of a sign on top that said, "Take one free."

As I sat on Harvey's couch, listening to the presses roll, I reflected on the problems of this particular form of journalism. The paper came out only when the editor in chief could get together enough paper and ink. This meant that there was a certain lag between the "news" and the time it hit the street. For instance the issue that had been available for the last few weeks was out-of-date.

That was the issue that Rhonda must have seen. I'd penned an item, "Which star on the education scene is having an artful relationship with an East Side beauty? Is this living up to his principles?"

There were a limited number of people in the city who had heard of the Simone School, much less knew who the principal was, and even fewer of them might put it together with Jana Crowley, but certain people would. Tony's wife had picked up the wrong piece of paper at the wrong time. Maybe she had just glanced at it while relining her parakeet's cage.

By the time that issue hit the streets, I already knew that the "affair" was over and that Tony's studly aura was a sham. The follow-up story was currently being printed. It was written in a similar style. I described the romance as a "flop" and said that " the artistic glamour girl has turned her sights to younger, greener, and possibly firmer pastures." Too bad Rhonda hadn't seen that before she decided to make a scene. I'd have to drop a copy near her apartment house.

Maybe that would fix her marriage. Unless it was too late. Unless she'd done something irrevocable in a fit of anger. Maybe something terminal, like killing Jana out of jealousy. That started the roller coaster ride in my head again.

So many suspects, so many motives. Thomas, Tony, Rhonda, Charlotte, Max, me, Jerry. Sex, humiliation, personal jealousy, professional jealousy. Throw Glenn Doyle into the mix and back out with the velocity of that car hitting him. Who had been in the car? Who were they aiming for? Over and over and over. It made my teeth hurt.

Harvey walked in, wearing a long woolen greatcoat that could have come from the estate of Hermann Goerring. His beard had frost on the ends, making him resemble a depraved Father Christmas.

He took one look at me and started rolling a joint. I accepted gratefully. This whole case had the feeling of unreality about it. Even seeing Glenn go through that window had been more like a bad trip than a real experience. As I held the smoke in my lungs, I could feel myself stepping into a space where I could make some sense of it all.

Harvey checked on the progress of the printing and then came out to join me on the couch. He also took the joint, for a deep inhalation. He nodded as an indication for me to begin and it all came spilling out.

I was able to get through it much faster than I had with Simon. Harvey knew what had been going on since Jana came back, so I didn't have to bring him up to speed. I just started with the murder and told him everything that had happened since, including the encounter with Glenn and its horrible aftermath.

He passed the pot back to me. It was a good high. I could see everything and still appreciate the seriousness of it. No stereotypical maniacal laughter or even giggling.

"So here's what I think, Harvey. I've got this horrible feeling about this Frank Polaris guy. What if he figured out what's going on with Jana and Glenn and he's the jealous type and he takes Jana out of the picture. Then he puts a tail on his boy who happens to be tailing me. He knows that Glenn and I made it, so I have to go too. Or maybe even both of us. I don't know. It's all too crazy. Someone had to be following us to know that we'd be right there."

"I don't know. I see wackos in cars all the time. Maybe someone just drove like a schmuck and didn't want to stick around to see the consequences."

"I think they were aiming the car. Oh my god. There's going to be a corpse in the morgue, just like Jana's. I'm the only person, except maybe the killer, who can connect them. I'm the smartest person in New York and I don't know anything."

"You know. You just don't know enough."

"And what about Gustave and Cleo?" I asked, as if Harvey knew, much less cared.

"What about them?"

"They were acting so weird."

"From what you've told me, they always act weird."

"Yeah. He's bizarre and she's—"

"A nutcase?" Harvey said helpfully.

"A very alluring nutcase."

"If you say so." He took a deep toke, the kind that keeps you from talking and when it does you can barely get the words out. "You know..." He tried again "You know what I think?"

We had achieved that level of communication that can only be achieved by intellectual equals at the same level of stoned awareness. I knew exactly what he thought and I didn't like it one bit.

"No, Harvey. Don't say that."

"Why not?"

"Because those two wouldn't be able . . . ."

"But the big guys might. You fucked with some heavy hitters."

"We still don't know that for sure. And what would it have to do with Jana's murder?"

"You know, Marti, the world didn't revolve around Jana Crowley."

"Mine did," I muttered. "Give me that." I took a hit. "Shit shit shit." That was the mantra for the whole case.

Harvey thought whoever was driving the car was out to get me, not Glenn. It would have been retaliation for a drug bust. The bust probably wasn't my fault, and even if it was, it wasn't.

Film criticism and slimy innuendo were so much fun, I had decided to expand my poison pen activities by writing personality profiles. I started by immortalizing my hairdresser, Marc Rappaport. I noted his status as stylist to the stars, as well as his tendency to be a prima donna. He was so thrilled that he offered to frost me for free.

A week into that hideous December, Harvey had turned me on to the biggest scoop of my journalistic career. A movie crew was filming in the city. A major Hollywood production starring Dudley Moore was being shot. That wasn't news. Mayor Koch was hot to get films made in New York. Good public relations, he thought, even after some thieves ripped off Warner Bros. to the tune of forty thousand bucks' worth of equipment.

The interesting thing about this particular film crew was the presence of Kirk Watson. When Harvey told me that, I gasped. It might not have impressed Abigail Beecher, my journalism teacher during a brief stint at UNLV, but to me it was like hearing that Superman or the Abominable Snowman was in the city.

I'd first heard of Kirk Watson as a whispered rumor back in 1969, when I took a cinema course at Quincy U. According to the myth, Kirk Watson was a guy who could get a job on any film being shot in any location

I WILL SURVIVE

that he wanted to see. He never picked up a camera or actually appeared on screen. He was hired and prized for his ability to score drugs anywhere in the world. He worked through a mixture of his own charm, a universal network of contacts, and the uncanny knack that dope fiends have to sniff each other out in a crowd anywhere from Brooklyn to Borneo.

I wasn't surprised that Harvey knew him, but it was hard to believe that Kirk would actually sit for an interview. Of course, I wasn't a typical member of the fourth estate. The official policy of *New York Night* was as fervently pro-drug as its editorial staff.

Kirk Watson wasn't his real name of course. Asking for that was strictly a no-no. There were other conditions. The interview took place in Central Park, by the fountain, where the conga players assembled every afternoon. The arctic spell was in full flower and my ears were burning with the pain of cold, but this was for journalism, after all. O.K., I admit it, I wanted to meet the guy.

The man who came up to me and said, "Let's get physical," which was not a come-on but rather an example of Harvey's deranged sense of humor in devising a code word, was nothing like what I expected.

I hoped my expression didn't betray the disappointment I felt. I'd been waiting for a counterculture superstar and instead I saw a middle-aged straight arrow. He had on a belted trench coat. His hair was red and not terribly thick. It was cut short. His face, an inverted triangle with a weak chin, was clean shaven. There were a few scars, but nothing that couldn't be explained from a life that might have included one or two youthful barroom brawls or service in the military. The sense of weariness might have come from a lifetime of commuting from some bedroom town in New Jersey.

Then he started talking in a hardboiled, staccato style that made him sound like he was chewing gum, even though he wasn't. His origins were an off-limits topic, and I couldn't pick out any particular accent. He just sounded tough.

The noise of the drumming was to thwart any potential snoops, spooks, or DEA narcs who might be inclined to put an end to his illustrious career. To the background of Latin rhythms, he told me about twenty years of circumventing the law, local custom, and the occasional bad mother-fucker, to provide the cream of the Hollywood crop with their favorite chemical divertissements.

He dished dirt on the stars that would have put Marc, John and every single one of the club kids I knew to shame. I had never imagined that Marisa Berenson did *that*. He knew things about stars and their habits that Miss Rona would have killed for. It was too cold to take notes, but this wasn't the kind of stuff I would ever forget.

He prided himself on never pimping for the celebrities. He said he was happy to get them heroin, pot, coke, or whatever else it took to get through the day, but they had to get their own playmates. Even the *wunderkind* producer who had offered him a percentage of the gross to set him up with a famous East German madam who was rumored to be former lover of highly placed members of Hitler's regime.

Kirk spoke most fondly of Bangkok. He went on at length about his adventures with a girl named Keiko from the House of the Blue Lantern who was also the mistress of his major opium connection in the region. The whole thing sounded mad and dangerous and full of intoxicated excitement. Kirk acknowledged trying and enjoying most of the goodies he had supplied to his clients.

It was getting dark and even colder. The drummers had left. We walked toward the 72nd Street exit on the west side of the park where the grim facade of the Dakota still haunted the landscape. He turned to me and asked casually,

"So, where do you get your stuff?"

I was surprised by the question. I was just a user and a small-time one at that. What connections could I have that weren't already in his little black book? It was time for me to get back to the East side and get dressed for an evening on the town with Jana, but Kirk had been more than generous with his time. How could I withhold information?

By then, I'd given up the thrill of scoring weed on the street for the ironic charm of "respectable" settings to get drugs. Dr. Max Jacobson had gone to that big dispensary in the sky, but the swanky neighborhoods had no shortage of expensively attired quacks with a quick draw on the prescription pad. Justin Vance, the young Dr. Handsome of Jana's circle, was providing me with Dexedrine (for weight loss) and Xanax (for insomnia), despite the fact that I wasn't fat and had no problem sleeping.

For those drugs with dosages of lines, hits, or doobies, I paid social visits to the Park Avenue duplex of Daniel Wilson, who had business cards that said "Social Worker." I'd heard that he never even finished his B.A. at Columbia, but with his lucrative practice, a degree wasn't necessary.

I mentioned those individuals to Kirk, who said, "Uh-huh, uh-huh," with a bored edge. I felt as though I was being asked to produce something really impressive. I thought I had something, but I was reluctant to give it, mostly because I hated the dealers. It was unusual for me to look down on anyone providing an illegal but necessary service, but Jesse and Heather were the kind of white trash who gave drug dealing a bad name.

"Here's the scoop," I told Kirk, whose features were melting into the deepening twilight. "There's this art gallery down in Soho. It's in a pretty seedy area. They have a permanent exhibition of Jana Crowley's pictures and a lot of really cheesy sludge passing for art. I call it Andy's leftovers, you know what I mean? It's run by this young fuddy-duddy named Nicholas who thinks that wearing tweed makes him look classy."

I went on to describe how Nicholas Wynn might have gotten away with this posturing since he had snooty manners, vests, and a wax-fruit Wasp demeanor. The giveaway was his receptionist, Heather, a young woman from someplace south of the Mason-Dixon line with a large butt and a larger mouth who never stopped yakking. You could hear her nasal twang over a whole room of art aficionados pretending to know what they were talking about.

The first time I walked into Nicholas's gallery with Jana, Heather had bellowed "Greetings and salutations" as if she were madly impressed with herself for knowing a word as long as "salutations." Her voice grated on every nerve in my body like the sensation of steel wool rubbing Ajax against a sink.

Within ten minutes she had attempted to engage me on such topics as college football, "One Life to Live," McDonald's vs. Burger King, and where I got my perm done.

"What perm?" I asked, hoping to shut her up, but nothing short of a nuclear attack at ground zero would have accomplished that.

It never stopped. She had an opinion on everything and the conviction that everyone in a two-block radius needed to hear it. Her favorite expressions, which I heard over and over until I had to write obscenities on my clipboard to keep myself from wringing her neck, were "I must say," "I am sure," "Would you believe it?" and "What was he thinking?" At least one of them seemed to apply to any conceivable situation.

I despised her. I detested Nicholas. I loathed his second-rate gallery, pompously named Art Attack. But

I WILL SURVIVE

I didn't know how much I could hate one human being until I met Heather's boyfriend, Jesse Wilcox.

I came out of a meeting with Nicholas and Jana to hear this booming laugh that existed only to advertise the stupidity of the freak who produced it. He had a glazed expression, long greasy hair, and a permanent halo from the Winstons that he never stopped smoking.

I was waiting for Jana to make her good-byes when I heard the clear sound of a fart. I shot a revolted look in his direction and he produced his other laugh, a sniggering monstrosity with the wet rasp of lung cancer waiting to happen. I couldn't get out of there fast enough and hoped I would never see him again.

No such luck. He lacked any sign of gainful employment and spent his days hovering around Heather as she did whatever an art gallery receptionist did, which, as far as I could tell, wasn't very much.

The main component of his vocabulary was the all-purpose adjective "trippy."

He was also fond of "cool," "freaky," "cosmic," and "swanky," which he deliberately mispronounced as "schwanky," which he thought made him sound hip. He wore a belt with shells on it. I was tempted to remind him that Jim Morrison was dead and so was that particular look.

I once asked Jana why she let Nicholas handle her work, when his place was so low class. She shrugged and said that she did it because Nicholas was a friend of her husband. I wasn't surprised.

As I repeated this to Kirk, I could feel myself being consumed with ugly hatred. Even Jerry had noted the unreasonableness of my feelings. I'd been in bed one night going over the events of the day, which had included a stop at Art Attack and an encounter with the gruesome twosome.

"He's such a repulsive excuse for a life form," I ranted. "I swear to god, Jerry, I believe in gun control to the living end, but all I need is four bullets."

"Is your aim that bad?"

"Two for the vocal cords, two for the balls," I crooned with a diabolical laugh.

Jerry looked at me.

"What are you looking at?"

"Has it occurred to you that this anger might be misplaced?"

"Not really."

"What did these people ever do to you?"

"They annoy me."

"I think you're overreacting. I think it's not really Jesse and Heather that you're angry at."

"Is this going where I think it's going?"

He sighed and I could see him deciding whether to continue.

"I think this is all anger that you really feel toward Jana, and you have every right to."

Jerry had made the wrong decision. That conversation ended with me sleeping on the couch. I shook off the memory and continued my narrative to Kirk Watson.

"Since it's so grubby down there," I continued, "the photographer from *New York Magazine* thought it would be a great location for scenic squalor." They spent a day shooting in and around the gallery, which meant I spent the day hanging out, holding my clipboard, and getting bored. I noticed that Heather and Jesse were both running in and out of the gallery a lot. At first I thought they were going out to smoke, but that wasn't it, because everyone smokes in there anyway.

"Then I saw Jesse talking to man in a suit and I spotted the hand-off. I made a nice little lookout for myself across the street and spent the rest of the day watching the business in action. I wouldn't vouch for the quality, but damned if those two cretins aren't dealing out of that place, right under Mr. Wynn's pointy nose."

I looked at Kirk and was gratified to get a smile. He

I WILL SURVIVE

took my hand. I thought he was going to shake it.

"I'll see ya 'round."

Then he kissed my hand and disappeared into the darkness of 72nd Street.

One week later there was a bust at Art Attack. Jesse was caught in a hand-to-hand buy. Heather had marijuana and crystal meth in her bag. They were arrested.

I knew that all the anti-drug propaganda which insists that marijuana causes paranoia was just that, but the longer Harvey and I sat on the couch getting stoned, the further into a vortex of fear and insanity our thoughts spiraled.

Was it thinkable that Kirk Watson was some kind of DEA snitch? Maybe he didn't exist and the whole myth had been made up to catch gullible former hippies like me. Maybe he did exist, but there was a fake Kirk on the market to root out information. Harvey said he knew him, but then admitted he had merely met him a few times under the kind of circumstances where you may not retain that many details. What did he look like? Average was all he remembered. That was a big help.

Maybe the timing of the arrests was coincidental. If I could spot what was going on, it didn't take the smartest patrolman on the force to figure it out. Even if it was a coincidence, I couldn't relax because Jesse and Heather didn't know that. They'd seen me hanging out. I hadn't hidden my contempt. They might think I'd fingered them out of spite. Jana had heard from Nicholas Wynn that they were out on bail, although he couldn't allow Heather to come back to work. He seemed saddened about this fact.

Harvey was happy to point out the possibility that whoever was supplying the Art Attack drug operation was holding me personally responsible for the bust and decided to aim a car at me. That meant they were following me. Maybe somebody tipped them off.

I stared at Harvey through the smoke and let my fears carry me all the way down.

Who could be involved? John the waiter in all his spiffy adorableness? Gustave and Cleo? Who was Gustave calling from the bar? I thought of Glenn. Could a boy with such a gentle face have been setting me up all along? I closed my eyes to examine the possibility and found myself falling asleep.

"Marti."

"What," I grumbled, wanting the raspy voice to go away.

"Marti, wake up. Or do you want to crash here?"

Crashing meant either curling up on the lumpy couch or taking my chances on the mattress on the floor.

"No. Can you give me a ride? I want to go home."

"Sure. I've got the cab outside. We could hit some clubs. There's a band from San Francisco playing at the Green Door. They're called the Plate Techtonics."

"No. I've got to get home. I told Jerry I'd be gone for a few hours."

"When was that?"

"At least twelve hours ago. Give me a few copies of the new edition."

I rode uptown with a pile of *New York Night* on my lap. Sleep was wrapping its arms around me ever more seductively. I wanted to be warm and safe and unconscious with my arms around Jerry.

My eyes opened with a jolt of fear.

"Shit, shit, shit!"

"What?" said Harvey making a sharp turn.

"I've been a bad girl." I said with the despair you get after the fun has long since passed and all you know is that you've fucked up.

I wanted to go upstairs and find Jerry already asleep so I could sneak into bed and get the rest I needed. I could feel the soft sheets. I could hear Jerry breathing. I was so focused on my fantasy of getting to bed that I was almost sleepwalking as Harvey dropped me off.

Sleep staggering was more like it. I could barely stand up in the elevator. I had a Queen song running through my head, but I didn't know if I was singing to myself or just hearing the memory of the tape from Glenn's bedroom. It was off key, so it had to be me.

"Another one bites the—" Before I could get to the "dust," the door opened and I found out the night wasn't over yet.

10

Jerry was waiting for me.

So much for the big sneak. I knew he was worried, but my glasses were back on Ninth Avenue and I was too bleary-eyed to tell if he was worried as in "Where have you been all day? I've been worried sick about you," or worried as in "Where have you been, you slut?"

He grabbed me into an immediate hug which was reassuring.

"Are you O.K.?" he asked, holding me almost too tightly.

Out of town doesn't count, I reminded myself.

"I'm O.K., honey, and I missed you. I've got a lot to tell you, but right now I am so tired you can't even believe it. Let's just go to bed and we'll talk in the morning."

I thought he might be so gracious as to carry me into the bedroom.

"Marti."

"Yeah."

"We have guests."

"Tell them to go home. The party was last night."

"No."

I WILL SURVIVE

Arguing with a New York City schoolteacher is not a good idea. He meant business.

If I were going to pick two people I had no desire to see just then, Paul Falzerano and Elisa Brinkham would have been high on the list, so guess who was sitting on my sofa? It made no sense for either of them to be there, much less both.

"What is this," I grumbled, "the children's hour?"

I marched into the living room.

"Aren't they up past their bedtimes?" I snarled.

"They've been waiting for you."

Was there an accusation in his voice?

"This better be good."

Jerry nodded at Elisa, who quivered as though I were going to dispatch her with a carving knife. Both children looked terrified. I glanced at the TV trays that had been set up. I could see the remains of chocolate milk and Oreos. I had a sudden attack of the munchies. I grabbed a cookie and jammed it into my mouth.

"I think my father killed Jana," she said in her pretty little British accent, catching me in mid-chew.

Jerry, Paul and Elisa waited for my reaction to this bombshell.

I finished chewing and then swallowed.

"Wait here," I said. "I'll be right back."

I ran into the bedroom, being careful not to actually sit down on the bed, lest I collapse. Strudel was in there wisely avoiding the scene in the living room.

I needed to get out of my clothes immediately, starting with those torture devices on my feet. Out of my closet came a dark blue garment that was either a short dress or a long sweater. Either way it managed to be comfortable while still having enough style to give me some authority.

My spare glasses were on top of a dresser drawer. With them on, the world snapped back into focus. My makeup was shot and I had no intention of redoing it, but I did run a brush through the hair.

With the outside taken care of, I had to deal with the fact that the great detective was about to go on duty with a body and soul that were both exhausted, not to mention a brain that was still impaired by Humboldt County's best. I was about to get vital information and I could barely keep my eyes open. I gave serious consideration to popping one of my dexies, but I settled for a Pepsi from the fridge.

I swaggered back into the living room ready to take charge. I was almost stopped in my tracks by the sight of my menorah, reproachfully unlit on the windowsill. I put that package of guilt aside for a moment when I had time to open it.

"O.K. Let me get this straight," I started, speaking to Elisa Brinkham. "You're supposed to be the sweet rose of England, transplanted to foreign shores who clings to her father and despises the wicked stepmother. In fact, this morning, I got the impression you were upset about Jana's death only to the extent that it affected your father. Now it's twenty-four hours later and you're here to accuse him. How does this happen? And furthermore, what does young Mr. Pudgeball have to do with it?"

The pudgeball flinched. Jerry shot a fierce look at me. He had a protective streak that was alien to me, even though I was a beneficiary of it as much as the kids were. He even nurtured their impossible dreams.

Elisa was afflicted with delusions of theatrical talent. She'd seen the movie *Fame*, and very much wanted to get into New York High School of the Performing Arts after she finished Simone. She tried out for every production that the Simone School had to offer. She often got parts due to Tony Falzerano's theories on fairness, which translated into keeping the parents happy by keeping their untalented offspring from being told how untalented they were.

Keeping Elisa happy was hard enough. She was too old for Simone, but the British/American educational discrepancies justified her presence. In other words, Daddy wanted her there, so there she was.

Jerry's sympathetic nature led him to offer piano and voice lessons. Once I'd heard Elisa tell Jerry how much she wanted to be in a professional show.

"I know where we can get a donkey," I muttered. Elisa either hadn't heard or hadn't understood. Jerry did hear and later told me that the comment was crude, even for me.

Elisa was like me at that age. Always wanting and never having. She was isolated by her accent and money. Even on the East Side, the Brinkham fortune was stratospheric.

"I knew she couldn't help," Elisa said to Jerry in a particularly snotty way, which reminded me why I didn't like her, even if I thought I understood her anguish. "I told Paul what I thought and he said we should go to Jerry. The first thing Jerry said was to wait till Marti gets home. She'll be here soon. I couldn't imagine why I should want to tell you anything. Now it's who knows how many hours later and the first thing you do is get in my face."

The juxtaposition of "get in my face" with her refined accent was ludicrous.

"I have half a mind to talk to the police after all," she finished firmly with a theatrical flounce.

I took a swig of soda. The voices in my head had a strategy meeting. Sure, I'd love to spend a few hours using these brats for verbal target practice, but I had a job to do. Finding Jana's killer was my primary goal. Being a bitch was just a hobby.

"I'm sorry Elisa," I said gently. "I didn't mean to snap at you like that. I'm very serious about solving this case and Jerry's right, I do have experience. If you've got information, I really want to hear it. Just one thing." I put some bite back into it. "Even if you do have half a mind, you don't have it to go to the police or you wouldn't be here in the first place, right?"

"Yes," she agreed reluctantly.

"So I'm going to sit down here and finish my Pepsi and have a few more Oreos and you're going to tell me why you think your dad offed my best friend."

The big chair matched the couch. It was comfortable, almost too comfortable. I started to close my eyes.

"I also think he killed my mummy."

That opened them in a hurry.

"Your mummy?"

"My real mummy. His first wife. Her name was Elizabeth. She was killed in a car crash, but now I think he killed her."

A sudden flash of Glenn going through the window.

"Why would he do that?" I asked sounding calmer than I felt.

"He married her for her money and then he killed her."

Her tone implied that it was so obvious I should have known.

"That is a bit of a cliché," I pointed out. "Do you have any proof of this?"

Her hair was pulled back in a ponytail with a ribbon, rather like a show horse. She tugged at the end of it.

"Well, mummy told me she was afraid of him. Her family did have lots of money. She was hit by a German tourist. That doesn't happen to anyone so he must have had her killed."

We had made a quick jump from "I think he killed her" to "I think he had her killed." Elisa's logic intrigued me, especially the fact that no one in England gets hit by a German tourist. Did that mean they might get hit by, say, a Swedish tourist?

"Proof, Elisa, proof. Did he ever hit her?"
"I don't think so."
"Threaten her?"
"No."
"Yell at her?"
"He never yells at all. It's just the way he is that's scary. You know that. Even Jana knew that." She made an especially broad sound in "Jana," just to show her contempt.

Jana wasn't scared of anything, I wanted to shout, except I knew it wasn't true.

She was afraid of being a starving artist again. She'd been a great waitress at Swenson's but she didn't want to go back. She was in love and she wanted her freedom, but not at the cost of poverty. That's why she'd had me recommend a good accountant.

Maybe fear was driving the extreme emotions of the previous weeks. What else was she scared of? Did she know about this German tourist crash?

"How long ago did this happen?"
"When I was ten. Almost five years ago."
"You've been playing the dutiful daughter all this time?"
"I didn't think about it," she said grandly. "I've always thought the world of him. I loved him. But when they found her last night, it all just jumped back at me." She put a dramatic hand to her chest. The girl was so hung up on being an actress that it was hard to remember that there was a scared child behind all the posturing.

I thought about what I knew of Post-Traumatic Stress Disorder. It sounded like that kind of thing. I made a mental note to call Dr. Karl Hammerschmidt, my favorite shrink.

"So you told him?" I said, jerking a finger at Paul.
"He's my friend," she replied pointedly.

The misfits had bonded into a friendship. I never had a friend when I was a miserable teenager.

"This murder is being investigated by the New York City Police Department, you know."

"Lot of good it does me. I know enough to know they're not going to listen to me against him. He knows people."

"Let's say he did kill your mother for money. He's got plenty of it now. Why should he kill Jana Crowley?"

Elisa opened her mouth and then closed it again. She didn't have an answer to that one. She pursed her lips.

"Well," she said finally, "Jana must have done something to set him off."

"Like what?"

"Maybe she was seeing another man," Elisa whispered broadly as if this was the most shocking thing she could think of.

"Like who?"

I finished off the can of Pepsi. While my head was tilted back, I caught Elisa trying to catch Paul's eye without my seeing it.

"Hey, Paul," I called out. "Look alive."

He just looked flustered.

"You're Elisa's friend. You came here risking all kinds of trouble at home to back her up. Is that right?"

"Yeah, I guess so."

I still wanted to smack him, feed him decongestant, and put him on a diet, but the only way I was going to find out more than I already knew was to treat him with a little respect. The things I had to do to solve murders.

"I really admire you for standing by her like that."

"Thanks."

I held his gaze. He didn't even twitch.

"If we agree with everything she's told us, then Jana might have been seeing someone on the sly, huh?"

"Yeah."

"Any idea who?"

His whole face spasmed violently.

"How would I know?" He said in his most childish whimper.

"Because I know, and Elisa here seems to know, so why don't you just tell me about Jana and your father?"

"I don't know anything."

"Sure you do. I'm giving you the best chance you're ever going to have to convince me that you might actually have the brains God gave geese. Jerry tells me you're actually pretty smart. All I ever see is this whiny brat, so I don't believe him. Which one of us is right, Paulie?"

I made it brutal. I figured he'd collapse into a pile of jelly and I'd have to take him home in a plastic bag. He surprised me.

"My mother sure thinks it is . . . was going on. I heard her on the phone to her friends and my grandma."

"You eavesdrop?"

"Yeah."

There was a twitch, but also shy pride. I rewarded him with a smile.

"Go on."

"They had a big fight before the party. They were both screaming. She said he was making a fool of her and she wouldn't stand for it. She said you told her."

"Me?"

"Yeah. She said Marti Hirsch told her."

I rolled my eyes. I didn't tell Rhonda anything, unless you counted her reading my *New York Night* column.

"What did your dad say?"

"He said nothing happened."

"She was pissed off, huh?" I said, being deliberately vulgar to encourage him.

"I'll say."

"Mad enough to kill him?"

"Yeah."

"Mad enough to kill Jana Crowley?"

"What? Uh. . . . oh . . . No . . . no . . . no."

"Stop whining."

"Sorry."

Elisa stood up to confront me.

She was wearing a white sweater over a long gray skirt, making her pale skin look almost translucent. She was taller than I was. An apparition of slender anger was standing over me. The late Elizabeth Brinkham must have been quite the exquisite Amazon.

"I don't understand you. I thought you and Jana were so close."

"We were," I said defensively.

"And you can't stand my father."

"True."

"So I tell you that he killed her and you just sit there like that?"

"Like what?" I said coolly.

"Like you don't bloody care!" she shouted.

I looked up at her with my best laconic tough-guy attitude. I held her eyes without saying anything, mostly because I couldn't think of anything. I didn't need to. As I kept staring, she started to tremble from the lower lip down. Finally she exploded.

"He's going to kill me next!"

The veneer cracked and she collapsed in tears at my feet. Jerry wanted to run over and comfort her. I put up a hand to stop him. Paul was working himself into a twitchy fit on the couch.

"Calm down, Elisa." The crying continued with her head in my lap. "No one's going to kill you."

If she didn't stop mewling, I was going to throttle her myself.

Finally she got control of herself and looked up at me with red tinged, watery-gray eyes. I smiled and indicated that she should return to the couch.

My body still wanted to head for bed, but my mind was going into high gear. Amazing stuff, that Pepsi cola.

"Jerry, we need to have a conference."

I WILL SURVIVE

He followed me into the bedroom.

As grim as the circumstances were, I had a good feeling about Jerry and me being on the same wavelength again. Two kids from Brooklyn out to save the world. The David Price murder had brought us together. Maybe Jana Crowley could save our marriage. She'd come close enough to destroying it. I struck my best insouciant Nick and Nora Charles attitude.

"Well, darling, what do you think?"

"I don't know. I know she's really scared. They both are."

"Yeah, I'm pretty terrifying."

"You know what I mean. Thomas isn't my favorite guy, but I just find it really hard to believe..."

"That he'd kill the first wife or that he'd kill Jana?"

"Jana..."

"O.K., let's put Jana aside for a minute. First wife. Car accident. German."

"We need more information."

"Absolutely," I agreed, trying not to yawn. I'll get on it in the morning."

"We'll get on it."

"Right-o."

"Could Elisa sleep on our couch tonight?" he asked.

"Probably, it's pretty comfortable. I just think if she's missing in the morning, that tips off Thomas and makes things worse."

Jerry looked unhappy about sending Elisa back to the dangers of the penthouse.

"Look, honey, even if all this is true, I don't think a man as fond of appearances as Thomas Brinkham is going to kill his own daughter in his own property. I mean, what's he going to do? Throw her out a window?"

"She's scared," he reminded me.

"I know. I'll take care of it. Let's go."

I went to address my small, waiting audience.

"O.K. Elisa, I've been suspicious of your father since

the minute I found the body, and you're right, I wasn't that crazy about him before. I spoke to a lawyer today who said that the DA always suspects the husband. I also talked to a..." I hesitated, "... a material witness who said that Jana was afraid of Thomas. I knew she wanted out of the marriage. I also know for a fact that she was involved with another man, and for what it's worth Paul, it wasn't your father."

The information didn't make him look any happier.

"Put it all together and it should spell murder. Unfortunately, Thomas is not our average husband suspect due to his height when he stands on his wallet. Also the cops are trying to pin it on me, but that's another story."

"So what do we do?" Paul asked. "I want to help."

"Do your parents know where you are?"

He shrugged.

"I left a note on my pillow. They don't check on me much." Even when I was fifteen and already convinced I was smarter than anybody else, including my parents, I never pulled that kind of stuff.

"O.K. I'm going to call them."

"No. Please. I can take a cab home and sneak back in."

"You're whining again."

He glared at me but still couldn't bring himself to tell me off. Rhonda and Tony had done a number on the kid. I felt myself moving from contempt to sympathy.

"I've solved two murders and I'll tell you what it's like. It's like putting on a show." That got Elisa's attention. "I'm the star of the show, but I can't do it without my singers and dancers. You guys are going to sing and dance and I'm going to nail Mr. Brinkham."

I knew had the kids in my pocket. Jerry was giving a look of admiration. He was probably amazed that I could produce such arrant bullshit with no preparation and no sleep.

"Elisa, I want you to be a great actress. Go home and

keep playing daddy's little girl. Meanwhile you're going to be my eyes and ears up there. Jerry's going to take you upstairs right now. If you run into your father, Jerry will tell him that if he even looks at you nasty, the Marti Hirsch hit parade is going to go in and mess up his hair."

It sounded ludicrous to me, but it went over like gangbusters with a couple of kids who were punchier than I was.

I had to make a very unpleasant call. I rang the Falzerano residence at an hour when it was likely that I would wake someone up and I did. I roused the slumbering Tony with the news that his oversized son was not safely asleep in bed, but was, in fact, sitting on my couch shoving an Oreo into his face. Luckily Tony was too out of it upon awakening to ask a lot of questions. He muttered and snorted until I got the important point through to him. Paul was with me and someone had to come get him.

I heard him yell something that was clearly intended for Rhonda. Even with a muffling hand over the phone, it was clear he had to yell into another room to reach her. I wondered how long it had been since they shared a bed. Finally, he said he'd be right over.

I usually shied away from waking people up, but the modicum of sympathy I'd developed for Paul gave me an impetus to annoy the parents who had created this craven slug. At least I knew that I wasn't parent material, and would never inflict my own insanity on a young life. Nobody had told the Falzeranos, and the soggy thing on my couch was the result.

We ate Oreos and watched each other warily. Jerry came down to report no incidents in the penthouse. Thomas had greeted his daughter with a warm parental hug and thanked Jerry profusely for being there to talk to her when he himself was still too distraught over the death of his wife to be the parent that Elisa needed. I nearly whooped my Oreos.

Not wanting to look at Jerry or Paul, I found myself staring at the windowsill where my menorah waited, its candles for the second night still unlit. It was too late to do much about it now. Jerry was the one who'd been concerned about us having a "real" Chanukah. Maybe he thought the ties of tradition were strong enough to bind us back together when so many things seemed to be tearing us apart.

The window itself had a craggy hole in it, covered with duct tape. Since Thomas was also the landlord, I hadn't been able to admit that I'd broken a hole in the window. Especially since it occurred during a fight with Jerry.

It was a Friday, specifically the Friday evening following the monthly staff meeting at the Simone School. Jerry hated those staff meetings. They were the main platform for inter-teacher conflict, inter-department war, race-baiting, finger-pointing and smartly dressed aggression. Every single one of those meetings made Jerry want to pack his bags and get a train, boat, or plane and take me and Strudel somewhere else. He'd set his sights on Los Angeles, a town I could not abide.

Jerry came home to tell me how unhappy he was. Furthermore he was unhappy being unhappy because he genuinely loved children. He wanted out. Palm trees and sunshine were the answer.

All I could hear was that he wanted me to leave Jana. He was upset that we didn't see each other enough. He thought Jana was a leech, draining me of time and energy. He didn't want to be beholden to Jana and Thomas.

It got ugly.

Jerry said I had sold my soul and he hardly knew me anymore.

I told Jerry that Jana thought he was a wimp.

He asked me why I couldn't write anymore. I told him that maybe I couldn't stand being trapped. He got quiet again and asked who had me trapped, him or Jana?

That's when I couldn't take it anymore. I ran into the bedroom to escape from the scene. I turned on my Toodleloop and out of it came the monotonous words "Let's get physical, physical."

That stupid thing had been on the top of the chart for weeks. It was driving me crazy. I picked up the doughnut-shaped radio and carried it into the living room. I turned up the volume as much as its puny motor would allow. Olivia was now moaning about getting into "animal," whatever that was supposed to mean.

"You hear this?" I screamed over the music. "This is what's wrong with the world!" With that I gave the blue plastic a mighty heave in across the room, hoping it would hit a wall and be destroyed. It went right through the window.

Jerry stared at the hole in disbelief. There were shards of glass all over the floor. The window faced nothing but a courtyard, so there was no danger of death by Toodleloop.

The outlandishness of the act dissipated the tension. Jerry sighed and said that I might want to cut down on speed, at least before eight.

We were left with a taped-up hole in the window and a hole in our marriage that wasn't so easy to repair.

The doorman called to let us know that Mr. Falzerano was there. I said to send him up. Tony Falzerano ready for his fans was always a well-turned out sight. Tony coming to get his son at one in the morning was nothing for sore eyes. Unshaven, unkempt, shirt untucked and tee-shirt showing underneath. He hadn't bothered with a tie. He fixed Paul with the twisted grin of a tyrant leading the vanquished off to execution.

"Come on son, let's go." The voice was still polished glass. He'd worked hard to learn that voice, and no middle-of-the-night surprise was going to drive the sound of the street out of hiding.

"Not yet, Tony."

He put his eyes on me, the way some men put their hands on your body.

"I'm not sure what's going on here or what this . . . what my son has been up to. I appreciate your calling me, but with all respect Marti, I have nothing to say to you right now."

"I think you do. We're going to talk about Jana. We can do it here or we can have a little privacy. Come on."

I led him into the bedroom, making sure I picked up one of my copies of *New York Night* on the way. I turned the page to my anonymous column.

"Here Mr. Principal. Read this."

I watched him read about how his attempted affair with Jana Crowley had fizzled out because of his inability to perform. His face blanched under the stubble. He shriveled onto the bed.

"You can't do this."

"I already have, but don't worry, most of the people who read this have no idea who you are or what Simone School is. Most of them wouldn't know Jana Crowley if they fucked her. Which is more than you could do, of course. I have lots of copies. You can give one to Rhonda. Then she'll know you were telling her the truth."

Tony desperately wanted to say something, but couldn't spit it out. Maybe it was that same thing he said when I first woke him.

"Jana told you?" he managed to get out.

Men are always surprised to find out what women really say to each other.

"She was my best friend. That's why I'm going to find out who killed her. Was it you?"

"Of course not."

"Do you have an alibi for the whole party?"

"Who are you to ask me this?"

I deliberately raised my voice.

"I'm the one who's going to personally put a copy of this in the mailbox of every Simone parent, every school board member, and every old goat on the board of trustees if you don't start answering some questions. I'm the one who's going to let everyone know you're not the big stud with the great marriage." I went even louder. "You'll be a laughingstock all over the East Side by the time I'm through with you. Mr. Would-be Philanderer who can't even get it up when one of the most glamorous women in New York is ready to do him in her own bedroom."

"I could have," he yelled back. "She just wouldn't give me time. I need time."

"Please Tony, spare me the sordid details of what's wrong with your schlong. Just answer the questions."

"I didn't kill her." He was practically sobbing.

"Why not?"

He looked shocked.

"I'm a Catholic," he said seriously.

"Oh yeah. So murder is out but attempted adultery is O.K.? Try selling it to the Pope."

"She promised she wouldn't tell anyone. Not for my sake, she said, but just to keep from humiliating herself. She said things . . . she was vicious . . . worse than you."

"Must have been pretty bad."

"I wanted to hit her, but . . ." He trailed off, putting his head in one hand to wipe away sweat.

"Alibi?" I demanded.

He shrugged.

"O.K. How about Rhonda?"

"What?"

"I know you two had a spat before the party. She thought you and Jana were actually an item. I can't imagine why she'd want to hang on to you, but she did.

She thought you were in love with Jana."

"Part of me was," he whispered.

I didn't want to know which part.

"So maybe Rhonda decided to have it out with her. It could have gotten out of hand. Or maybe she just snuck up and strangled Jana for the love of you."

He muttered something.

"What?"

"She wouldn't do that."

"Don't tell me. Catholic."

"Just too nice. Too good. Too good for me."

I wanted to tell him that his whole family was sick and that a good shrink could do wonders. I wanted to tell him to treat his son better, just so I wouldn't have to see the twitch anymore. I wanted to tell him exactly what kind of scum I thought he was. I settled for walking to the bedroom door and opening it.

"Good night, Tony."

He looked me over and thought he was getting off easy. He got up and walked out, regaining a bit of his accustomed swagger.

"You hair looks great," he said as he passed me. It was the same flattering tone he would have used on a Simone mom. "Let's go, son," he said to Paul.

Paul looked up at him. He was still fat and afflicted by a twitch, but there was some kind of strength that hadn't been there before. He'd heard me call his big, strong father, a weenie who couldn't get it up and heard his father admit it. Kind of a primal scene in reverse. Tony sagged a little before the power of that look.

Jerry was smiling at me as the door closed behind them.

He put his arm around me. I rested my head against his shoulder. Maybe the night was coming to a close after all. Jerry started cleaning up the cookies and milk. I was hoping for some much-needed sleep when there was a firm rapping on the door.

"What's the matter, you want an extra copy? Oh. Hello, Detective Warner."

I stood there staring at her. Why was she there? It must have been connected to Glenn. My stomach started churning. How could I have run away without finding out what happened to him? At least now I'd find out.

He must have ended up in the hospital or the morgue. They'd gone through his possessions. Had his wallet survived the fire? Which address was on his ID? The one in New Jersey, no doubt. They'd gone to tell the mother. That must have been a scene. Poor Mom. Then they went up to his room. Found the letters. They were signed by Jana. Was it Sharon and Johnny on the Glenn Doyle case, or had another cop made the connection? The same picture on the easel and in the envelope. Glenn to Jana and back to me.

Another way: same body, no ID. Case the area. Ask around restaurants. End up at Serenissima. John tells them I was there with Glenn. Sharon's here asking how I happened to be eating dinner with a guy who just got hit by a car and went through a window. If I was at the scene, how come I hadn't stayed around to answer questions?

Or maybe the ID leads them to Frank Polaris. Has Frank been following his protégé? Does he mention Jana Crowley or me?

I was trying to play chess against the cops and think twenty moves ahead. The trail that had brought Sharon there would determine what I should say. I never did like chess. I'm more of a Scrabble person. I like to play skill and luck together. I like it even better when it plays to my strengths.

Sharon hid me in a moment of weakness.

"Can I come in?"

"Yeah. Sure. Would you like an Oreo?"

"No," she said slowly, "that's O.K."

Oh great, I thought. Now she knows I've been smoking pot and I've still got the munchies.

Jerry was in the kitchen putting away the milk.

"What can I do for you?" I asked, feeling like the celebrity killer in an episode of "Columbo" who's about to blow it in the first line.

"I want to talk to you about . . ." I just knew she was going to say, "Glenn Doyle." ". . . about your haircut."

"You can't afford it, and I don't think it would look that good on you."

She walked inside and made herself comfortable on my couch. Then it registered on my brain that she had just asked about my haircut, not about a certain twenty-three-year-old with a great smile.

"My haircut. What about my haircut? Who cares about my frigging haircut?"

"Sit down, Ms. Hirsch."

"Thank you. Don't mind if I do."

I sprawled in the big chair. I wanted Strudel with me, but it wouldn't be fair to wake her.

Detective Warner had her notebook out.

"I've talked to twenty-four people who were at the party."

"You poor thing."

No wonder she sounded hoarse. The sound of her voice made me want to offer her a Sucrets.

"Most of them were pretty nice and the coffee was better than what I usually get offered on these things. Since my partner has a bug up his ass about you, I made sure to ask everybody about you. Did you seem upset? Were you mad at Miss Crowley? Things like that."

I held my breath. Which one of those upper-class creeps was trying to sell me down the river?

"And," I said between clenched teeth.

"And six different people mentioned your hair."

"Were they fer it or agin it?"

"I don't think they felt strongly either way. They just

thought is was different. Two of them said the same thing, from the back, they couldn't even tell it was you."

"So what?"

Sharon was starting to show the exasperation of a long day.

"Ms. Hirsch, I am doing my best to find out who actually murdered your friend. I'm pretty sure it wasn't you, no matter what Johnny thinks. I know you're playing your own game, so I'll work around you. But cut me some slack here. Tell me why the hell you got your hair cut."

"I was having a party for crying out loud. Don't you get your hair done before a party?"

I could hear my voice rising into the hysteria zone.

"Done, yeah. But not chopped off like that. I would never do that before a party. If my girl tried to do something like that to me before a party, I would feed her ass to the dogs."

"Well that's just ducky," I snapped. "Maybe you don't have a prima donna hairdresser who can push you around." I started going louder and faster. "And maybe you're not going crazy like I was, so that I felt lower than whaleshit and didn't have the strength to say 'no' when the goddamn prima donna told me my hair wasn't doing anything for me. I wanted to feel beautiful again. I wanted my hair to do something for me. That's what being Jana Crowley's best friend in the whole wide world makes you do." I was screaming at the top of my lungs. "Get your hair chopped off before a big fucking party, O.K.!" I realized I was losing it and I couldn't stop myself. "Oh my god." I sobbed.

Jerry flew in from the kitchen to put his arms around my shoulders. Sharon Warner had the look of a detective who had gotten more of an answer than she intended.

"Are you O.K., Ms. Hirsch?" she asked finally, in a much smaller voice than she had been using before.

I managed to stifle the tears and wiped them away

from alternate cheeks with the top of my arm.

"Fine," I said, with a deep breath.

"The only reason I was asking had to do with a theory. When I talked to people and they mentioned your hair, they kept saying they couldn't recognize you from the back."

"Yeah. O.K. So they're a bunch of idiots."

"And you were wearing a very similar dress to Miss Crowley's."

"You couldn't afford that either."

"I'm starting to understand why my partner wants to get you. You got a smart mouth."

"That's what my mother always says."

"Well, if you'll manage to shut it a moment, I might tell you something you actually want to know."

"Such as?"

"Autopsy report."

"My lips are sealed."

"Good, keep them that way. She was strangled."

I opened my mouth to make a smart-ass comment about how I knew that already. She stopped me with a glare.

"There were fibers found on her neck. Blue silk."

"Man's tie?" I blurted out before I could stop myself.

"We think so. Good-quality stuff."

My mind immediately went back to the night of the party. How many of the men had been wearing ties of blue? How deep is the ocean? How wide is the sky?

"Nothing under her nails. No sign of struggle except . . ."

I kept my mouth shut, but begged for the next words with my eyes.

"Except her lipstick was smudged and her panties weren't all the way on. Like she'd been putting them on or taking them off."

I nodded and tried to look surprised.

"Rape?" I asked, wide-eyed.

"Not from the lab reports. Autopsy showed alcohol in her bloodstream. Traces of cocaine. There was also residue in her nostrils."

I made a show of exaggerated shock.

"You know anything about that?"

I shook my head solemnly.

"Yeah. We'll drop that for now. Here's my theory. Killer goes down there. He sees her from the back. Black dress, long hair. He goes in with the tie, gets her from behind, and does it hard and fast. She never has a chance to fight back. He never looks at her face till it's over. Then he gets the big shock."

"Mother may I speak?"

"Yeah. Go ahead."

"What's the big shock?"

"The big shock is that it's Miss Crowley. What if the killer thought it was you?"

I looked at Jerry, who'd been standing by patiently. He looked at me and at Sharon with an expression of incredulity, an expression I'm sure I shared. First of all, even from the back, I doubted anyone would mistake me for Jana Crowley. Then there was the main point.

"Who would want to kill me?"

"I don't know. Why don't you tell me?"

"Aside from some particularly deranged movie fan who took the trouble to write a two-page, double-spaced letter explaining why I was a moral leper because I preferred *Apocalypse Now* to *The Deer Hunter*, I'm universally adored."

"You've haven't talked to the same people I have today."

"They didn't like the party?"

"Nobody wanted to say bad things about the victim, but lots of them had a bone to pick with you. I heard the word 'bitch' several times."

"I'm devastated. The cream cheese of the Upper East Side doesn't love me."

"Not to mention a Mr. Washburne."

"Oh you found Max. Why should he be mad at me? Jana was the one who signed the letter calling him a washed-up parasite."

"He thought maybe you wrote it."

I tried to wipe the grin off my face. My literary talent was appreciated.

"Look, Detective. I was a bitch so Jana didn't have to be."

"Maybe she ended up paying the price."

I tried to push the concept into my brain so I could work with it. The implant wouldn't take. Sharon might have been a good cop and even a good soul, but she was rowing in the wrong direction. I wanted to correct her course, but I couldn't give her my own compass. I was drowning in watery metaphors when Jerry spoke up.

"What about the wackos?"

"Yeah, the wackos," I chimed in.

"What wackos?" asked Detective Warner, seemingly reluctant to give up her pet ideas on the crime.

"Wait a minute." I got up and went into the bedroom. I had the wacko file in a pink shoe box that had previously held a pair of Italian pumps. The box held the ravings of a certain segment of Jana's fans. Loonies, lovers, liars, buffoons. I called them wackos and put them in the pink shoe box. They wrote on floral stationary, on lined notebook paper, on construction paper meant for a fourth-grade art class. Writing implements ranged from magenta crayons to number two pencils to green calligraphy pens. They all had something to say to Jana Crowley. Almost none of them mentioned art. Most men who saw Jana in person fell in love with her. I'd gotten used to it. Certain men who saw her from afar, or on the pages of *New York Magazine* lost their senses all together.

Jana made them want to marry, ravish, kill, photograph, maim, and eat fresh figs off her back. They rarely signed their names, and return addresses were never included. Jana and I would take out the shoe box and giggle from time to time. It made an excellent diversion when it was too late for another party and the coke hadn't worn off yet.

I brought the box into the living room and handed it to Sharon. She started reading the first letter, and her thin, crescent-moon eyebrows went jumping in the direction of her forehead. She shuffled through a few more. Her nostrils flared.

"Did it ever occur to you that this stuff might be a reason to call the police?"

I shrugged.

"I know it's scary, but we figured they were just lonesome losers. It didn't seem very real or serious. Just proof of her beauty."

"I'm going to take these all downtown."

"Uh... You know, they're covered with my prints. Jana's too. Probably not much for your forensics people."

"I was thinking of the criminal psych guys." She gave me her best stern-mother look. "Is there any other information or evidence that you're withholding?"

Here was my big chance to come clean. Tell her about Jana's relationship with Glenn Doyle and find out what happened to him. I arranged my features into the soul of candor.

"Have you talked to Charlotte LaFayette? She had a hate-on for Jana you could feel across a crowded art gallery any day of the week."

"She's not exactly a member of your fan club either. She's been questioned. Her alibi checks out."

Sharon got up. She looked almost as tired as I felt. I could see bags under her eyes. Jana would have painted her in shades of black and brown, with a brown/pink color mixed specially for the freckles. I caught her stifling a yawn.

"You should get some sleep." I said, showing her to the door.

"That's what my husband says. I'll sleep when I know who killed Jana Crowley."

Now there were two obsessed women working on this case.

This obsessed woman was determined get some shut-eye. Sharon's yawn had been contagious. It was after 2 A.M. I'd been awake for nearly twenty-four hours. I hated to admit it, but I couldn't handle that as well as I had a few years back. I traded my sweater-dress for a long flannel nightgown.

Jerry had put on white pajamas in deference to the frigid temperatures that still managed to infiltrate our apartment despite the best efforts of a musty-smelling radiator. We snuggled into the bed, under the comforter. I took off my glasses and put them on the nightstand. I wanted to dive into the warm ocean of unconsciousness and float there as long as possible.

"What happened to your glasses?"

The words came floating toward me, as though trying to find me in the tunnel of love. I couldn't hear them at first. Then I didn't want to hear them.

"What?"

"Your glasses. You came in with no glasses. You put on your second pair. What happened?"

It was a reasonable question. My reluctantly guilty conscience heard only an accusation. Without realizing what I was doing, I got out of bed and went into the living room. I wound up tossing and turning alone on the living room couch with a thin blanket. I managed to get some sleep, but it wasn't good sleep and it wasn't enough.

11

Life is not fair, as a wise man once said, and you can't always get what you want, in the words of two others.

I woke up with a headache which I traced to the bump on the back of my head from when I'd hit the ground the night before. That was just before Glenn Doyle hit the window.

It was Monday morning. Some folks were getting up and going to work. Most of them didn't live on the Upper East Side. How many parties and openings had I been to on Sunday nights? It was as if the beautiful people and their friends deliberately scheduled functions for Sunday nights, as if to emphasize the fact that they didn't have to get up on Monday morning.

I couldn't stop reliving the whole sequence of events on Ninth Avenue. I saw the car coming and Glenn pushing me out of the way. I heard the crash as he went through the glass. The worst part was that indefinable popping sound as he hit the tree and the wiring shorted out. My hands were still scratched up from my backward crawl on the cold pavement. I didn't need the throbbing pain to tell me I was in over my head.

When I added Elisa Brinkham telling me that Thomas

had killed his first wife, I felt completely overwhelmed. Even if it was true, he was the kind of guy who could make witnesses disappear and cops look elsewhere. I still had Johnny Rostelli out there trying to nail me, just because I'd made him look like a chump and put his crooked partner out of business for good.

On top of that, I was on the couch and Jerry was in the bedroom. I loved Jerry. It hurt to be away from him. I should have just told him about Glenn and the fire and found a way not to mention what had happened in Glenn's bedroom. I couldn't tell Jerry the truth, especially considering how much I enjoyed it. He might forgive me, but his hurt would kill us both.

Why couldn't I just go to the movies? I'd escape from this whole sordid mess in the refuge of a theater. I could write some reviews for *New York Night*. That's it, I thought. Go back to sleep. Wake up later. Go to the movies. Deal with Jerry later.

It was a good plan, but Strudel had other ideas. I realized that she was sitting on my chest and digging her nails into my nightgown. When I raised my head slightly, she pushed her chin down on my forehead. There was a deserving page of the *Post* spread out for her in the kitchen, but she wanted me to take her out even though it was freezing. I tried to form a simple "no," but when she licked my face, it was all over.

"O.K., O.K.," I said, rubbing her smooth, brick-colored trunk. She knew she had me and started wagging her tail enthusiastically. "You are no good for my image," I told her as I grumbled and bundled. "How can I be the toughest dame in town if I let you walk all over me, huh?" The dachshund didn't care. She was just happy to get her own way. We had a lot in common.

Jerry was still sleeping. I let him stay that way.

I put on a suitable number of layers, including those ludicrous toe socks and a pair of comfortable sneakers. So what if I looked like a bum? Reporters wouldn't be looking for a pile of laundry. Strudel went into her sweater. I got the leash and we were on our way.

There were no reporters in sight.

Jana Crowley's murder was yesterday's news and the vultures had moved on to something else.

I took Strudel toward the park. We'd gone about a block when I heard huffing and puffing behind me. I turned around to see an extremely tall man running to catch up with me. This should have been a signal for me to bolt, but I didn't because the man also had a dog.

It might have been part poodle, but it mostly resembled a dust mop. It was hard to be frightened of a man with such a cute dog. Also, the man himself was hardly threatening. When he caught up and stopped, he was panting to catch his breath. His face was lengthened by his chin, which seemed to be aiming for the ground. A broad mouth cut his face in half.

"May I walk with you?" he asked.

"Why?" I snapped.

"Company."

I put up my hand to show him my wedding ring, forgetting that I was wearing gloves.

He smiled, which make him look goofy.

"Oh, what the hell."

Our dogs were making their own introductions. Whatever they sniffed seemed to agree with them. The new dog was slightly larger than Strudel. It was gray and shaggy. As we approached a tree, he did a little marking.

"Larry Ramsey," his owner said.

Where had I heard that name before?

We shook gloves and proceeded toward the park. It was another cold morning. The air escaping from my scarf made smoke in the air, but it wasn't as cold as it had been. If only by a few degrees, it was getting warmer. That, or I'd lost my mind all together.

I tried to let the murder leave me alone for a while. I wanted to enjoy invigorating air, the barren vistas of

Central Park, the frolicking of my dachshund and his whatever-it-was.

"What's his name?"

"Bandit."

When you're on the case, the case never goes away and in this case it surely hadn't.

"Would that be Larry Ramsey of the *New York Post*?"

When he stopped smiling, the long drooping mouth made him look mournful.

He nodded his head and shrugged.

"You were going to try and get me to talk by using your dog? That's low."

"Nothing else was working."

"Why should it? Look pal, you may have a cute little Bandit there, but you're also getting information from a cop who's out to get me. Let's talk about that."

The ugly bare trees of Central Park were a fitting backdrop for an ugly conversation.

"Johnny's not such a bad guy."

"Here, Strudel," I said, giving a firm yank on her leash and preparing to walk away.

"Johnny and I go way back," he said plaintively.

"You don't sound like you're from Brooklyn."

"Not that far back. We were in the police academy together."

"Now I'm definitely leaving."

"Hey, I grew up in Irvington, New Jersey. I wanted to be cop."

I gave him a look.

"You watch enough *Dragnet*, it can happen. It doesn't matter, 'cause I washed out of the academy. Johnny did everything he could to help me. I just wasn't police material. Now I'm a reporter with a great source."

"You're out here trying to get me to talk when everybody else is on to bigger and better things. Why?"

"I started this thing. My editor wants me to finish it."

"How much has Johnny given you?"

We had to keep walking to stay warm, but we couldn't go much further north without straying into dangerous territory above the reservoir.

"You're playing games, Ms. Hirsch."

"I'm trying to save my ass. I'm also going to solve this murder. Don't be a schmuck, Larry. I didn't do it, but I know more about it than you or Johnny, the not-so-bad guy. If you want something that's going put you back on page one, you're gonna play ball."

I turned around. Strudel was ready to go too. She'd lost interest in her new acquaintance.

Larry was wearing a long muffler that wouldn't stay wrapped around his neck. I could hear it flapping.

"I think Johnny's O.K., but he's been different since that shit went down on the David Price case. Cops and their partners, you know?"

"I'm the one who broke that thing. That's why he hates me so much."

"If he gets wind of my getting chummy with you, he'll hit the ceiling."

"I won't squeal, if you won't. Tell me what you've got."

"Not much. Just what Johnny told me the first night, which pointed to you. Late last night he called me with the autopsy report."

"Blue silk fibers, cocaine, etc., etc."

His face fell again.

"What do you need me for?"

Even bandit looked droopy under his heavy coat.

"Cheer up. I've been working my own sources, but I definitely need some help. What do you know about her husband?"

"Thomas Brinkham? He's rich, he's British—"

"And he's got a good tailor." I interjected. "Anything else?"

"Not really."

"Try this one on for size. How do you like him for the killer?"

His goofy grin came back. He threw one end of the muffler around his neck. I think he was trying to look jaunty.

"Aside from the fact that he has an alibi and no motive?"

"Scoop number one, Jana Crowley was in love with another man and looking for a way out, so don't give me the 'no motive' bullshit. As for the alibi . . . let's just ignore that for the time being."

"Could be. Husband is always the first suspect."

"Right. And this one acts plenty suspicious. Do some digging. Every piece of dirt you can find on Brinkham. How exactly did he get so stinking rich? What was the deal with the original Mrs. B.? Stuff like that."

"Why am I going to do this again?"

"Your editor wants you to finish the story."

"For all the good it's going to do. All they're talking about in the newsroom today is the fire last night."

"What fire?" I said nonchalantly, throwing Strudel a yummy.

"Some dirty bookstore went up last night. A couple of guys got caught with their pants down and got some very interesting burns."

"I'll bet. Do they know what started it?"

"They think it was arson. Molotov through the window, maybe."

Molotov my ass. The only thing that went through that window was Glenn Doyle. Was I the only person who saw it happen?

"Was anybody hurt, I mean, anything worse than burns?"

"No word on casualties from the cops."

"Shocking."

"Yeah, well, weirder things have happened. I'll call

you later on this Brinkham stuff. Do you think you can prove he did it?"

"Weirder things have happened."

I watched his long legs stride off with his muffler flapping in the wind and Bandit shuffling behind him. I wondered who was conning whom. It had taken more self-control than I thought I was capable of not to tell him the real story of the fire at Ernie's.

Poor Glenn. Talk about being in the wrong place at the wrong time. I couldn't get his face out of my mind, especially his smile. If I felt guilty for cheating on Jerry, it was nothing compared to the pain of feeling I was responsible for this horrible thing.

Please dear god, let him be alive.

Glenn wouldn't let me go home. Strudel had done everything she needed to do, but I had work ahead of me. I knew she was getting tired and wanted to go inside.

"Come on, honey. We're going to the West Side."

If she got too tired, I could always carry her. That was one of the advantages of being stepmother to a small breed. It was a long walk at the time of day when the park belonged to those on the go. Joggers, cyclists, roller skaters, and the occasional business person whose commute consisted of changing sides of town.

Going to the West Side put a bounce in my step, even if I was going on serious business. I'd never felt comfortable among the high and mighty in their towers. Even though the Upper West could be just as ritzy as the Upper East, it had a *haimisch* feel to it. Brownstones instead of gray towers. The West Side had all those funky shops on Columbus and Amsterdam. The West Side had noise. Those same trucks that seemed to have been banned from East 65th were happily making traffic on the other side of the park. The West Side had Lincoln Center, The Beacon theater, Cafe des Artistes, St. John the Divine, and Zabar's. I scooped up Strudel and told her we were going to Zabar's.

I practically jogged to Broadway, despite my esthetic revulsion for the sight of East Siders in silver tights and pink leg warmers running laps and putting their hands on their necks as if they could actually feel their pulses. Zabar's was worth running to.

Since it was a weekday, the line was out the door, but not all the way around the block to 80th. Soon I had a poppyseed bagel with Nova lox. I fed a little to Strudel, who enjoyed it immensely, proving that she really was a Jewish dog, despite her German heritage. I washed mine down with a Dr. Brown's Celray and started looking for a pay phone. That was easy enough. The tricky part was finding one that actually worked. Legible graffiti was optional.

I wound up in a diner around 95th Street, which had a phone in the back. Frank Polaris turned out to be unlisted. That was to be expected, even on the West Side. The waitress didn't want to be bugged by the likes of me, but I bugged her anyway. Three angry-eyed businessmen waited for coffee while she dug up a Yellow Pages. My fingers did the walking while my dog cowered at my feet, visibly disturbed by the cacophony coming from the kitchen.

He wasn't listed under Furniture, Imports, or Exports. I was getting worried. What else did I know about Frank Polaris? The Yellow Pages didn't have a Sugar Daddy listing. Wait a minute. What had I said when I busted Glenn? Rich old queen. Old. Antiques. I looked under Antiques. "Frank Polaris. Antiques and Collectibles. By appointment only."

I dialed the number.

"Frank Polaris."

"I'd like to make an appointment," I said in my best social secretary—artist's flunky voice.

"All right. I could see you this afternoon."

I WILL SURVIVE

"Sooner is better. It's kind of an emergency."

"I'm not a doctor, you know."

"Call it an artistic emergency."

"All right. Come on over." He gave me an address on Amsterdam Avenue near 65th Street. That was why Glenn had been walking dogs in the park so close to us.

"Can I bring my dog?"

"I've got a Rottweiler here."

I didn't tell him that I already knew about his Rottweiler.

"We'll see how it goes. My dog is pretty cool."

"O.K.. What's your name?"

"Marti Hirsch."

There was a pause.

"I'll see you in a little while, Miss Hirsch."

Maybe it was the brisk walk, but I really was feeling warmer. Maybe God had punished us with cold long enough. It seemed odd to get sunshine as a Chanukah present, but there it was. The stores on Amsterdam were beautifully decorated. Not that gaudy downtown "throw in everything but the kitchen sink" look, but tastefully done tableaux in gold and crystal. I found myself feeling downright festive, in spite of the emotional weight I was carrying.

Before I could start regaling passers-by with "Silver Bells," I put my mind back on the matter at hand. Frank Polaris. His voice was soft, but it had warmth to it and just the hint of a Southern or Western accent. I tried to envision him. I kept coming up with Tennessee Williams, except that it occurred to me I didn't really know what Tennessee Williams looked like either.

The sign was modest. F. POLARIS. The window was full of Victorian dollhouses covered with fake snow. The man was not what I expected, which was my fault for dealing in the stereotypes that went along with phrases like "rich old queen."

He was only old compared to twenty-three. I guessed

late thirties. His exact age was difficult to determine because he had a closely cropped beard covering the bottom of his face, but neither head nor facial hair showed any gray. He was a tall man, with long legs, wearing khaki slacks and a brown shirt. His posture was relaxed. Even his cigarette smoking happened at a calm pace.

At the same time, there was a tautness about him. The tightly clipped hair and beard made me think of discipline. The shirt looked soft, but it was tucked in and belted. I didn't see any telltale flab.

I was so busy giving him a thorough looking over that it took me a while to notice that he was looking at me. I got the impression he didn't think I was the right caliber of person to be calling him for an artistic emergency appointment. I was ready to invoke my Brooklyn roots and ask what the hell he thought he was staring at, until I realized that I still looked like a laundry pile with a sealskin on top of it. I hadn't even brushed my hair.

"Hi, I'm Marti Hirsch. I didn't realize that it was going to be warm today."

"A pleasant change, isn't it?"

"Yeah."

"Well come on in."

"Quite a place you've got here. Look at all this stuff."

"It's just a matter of knowing what things are worth."

The store was a typical artsy antiques place, with the requisite amount of dust. I could imagine spending hours there, decorating the loft of my dreams. The heat was on and I immediately had to peel off my top layer of coat and scarf.

"Mr. Polaris, I came to talk to you."

He nodded and continued to smoke his cigarette.

"We'll talk in the back room."

I made my way through the array of clocks and cabinets and lamps and tables, carrying Strudel in my arms. She started barking as we came into the back room, which was white and sparsely furnished, compared with the clutter on the outside. There was a low growl in response. That would be Frank's Rottweiler, Judy.

I told Strudel to calm down and Frank tried to talk sense to Judy. I put the dachshund down. The barking and growling continued, but seemed to be mostly bluster on both sides. Neither dog made a move. Frank leaned against the door.

"Miss Hirsch. I made a few calls. I know who you are."

At least someone did. I was thirty-two and I wasn't quite sure.

"I was sorry to hear what happened to Miss Crowley, but I want you to know, I'm an antiques guy. I don't handle paintings, even though I'm pretty sure her stuff is going to be worth a pretty penny real soon. I'd sooner take on the First Airborne than deal with the art dealers in this town."

"I'm not here to talk about paintings. I'm here to tell you that Glenn isn't coming home."

It took him a minute to be surprised that I even knew who Glenn was. He stubbed out his cigarette and then ran a hand over his bearded chin.

"He's staying with his mother for a few days."

"He's not going to be there either."

"I see. We're talking about something serious then."

"Very serious."

Frank Polaris sat down in a straight-backed chair.

"You pick 'em up, you keep 'em awhile, then they go away. You always think it won't matter. But..."

"But Glenn was different?" I finished for him.

"You know him then. Are you the one who's taking him away from me?"

"No. That was Jana. It started a few weeks ago. Did you know?"

He shook his head vigorously, then stopped himself.

"I made the mistake. I fell in love with him. Of

course I knew. I didn't know who, but I knew something was different. It was just a matter of time." He lit another cigarette from a package of Kools. "Jana Crowley? I wouldn't have guessed. A little old for him, isn't she?" He said archly before correcting himself. "Wasn't she? But she was killed. Do they think Glenn was involved? Is that why he's hiding out?"

This was getting difficult. I felt a craving for one of those cigarettes and I didn't even smoke tobacco.

"O.K. Frank, I need you to slow down and listen up. The cops don't even know about Glenn and Jana yet, but that could change any minute. Glenn was involved in the murder to the extent that Jana was in love with him and might have left her husband, if she could do it without getting screwed financially. On the other hand, Glenn wasn't in a big hurry to tell you."

"Of course not. He isn't an idiot."

"No." I agreed. "I still don't know if it's 'isn't' or 'wasn't,' but I'm not hopeful."

"What happened?"

"You heard about the fire last night?"

"The porno place? He wasn't there . . . he was in New Jersey . . . wasn't he?"

"He was with me." I let that sink in, with whatever interpretation Frank wanted to put on it. "I'm looking into the murder on an independent basis. I don't trust the cops," I said simply.

"I understand."

"Glenn was hit by a car. He went through the window and that's when the fire started. It looked real bad. He's either dead or in the hospital wishing he was."

"Oh god." He closed his eyes and bent over. "It can't be. He was so . . . alive. I don't believe it."

Why did I always have to be the bearer of bad news? Frank was starting to cry.

"Frank, I know this is really hard. I don't know who that car was trying to get. I think it was me, but I don't know. Did anyone have a reason to kill Glenn?"

"No. No. No."

"Does that mean no?"

"Why are you making jokes?" he demanded harshly.

"Maybe because I feel guilty as hell. He wanted to help me to find out who killed her and now he's dead. He got killed and I don't know why."

"I don't know either." He sobbed quietly.

We sat there in mutual gloom. The dogs had chilled out. They watched each other warily.

Frank broke the silence. He had gained control of himself and was looking at me.

"He really got to you, didn't he?"

"I guess so." I found myself telling Frank Polaris more than he probably wanted to know. "It was my high school moment. You never get over high school. I didn't anyway. Even at twenty-three, he was all the boys who didn't want me. I'm sorry. You don't want to hear this shit. You don't even understand."

"Try being queer in Alabama. Hell. Try it at Fort Hood, Texas. I know where you're coming from. I wish I could help you, but Jana Crowley's just another overrated painter to me."

I had to defend Jana's talent.

"She was pretty good."

"And Glenn was a pretty good actor. Don't forget that, Marti. He was an actor first and foremost. He was always playing a part in someone else's play."

That was either stupid or profound. I was trying to decide which one, when the air was split by the longest, rudest buzzer I had ever heard.

"Another appointment?" I asked.

He shook his head.

"Nothing on the books till noon."

"Well, I'll be leaving anyway. I appreciate your time. I'm sorry."

"I still don't understand this, but I suppose it's better

to hear it from someone who cared a little."

The buzzer was still going strong.

I picked up Strudel. Judy followed Frank back out into the store and to the door.

As Frank opened the door, I saw the leather jacket, goatee, and badge. I knew I was in trouble. The dogs knew it too. Their differences were forgotten in a mutual chorus of barking and growling.

"Mr. Polaris? I'm Detective Rostelli. I'd like to ask you some—" Then he saw me and the professional politeness evaporated. "What the hell are you doing here?"

"Hi Johnny."

"Don't give me that 'Hi Johnny' shit, you... you..."

His hatred for me couldn't be summed up in the epithets that might be thrown at the average miscreant. I was something he didn't have a word for, but it was something that pissed him off a lot. Frank Polaris was forgotten. His laser beam blue eyes were focused solely on me.

"You think I ain't got enough problems right now, Marti? I've got the Crowley thing with her husband calling the mayor's office every day to find out what's going on. I know you were involved because I got a bunch of statements from your pals saying how much you hated her guts. Then it turns out that instead of dogging your ass, like I told her to, my partner is out all night on a wild goose chase on a pile of shit that you gave her. Now I got a stiff in New York Hospital that's so crispy it barely looks human."

I thought my chest was going to explode.

Johnny was so caught up in his tirade that he didn't even notice the look of horror on Frank's face.

"The only reason we know who it is, is because he had a wallet that didn't get burned all the way, he had a guild card in there, so I knew he was an actor. We blew up the picture and start casing the neighborhood. I end up at three in the morning talking to a waiter who tells me that this guy was in his restaurant with you. That's one hell of a coincidence, ain't it. This same waiter said that the soon-to-be-deceased was a friend of Mr. Polaris."

Thanks a lot, John, I said to myself. See if I go to your restaurant anymore.

Johnny was practically frothing at the mouth.

"So I come to see Mr. Polaris and look who's here? I've put up with just about enough of this."

Johnny was pulling his fist back, presumably to belt me one. Frank Polaris stepped in front of me and with a single fast gesture, he blocked the punch and pushed Johnny back against the door.

"No way," he snapped. "You ain't messing with a lady here."

He held him back until he was convinced that no further violence would commence on his property.

"O.K., fine. We'll do it that way. Let's go, Marti. Downtown."

"Where all the lights are bright?"

"You have the right to remain silent..."

Johnny spat out my Miranda rights, while keeping a hand clamped firmly on my shoulder. Making a break for it didn't seem likely.

"Uh Frank, I need you to do me a favor." I gave him the end of Strudel's leash. "I'm going to be unavoidably detained for a while. Could you get her home for me?"

"Sure. Do you need me to call a... cop or something?"

"Nah. I can handle this."

With that Johnny dragged me outside. My coat was still in Frank's back room. It was warmer than it had been in days, but it was still too cold to be outside. Johnny solved that problem by shoving me into one of those nondescript heaps of unmarked police car that never fools anybody.

While he was gunning the engine and I was practicing my performance of "I want to see my lawyer," a big car pulled up alongside us. I saw a familiar face in the passenger seat. It was Heather, yammering away as usual. Then I saw something in the driver's seat that scared the shit out of me. Jesse Wilcox had looked merely ugly with his long hair. Now his hate-filled face stared at me with barely a week's growth of prickles. They must have shaved him in jail.

"Fucking bloody hell."

"Watch your language," Johnny shot at me.

Then we saw the window roll down and a gun being pointed. You never get used to the sound of one of those things being fired. The asshole trying to shoot it missed and put a hole in the back window.

"What the hell?" Johnny exploded. "Freeze, you son of a bitch. I'm a cop."

The befuddled face driving the other car registered an expression of "Oh shit" and tried to drive off into the middle of Amsterdam Avenue.

Johnny peeled out and started chasing them. I didn't have my seat belt on. I couldn't even find it.

"Johnny, stop, the car. Let me out. Oh my god!!!! Stop!"

The whining was unseemly, but Johnny was driving the car like a speed demon, ignoring the presence of other cars, red lights, and pedestrians. The big black car wasn't obeying the rules of the road either.

I closed my eyes. Bad idea. Jesse tried to get away by turning, Johnny followed him and I nearly lost my bagel.

I opened my eyes and focused on the license plate in front of me.

"It's a New York plate. PR5 887. You can just go to

I WILL SURVIVE

the station and run it down. Please stop. Call it in now. Get help. Just stop the car."

We were now tearing down Broadway.

"Who is that Marti?"

I was beyond clamming up or playing games.

"Drug dealers. Jesse Wilcox and Heather somebody. They were busted a few weeks ago outside an art gallery in Soho."

"They fucked up my car."

"It's the same car that hit Glenn. The guy that burned."

Fifty-seventh Street. Another sharp right and we were crossing Columbus circle against the light. Cars were skidding around us right and left. I didn't think Jesse could drive well enough to keep this up much longer. I wondered what had gone down over in the Tombs, besides the shaving, or maybe that was bad enough. Maybe that was why he didn't want to deal with the police again, no matter what.

"Why are they after you?"

"Maybe they think I set them up. Maybe a connection to Jana. I don't know."

"Sons of bitches."

"Daughters too," I agreed. "Please stop the car." We were going into the park, but not on a car path. Someone was going to die. Over the grass, barely missing trees, roller skaters careening off paths to avoid two cars being driven by lunatics. I thought I heard more gunshots, but I wasn't sure. Crying tires. Busted glass. More screaming. "Oh my god, Jesus Christ," I screamed with the conviction that only a Jewish atheist can manage.

We came out on the east side of the park, which would have been a perfect opportunity for Johnny to drop me off at home. Instead he got close enough to actually hit the rear bumper of the car. That seemed to spur Jesse to get even more power out of the sedan so the chase continued up Lexington Avenue, where there were no trucks, but plenty of baby carriages, aristocratic dogs, and their guardians.

Everyone who saw us coming knew to get out of the way. Most of them approached the experience with that New York nonchalance. Freezing temperatures? Bundle up. High-speed car chase on Lex? Jump for your life. No big deal. It's a hell of a town.

They were putting too much space between the cars as we crossed 110th Street, so Johnny pulled his gun. I thought he'd have to roll down his window and shoot from the side.

"Cover your eyes," he ordered.

For once in my life I complied with a police demand and put one arm up to shield them. I heard a sound that made me feel like my head was exploding from the inside out. My ears rang. I thought they were bleeding.

When I lowered the arm, I saw shards of glass everywhere and realized that the front window of the car I was in had shattered into nothing because the crazed cop who was driving it had shot through it, to get through the back window of the car in front of us. The bleeding I felt was a nick on my left ear where one of the pieces had gotten me. I lost control of a bodily function, but I figured it didn't matter, because I was dead meat on a slab anyway. Johnny was driving by looking through a hole in the glass, and still Jesse kept going.

Is this trippy enough for you, scumbag?

Good-bye Upper East, hello Harlem, where the inhabitants seemed even less perturbed by our activity or even the sight of cars with large portions of glass shot out.

Lexington gave way to the Harlem River Drive. I started to relax a smidgen, as the terror of hitting a major obstacle subsided. Then I panicked again, because the speed was increasing. We were on a regular highway now, where Johnny could channel whatever *Bullitt/French Connection*/Le Mans fantasies he had into capturing those two worthless pieces of shit in the car in front of us. I thought I saw a reddish tinge to the broken glass in their rear window. Someone was bleeding. I could hear sirens behind us. Maybe a black and white was coming to end the insanity. They had to catch us first.

You know you're having a bad day when you're about to die in a car chase with a psycho cop who hates your guts. The only thing that could make the situation worse would be to turn on the radio and hear "Physical." I decided not to risk it.

Johnny was grasping the steering wheel with a white-knuckled death grip as he pushed down on the pedal to get more speed out of his piece of Chevelle. At that same moment there was a perceptible slowdown of the black box.

"I've got you now, you bastard," Johnny crowed.

He pulled to the left side of the car, expecting it to stop as it hit the guard rail of the Harlem River Drive. Instead it sheared through as though it were a blow torch and with a *pop* that was horrible in its lack of volume, it went over the side. I didn't hear any splash because I was bracing to follow it and screaming my lungs out for no reason except that I couldn't stop myself.

"Will you shut up?" said Johnny, braking the car with a squeal as we stopped just in front of the hole in the guard rail.

But I couldn't stop. I couldn't stop crying or shaking. I had almost died and I hadn't faced it particularly well. I'd betrayed my image of myself. My legs wouldn't stop trembling. I tried to steady my knees with my hands, but every time I took the hands away the legs started shaking like a pneumatic drill.

Other policemen had arrived on the scene and a few fire trucks for good measure. Johnny was conferring with his fellow swine. They were staring at the sinking car, waiting for a diver to go in after it.

I was bruised from being bounced around the car. I was bloody from flying glass. I had soiled my clothes out of fear. I could barely control my muscles.

On the other hand, I had no intention of waiting around for Johnny to take me back to headquarters. He'd never cuffed me and no one was paying any attention.

I opened the door and got out. It was a slow, laborious process and every second, I expected my legs to collapse under me, or one of the cops to pull a gun and add me to the body count. With time passing in the slowest of motion, I walked away, leaving a gaggle of fuzz behind me, with their eyes on the Harlem River.

The wind howled off the water and I was acutely aware that my coat was back in an antiques shop on Amsterdam Avenue. The shock of cold made me tremble more, but also helped me focus on getting away.

I managed to get across the highway without getting run over. Then I had to climb a hill. It wasn't particularly steep, but I found myself panting as if I were tackling Mount Everest. Houses. Neighborhoods I didn't know. Suburbia in the city. Laurel Hill Terrace. Had I been walking for minutes or hours? I couldn't tell. And then thank God, although I wasn't sure why, Yeshiva University. Someplace a Jewish girl could feel safe to rest for a minute, although I couldn't study there.

I didn't want to study. I just wanted to curl up on a stone bench and finish the crying and trembling that had been curtailed back at the crash site. It was quiet there. A good place to cry and I did so, until I felt like it was out of my system. My eyes were tender and my jaw hurt. I was still humiliated and I knew my undies were a mess, but I felt peace. I closed my eyes and practiced the deep breathing as self-hypnosis preached by my former semi-shrink.

"Hey you! What are you doing here?"

I opened my eyes and saw a vision in black.

Black coat, black beard, and the broad, flat-brimmed

hat of a Chasidic Jew. Maybe a rabbi, as I assumed the university students must be on vacation. The man was looking at me quizzically. I realized I looked like a bum and probably smelled like one too. I needed to establish my Jewish credentials immediately.

"Happy Chanukah."

"And you also."

I sat up.

"Is there a subway stop around here?"

"Two blocks that way." He pointed.

"Thanks."

"You shouldn't be here."

"Tell me about it," I said, getting up to leave. I didn't know if he was speaking deep Talmudic wisdom or just telling me to get the hell off his campus.

12

I got home tired and smelly, but happy to be alive.

I had the funk so bad, I even got a funny look from the doorman who was supposed to accept all manner of oddness as long as it came from rent-paying occupants.

I stopped to pick up the mail. Our box contained holiday cards, including one from my mother, which no doubt included the usual check for twenty dollars, as if she didn't believe that I might actually be solvent.

Out of habit, I started to open the mailbox marked *P* to extract any mail addressed to Jana. Mail collection had been one of my duties along with clipboard holding. I hesitated and then decided to do it anyway. I was still on the job until I finished "taking care of it."

She had gotten a bill from Saks Fifth Avenue. Some envelopes were obviously Christmas cards. Those were addressed to Mr. and Mrs. Thomas Brinkham. There was another envelope from Samuel Rubinstein, CPA.

Sandy Rubinstein was a friend of my dad's from way back. Lots of Maury's clients had been old-timers, and Dad would send them to Sandy to make sure their assets were well protected. Sandy had been at the funeral, but I was too overwrought to acknowledge him. However, when Jana Crowley told me she needed financial advice, I gave her Sandy's name and phone number. Apparently she'd used it. I wanted to look at the other envelope first, but I realized it was still in the pocket of the coat that I'd left at Frank Polaris's shop.

I opened the new one, shielding myself from the possible gaze of nosy doormen.

"Holy shit."

I looked around to see if anyone had heard me.

In front of me was a complete report provided to Jana by Sandy's agency. The letter said that this was the additional information she had requested. It wasn't about dollars and cents. That may have been in the first letter. Sandy had sent a complete report on Thomas Brinkham as researched by Chuck Camaro, a private detective.

Investigations by a private detective weren't usually a part of Sandy's service, but could certainly be procured by a client with money to spend.

I staggered to the elevator and forgot to push a button. I didn't notice.

Thomas was born in Sheffield, England, in 1935, making him even older than I thought he was and certainly older than he'd told Jana. Dad was in steel and Thomas inherited the factory when the old man died young. Met Elizabeth Winterwine on holiday in Athens in 1955. She was old-money rich, with a father in the House of Lords.

Thomas had married up and been widowed lucky. The report didn't have details on the famous accident; apparently Chuck had been sidetracked from his English investigation to an Asian connection.

Practically everything that Thomas inherited upon Elizabeth's death got invested in his Hong Kong operation. That's when he went from Well Off to Filthy Rich and maybe crooked. Mr. Camaro was said to be following up on allegations of involvement in international money laundering and drug trafficking.

Further information would be forthcoming as soon as Mr. Camaro had completed his investigation.

The elevator finally came, only because someone came down from the fourth floor. I got on in a daze. I didn't know which was more shocking, that Jana was having Thomas investigated or the results. Drug trafficking? Thomas, I didn't know you had it in you.

Then I saw the pink envelope still in my hand, addressed to Jana Crowley. I recognized the writing, done in thick green ink, with an assertive calligraphy pen. There was also the smell. It was like a fruit salad that had gone bad.

Jana and I had spent a lot of time contemplating the identity of that particular correspondent. I'd have to call Detective Warner and tell her we had a new addition to the wacko file. I'd also mention that her partner had gone further over the edge than either of us had realized.

When I got upstairs, I was happy to notice that Strudel had arrived safely and that Jana's coat, which I had started thinking of as mine, was draped over the back of the couch.

Jerry was playing the piano. It was the song that had been recorded by Vicky Dell. How can you truly love somebody if your happiness for their success is drowned out by anger at your own failure?

He looked adorable. I really do love him, I thought. I loved his fluffy blond hair, big nose, and blue-gray eyes. I loved his sweetness and his music and his sense of humor. But most of all, I loved how he loved me. So why did I do things that might hurt him? To prove I could? Because I wanted to? High school?

I walked over to the piano and touched his hair. He stopped playing. He looked up and smiled at me. Then he wrinkled his nose. I must have been a sight.

"You're bleeding!"

"And I smell bad."

"That too. What happened?"

"There was this car chase," I started feebly.

"You don't drive," he pointed out.

"That was the cop who arrested me."

He got up to hug me, a brave move under the circumstances.

"If you got arrested, what are you doing here?" he asked reasonably, rather than showing any panic about the situation. He knew about Johnny, so he could fill in some of the holes himself.

"I walked away," I said, suddenly realizing the severity of what I had done. "I think I'm in a lot of trouble, but all I want to do right now is sleep. Really sleep. In my bed. O.K.? I'm going to take two happy pills. If I'm lucky, I won't wake up."

"Marti." He sounded upset. Then I realized I sounded suicidal. Maybe I was.

"Don't worry about it, Jer. I've been rolling snake eyes since this thing started, I'll probably be up in a few hours to tell you all about it."

"Everything?"

"Everything," I promised, with a mental image of fingers crossed behind my back.

"O.K.," He kissed me softly on the lips. "Maybe you should take a shower first," he said with Brooklyn bluntness.

He was right. I retreated to the bathroom. Those jeans were destined for the incinerator. I'd had guns pulled on me and held up better than that. Under the hardest, hottest spray I could stand, I tried to wash the whole horrible morning away. I took those pills to make sure I slept, but also to forget. I wasn't much of a detective. All I'd done was wreak havoc without getting closer to a solution.

The unconscious is a tough little bastard, as Dr. Karl Hammerschmidt once told me. Drink yourself into oblivion, take drugs, practice any form of escapism you like, and it's there, ready to pop up as soon as your head hits the pillow.

Sleep I got. Escape from my problems, nada. Dreams of failure and persecution. Jana was telling me to take care of it and I couldn't. The killer was right in front of me and I couldn't see him. Paul Falzerano was laughing at me with his congested wheeze. Cops were chasing me in cars and I was crawling in slow motion. Men in suits with oversized ties and bald heads were throwing me around like a bean bag. Then I saw myself in a corner trying to write about it, but all I had was a pencil that wasn't sharp enough.

I woke up in a sweat knowing I had to call my lawyer. I squinted at the clock next to the bed. I'd been out for about three hours. Call Simon now, I told myself. You're a fugitive from justice. They could put out an APB and call you armed and dangerous. I tried to laugh at the irony, but found my mouth too dry even for that. I went to the kitchen for a soda. On the way, I noticed the bouquet in a vase sitting on top of piano, where Jerry was still playing. He had a pencil in his mouth. He was composing something new.

"What's that?"

"Flrs," he muttered around the pencil.

"Pretty. For me?"

"He nodded.

"Thanks."

He took the pencil out of his mouth.

"They're not from me."

"Oh. Who sent them?"

Jerry shrugged.

"The card has your name on it."

"Oh come on, Jer. You should have looked. I've got no secrets from you." He cocked his head and gave me a skeptical look. "I'm getting a Pepsi, you want one?"

"Sure."

"Just read the card to me."

I went into the kitchen and opened the refrigerator.

"Great party. Thanks for having us."

I came back into the living room.

"Who signed it?" I asked, popping the top on a Pepsi and handing it to Jerry.

"Annette Abelman?"

"Annette? Mrs. Jap Supreme? I didn't know she was there. Didn't she have to stay home with the kid while Jake was whipping up the latkes?"

"She must have had a baby-sitter."

"I didn't even see her upstairs."

"She was here most of the time. She was a big help with the kids."

"Isn't that nice," I said as snidely as possible. She probably sent the flowers as a sneaky thank-you for my not going to the house yesterday. Maybe she was in cahoots with Simon and knew that I'd been told to back off.

I ran a hand through my hair. The sensation of not finding my long mass of curls there was disturbing. It made me think of the hideous sight of Jesse's malevolent face and his gun and the ugly skull. Then it reminded me of Sharon's theory that someone could have been gunning for me and gotten Jana by mistake from behind.

"What if . . . what if . . . ?" I said out loud, hoping that I could verbalize an end to the question.

"What if what?" Jerry asked.

"Why would anyone want to kill me?"

Jerry gave me a knowing smile.

"Aside from that . . . why would Annette want to kill me?"

Same look, only with a raised eyebrow.

"You don't understand. Blue silk fibers, so it has to be a man with a tie, right? Wrong. Could be a woman with a man's tie or something else, a scarf, a sash, something like that. But why would a woman kill Jana? Why do women kill women? Because they're scared. One of the great failings of the feminist movement is that women still hate any woman who could take their man, and Jana could have any man she wanted. Someone was jealous and scared."

"So you're back to Rhonda?"

"Help, help me Rhonda? No. I don't think so. She may have been mad and hurt, but she had to know that Tony needs his image more than he needs any nookie. Maybe she even knew that her good Catholic boy couldn't get it up with another woman anyway."

"Marti, you're losing me."

"Really?" I asked, not talking about the murder anymore.

"That's up to you," he said solemnly.

If I stayed in that room with him another minute, I'd wind up spilling everything and begging for his forgiveness. I'd probably throw in the guitar player's girlfriend in Topeka just for good self-abasing measure.

I decided to call my lawyer instead. There was a perfectly good phone in the living room, but I took the opportunity to retreat to the bedroom.

I placed the necessary call to Simon Abelman in Manhasset. He didn't sound particularly happy to hear from me and he was even less thrilled when I conveyed the information that I had been arrested and then escaped.

"What?" he yelped, as though someone had just wrapped their hands around his testicles and squeezed hard.

"You heard me. It's not that bad. I didn't shoot my way out or take hostages or anything. They were at least ten cops there and they were all so excited about having a car in the river that they didn't even notice me leaving."

"I don't care if you left a card and roses. You don't walk away from police custody without permission. They get a little testy about it. It doesn't make them look good, and from what you've told me about Detective

Rostelli, that's already an issue with him. You've got to turn yourself in immediately. I'm going to call the cops right now. I'll tell them you're at home and ready to surrender. You stay there. Don't move. Don't go out. Not for anything. Do you hear me?"

"Yeah. I hear you. I'm staying put. Just tell them to come and get me."

"I don't believe this," he said in disgust. "If your father was here to see this . . ."

"I'm sorry, Simon. Will you meet me at the police station?"

"Call me as soon as the police get there."

He didn't sound enthused about it, but I'd kept my side of the bargain. He didn't have a choice.

The phone was still in my hand. I needed to talk to someone. I dialed a number in California. Since it was in Hollywood, I had to get through a receptionist, a secretary, and some self-important flunky before I heard the familiar voice of Dr. Karl Hammerschmidt.

"Hello M-M-Marti."

"Hey, Doc. How's it going?"

"C-c-considering where I am, it's not half bad."

Where he was happened to be the heart of lightness. Karl Hammerschmidt was a respected psychologist who'd made a public name for himself by publicizing his theories on Post-Traumatic Stress Disorder. He'd never been my official therapist, but we'd had some kind of relationship since 1977.

He was in Hollywood because a television producer with dreams of art had seen one of his appearances on the Phil Donahue show a few weeks before starting production on a new cop show. The idea of a police drama with anything new to say was ludicrous, but it's amazing what happens to people given the right combination of sunshine and cocaine. The inspiration he'd had was to make this particular cop a Vietnam vet. He wouldn't necessarily be suffering from PTSD, but he would have flashbacks and be a troubled character. I suppose it was more interesting than a cop with a cockatoo, but barely.

Mr. Producer had offered Karl an obscene amount of money to be a "technical adviser" on the show. He got suckered with promises of "input" and "honesty." I'd had my doubts when he told me about this, but it was the kind of scam I loved, so I told him to go for it. Even if the thing got canceled in thirteen weeks, he'd have enough scratch to do more research and write another book.

"Input" and "honesty" got thrown out the window after the Neilsen ratings came in for the first three shows. The cop stopped having flashbacks and was given a goldfish to talk to. Karl wanted to cut and run, but the producer liked the prestige of having an actual shrink on the credit roll as a technical adviser.

The star of the show liked it too. His name was Steve Logan. He was one of those conventionally handsome actors who hang around Hollywood for years waiting for the big break and sometimes never get it. He knew that this show was his last chance because he was approaching the ripe old age of thirty-six. He'd acquired twenty years' worth of insecurities, but never wanted to admit his weakness by seeking help; however, with Karl on the set in his "technical adviser" capacity, he felt free to invite Karl into his trailer for long rambling talks.

Karl was good at what he did, although he would rather have been dealing with veterans who couldn't function due to the horrors they had seen in war. Instead he had to listen to this aging pretty boy rail about the indignities of being passed over for the part of a wacky neighbor in a sitcom that he was sure could have made him a star three years earlier.

Steve told his friend Patrick about his stuttering shrink. Patrick was semi-successful standup comedian who was getting tired of the clubs and had made three pilots in four years, none of which had sold. Karl Hammerschmidt soon became the therapist of choice for a whole cadre of second-string celebrities. He bought a house in the hills. He wasn't getting a lot of research done. The last time I had spoken to him, I'd told him how much I hated myself for selling my soul to Jana Crowley and her husband's money. Karl had been very quiet.

Now I found myself pouring out the insanity of the last forty-eight hours. I told him everything, trusting my husband not to eavesdrop. I just needed to get the whole thing off my chest where it had been lying like a hot rock, burning and suffocating me. It took a long time to tell two days of activity and I was going at breakneck speed, as though I were narrating the whole thing while still stuck in Johnny's car during the chase.

"And now I'm here and the cops are going to come and I still don't know who killed her and I wish I were dead."

"S-s-stop right there. You don't really m-m-mean that."

I took a deep breath and sighed.

"No. I guess not. It's just . . . I don't know. How could I know so much and not know who did it?"

"It's quite a story."

"Maybe they could use it on your show."

"Reality is the last th-th-thing they want." He sounded disgusted. "Snappy d-d-dialogue and a facile solution. Sell c-c-cars."

"Snappy dialogue I can do."

"H-h-hatred."

"What?"

"Wh-wh-why do you hate so hard?"

"Family trait. Dad was a good hater. Mom too. She never forgave anyone who got a part she wanted. Why do you ask?"

"Those two who got arrested and were in the c-c-car. You sound so vicious."

"Why the hell shouldn't I? Those two worthless pieces of shit killed Glenn and they tried to kill me. That's worth a bit of viciousness."

"But you hated th-th-them before."

"Stupid, noisy, ignorant, fucking cretins."

"Exactly. Self-hatred turned outward?"

"I don't think so."

"You might want to l-l-look a little closer."

"And I might not. You got any ideas about this murder?"

"I only know about killing in war. I d-d-don't know about murder. Steve could solve it for you in forty-eight minutes. What about this G-G-Glenn?"

"What about him? I shouldn't have done it, but when I was there and he touched me, nothing, and I mean nothing in the world could have stopped me. I had to do it."

"And n-n-now you have to deal with the consequences."

"You think I don't know that? I wanted to talk to you to feel better, not worse."

"It's a painful process."

"What?"

"G-g-growing up."

"If I wanted to hear that, I'd call my mother."

"You probably should anyway."

"Karl, what am I going to do?"

"If I know you, you're g-g-going to solve the murder."

"How?" I whined.

"Em-m-motion. I don't think someone strangles over a small emotion. It's pretty strong stuff, d-d-on't you think?"

"I do think. I think it's fear and jealousy and I can't help thinking it was a woman, even though there's practically a neon sign pointing toward the penthouse, especially since it turns out that Thomas is even less of a choirboy than we thought. Now I just have to figure out which one and prove it before the cops put me in the slammer and throw away the key."

"I have f-f-faith. When it's over you should come out h-h-here."

"Don't you think I should stop running?"

"It's about eighty d-d-degrees today."

"Meet me at the airport."

"I'll bring Rebecca."

"Is that a new dog? What happened to Effie?"

"Effie's right here. Rebecca is my g-g-g... she's someone I've been seeing."

It was a strange term for a blind man to use.

"Really?"

I didn't want to sound too surprised.

"You're surp-p-prised, aren't you?"

"Slightly."

"You'll l-l-like her."

"What does she do?"

"Weight loss therapist."

"Right. Karl, if I survive this, I'll take you up on your offer. If not, feel free to write me up as a case study and cautionary tale."

I hung up. Karl had a girlfriend. I wondered how Effie felt about it. It felt nice to worry about someone else's life for a change, especially when the someone was very far away and didn't have the kind of problems that could get him killed.

Before I could enjoy the distraction too long, the phone rang.

"Hello."

"Marti?"

"Yeah."

"It's Larry."

"My favorite muckraker." I'd been too busy to see a paper. "What's the headline today?"

"Many are cold, few are frozen."

"Yuck."

"Especially since it went all the way up to thirty-six today."

"It's like a heatwave burning in my heart. What did you find out about Thomas Brinkham?" I asked, not letting on that I already had a detective's report on the topic.

"The first thing I found out is that a lot of people didn't want to talk about him."

"Because they're scared or because they don't know anything?"

"Some of both. You'd think when someone's got that much money, people would want to gossip just for the hell of it. Brinkham, almost nothing. He such a globetrotter than no one really gets a fix on him before he moves on. The New York crowd thinks he's not much in the personality department, but he's rich enough to make up for it. Marrying Jana Crowley was kind of like a personality implant for him. Everybody loved her."

"Except the ones who hated her."

"None of the power brokers wanted to give me dirt on Brinkham. He's spread a lot of that dough around. Not just here either. He's been to D.C. a lot. I don't think he's met Reagan personally, but he's been by the commerce department a few times. He knows how to make friends."

"And buy influence?"

"Let's say his projects don't get tied up in too much red tape."

None of this was mentioned by the accountant's letter. Maybe Chuck Camaro had been looking for a forest in Hong Kong and missed a tree in England.

"I read you. So where did he get all this money?"

"This is where I really got into trouble. I had to call England."

"The *Post* can't afford long-distance phone calls?"

"It's the middle of the night there. I woke up some friends of mine. They weren't happy."

I had forgotten about the time difference between the U.S. and the U.K.

"After you pissed them off, did you get any information?"

"Has anyone ever told you that you are really pushy?"

"Who, me?" I asked innocently.

"Who am I to talk? Anyway, Mr. Brinkham isn't quite the self-made man he'd like everyone to think. First of all he inherited a bit from his father who started a steel factory in Sheffield. Everyone you talk to says he's smart. He knew when to invest and when to sell. He started taking his money out of Britain as soon as possible because of taxes."

"How about his first wife, Elizabeth?"

There was a numb silence.

"I get cursed out transatlantic and you're ahead of me all the way. I'm starting to think Johnny's right about you."

"That I'm a bitch or a murderer?"

"Are you this tough or is it all an act?" he asked, dumbfounded.

I thought of myself during the car chase, heaving my guts out from fear.

"I'm really this tough. Tell me what you know about Elizabeth."

"She was rich."

"Very rich?"

"Old money. Most of it in property. Nobody I talked to would come out and say he married her for money."

"How about murdering her for it?"

"That's what you think?"

I could imagine his broad mouth making a shoe face of disbelief.

"It's one of several competing theories."

"Well you can scrap it. He wasn't even in the country when it happened."

"She really got hit by a German tourist?"

"I heard Dutch."

"Anything else?"

"You're worse than my editor. That's all I've got for right now. I've got one guy who said he thought he remembered something about the accident. He said he'd call back at a more a civilized hour. I'm not sure what he meant by that. My editor wants to know when I'm coming up with something on the Crowley murder. Give me something Marti, or I'm going to be covering traffic court."

"It's your lucky day. Detective Johnny Rostelli made an arrest this morning in the Jana Crowley case. The suspect escaped, but is expected to be back in custody later this afternoon. There was also a car chase, but that wasn't part of the arrest, strictly speaking."

"Who's the suspect?"

"Me."

"I was wrong. You're not pushy, you're just nuts."

"Thanks, Larry. Call me if you get any more information."

"Will you be there?"

"Unless I'm in jail. Later, friend."

I put down the phone and closed my eyes. Where were the police already? The sooner I got processed, the sooner my lawyer could spring me. I went back into the living room. Nothing had changed. Jerry was still playing the piano. Strudel was sitting on the couch. I put on the TV set and sat down next to her. "Edge of Night" was on. For a soap opera, it was classy, well acted, and brilliantly written. Besides, I had a minor crush on the actor who played Miles Cavanaugh.

I was happily absorbed by the doings in Monticello for a blissfully phone-free half hour. Strudel had moved her head onto my lap. I stretched my legs out on the couch and dozed off again, pondering the great truth that life is a soap opera.

I WILL SURVIVE

I was frustrated to find that instead of dreaming glamorous "Edge of Night," I was stuck in "General Hospital," a show I was never very fond of, and what was worse I was stuck in a shouting match between the truly repulsive Luke Spencer and Dr. Noah Drake, whose hair was a lot more interesting than his acting. It was awful. Then I realized they were trying to tell me something about Jana Crowley, but they were both yelling so loud that I couldn't hear what it was.

A ringing was added to the cacophony. I wanted to push it away, but it went on and on until it stopped. I felt a hand on my shoulder and realized it was a real hand. Jerry's soft voice was trying to wake me up.

"Marti, Marti, get up."

"What is it?"

"It's the police."

I tried to shake my head out of the mist.

"O.K. Tell them I'll be right with them. I just want to brush my teeth. I shouldn't go to the police station with bad breath."

"On the phone, Marti. It's Sharon Warner."

"Oh. O.K. I'll take that in the bedroom."

Back in my "office" I picked up the phone and listened to the click as Jerry hung up the living room line.

"Hey, Detective Warner. What's the good word?"

Detective Warner was in no mood for my joviality.

"Don't give me that shit, Ms. Hirsch. What the hell have you been doing on that phone? I've been trying to get you all afternoon."

I stared at the phone for a second. Didn't she know?

"Don't you know?"

"Know what?"

"Johnny arrested me. I got away. My lawyer blew a gasket and now I'm sitting here waiting for someone to come and take me into custody. I'm trying to decide what to wear at my arraignment. Didn't you hear about the car chase?"

"I've been busy with those damn letters."

"But he's your fucking partner!"

"This ain't 'Dragnet.' "

"That's for sure," I said.

"Now can we get back to those letters?"

"Sure," I replied with a mental shrug.

"I'm at Bellevue."

"I'm not surprised."

"I gave those letters to these guys I know who specialize in criminal psychology."

"What did they say?"

"Well, first they said that they wanted to meet Miss Crowley."

"Too late."

"If I say right now that I think you're funny, will you stop trying to prove it?"

Ouch.

"Yes ma'am," I said contritely.

"Then they divided the letters up. Sick, but harmless. Sick, but probably harmless. Sick and dangerous. Then they put together one pile and both of them agreed that whoever wrote them was so sick and so dangerous that the person who got the letters should call the cops and leave town on a long vacation. Guess which ones?" she ended on a note of teasing triumph.

"The guy with the crayons who wanted to carve her up and make sculpture."

"Nope."

"The whipped cream fantasy? That one always gave me the creeps."

"Wrong. It's the stinky ones."

Goosebumps jumped up all over my body.

"Oh my god," I said slowly. "There was a another one in the mail today. I was going to call you. Wait a minute, it's right here." I'd still had it in my hand when I fell asleep earlier. It had gotten into the bedclothes somewhere. I straightened out the blankets and the letter wound up on the floor. I reached over to get it. "Sorry, here it is. Stinky is right." Where else did I know that smell from? It was like that horrible moment when you get a snippet of a song stuck in your head but you don't know where it's from.

"Are you sure it's the same guy?"

"Pink envelope. Dark green ink. Calligraphy. It starts "Dear Liebchen.""

"And the smell, right?"

"Yeah."

"I'm taking them down to the lab after I leave here. Maybe we can get a name and start from there. Maybe it's a perfume or an aftershave or something."

"Whore bait," I said, using a favorite expression of my father's.

"Is there a postmark on the letter?"

I looked at the envelope. "December sixteenth."

"And she was killed the night of the eighteenth. Maybe he went over the edge. Read me the letter. I'm going to copy it down and give it to Sam and Mel."

" *'Dear Liebchen. Soon we will be together forever. It will be the best of all holiday presents when I am freed from my current entanglements. You are the queen of my life, my soul, my dreams.'* "

"Nice guy."

"Wait, there's more. " *'I will personally take revenge on those schweinhund from* New York Magazine *who dare to cast aspersions on your honor. Their lenses cannot see your beauty the way I can. I will leave everything behind as I know you will too. Our great talents will be multiplied. Auf Wiedersehen'.* "

"No name, huh?"

"You know how these psychopaths are. Especially continental ones."

"Yeah. Sam and Mel think that's important. The German."

"They must be Jewish."

"One of them, but that's not why. They just think it tells a lot about the writer. Cultured, educated, maybe from Germany or somewhere in Europe."

"That narrows it down." There was a chiding silence. "Sorry."

"Ms. Hirsch, I don't like asking for help from civilians. At least Sam and Mel are city employees, but you're practically an enemy of the state." I restrained myself from thanking her. "If this goes sour and my captain finds out about it, I'm going to be walking a beat in Bed-Stuy. I've talked to a lot of people who knew Jana Crowley. I've got three notebooks full, and so far I don't know anything important except what I've heard from you and Mr. Brinkham. It looks like you spent the most time with her."

"Right." I didn't bother to remind Sharon that I was Jana's best friend.

"So tell me, Ms. Hirsch, who do you think wrote the letters?"

"I don't know. Really. The German thing is important, but it makes it harder. She grew up all over the world. She was an army brat. Her dad was attached to the state department. So maybe she had an old admirer who's recently bloomed into full-fledged nuttiness. She was overseas after David Price got killed and I wasn't near her then, so I don't know what particular Eurotrash she might have attracted. We know it's someone who's in the city now. We need someone arty, smelly, and foreign."

Suddenly, I knew who it was. I restrained myself in mid-gasp. Sharon heard me.

"What?"

"Nothing," I said quickly and then improvised to cover. "I was just thinking that Major Crowley should be coming to town soon. I assume Thomas called him. He might have more information."

"That's good. We'll talk to him. Stay put."

"Should I tell Johnny you said that when he comes to get me?"

"If he shows. You gotta go, but no matter what, keep thinking about the letters. It's there. It's him. We have to find out which one it is, and you're going to help me."

"Yes ma'am."

"And don't give me that attitude, O.K.?"

"O.K."

I could hardly wait to get her off the phone. Arty, smelly, foreign. That particular scent. Gustave Klausman.

It had to be him. I couldn't confront him, of course. He gave me the creeps too bad. So why hadn't I told Sharon and let her sweat him out? Because I was going to solve the damn case. Not Johnny, not even Sharon, kind and reasonable as she was. Not Larry Ramsey. Me. Me. Me. The only way I was going to throw off the indignities of the past six months and walk away with my self-respect was to personally bring down Jana's killer.

For a second, I tried to stop myself with the nastiest thing I had in my mental arsenal. You just want to write another book, I sneered at myself.

The public defender in my skull came back with a devastating riposte: for what? I couldn't get it published if I wanted to. It's not about fame or fortune. It's about becoming myself again, so that no one can bully me into getting my hair cut.

Speaking of hair, It was time to talk to Marc Rappaport, stylist to the stars and big-time fink. It was getting late, but I figured I'd try his salon anyway. The beautiful people needed special services before they hit the night, and the holiday party circuit was in full swing. I was told he was in with a client. I told the prissy thing who was answering the phone to tell Marc that my dye job had just turned fuschia and I was going to sue him, so he'd better get to the phone. That produced results.

"Is that you Marti?" he asked with amused annoyance.

"How did you know?"

"My dye jobs never turn fuschia. Puce maybe, but never fuschia. Did you want an appointment?"

"I think you've done enough damage for the time being."

"You'll get used to it. I've got a Tony winner in for a perm and if I leave it in too long she's going to look like Angela Davis."

"I love Angela Davis."

"I love Bette Davis, but that isn't why you called."

"I called to tell you that you're a rat."

There was a pause. Miss Tony Winner was in for a big old 'fro.

"I don't lie to cops. I wouldn't tell them about somebody's roots, or fake boobs, or something, but I wasn't going to lie to guy who was on a murder case, especially when it was something he was going to find out anyway. It's not like you killed her or anything right? I don't like trouble with cops. I've been on the wrong side of vice a few times. It's not pretty."

"And your friend John is a big rat too."

"Don't do this, Marti. We all have to cover our asses."

"I'll bet. You thought Rostelli was a hot number, didn't you? He's not my type with that little excuse for a beard, but he might just appeal to you."

"That's cold. You know I'm serious with my John."

"And you never, ever trick out, huh?"

"Not with straight cops, thank you very much. He did have nice eyes though."

"Here's your big chance to make it up to me."

"Free dye job. You could be a blond."

"And have it turn puce? I think not. I want a phone number."

"Whose?"

"Cleo Coltraine's."

"I can't give you that," he declared adamantly, but he couldn't resist the opportunity for gossip. "What do you want it for?"

"I want to write a profile."

"She's a too big for your little rag, don't you think? Besides, Gustave controls all her publicity. He controls everything. Her number is his number. You'd never get past him."

"Watch me."

"You're going to try and date her? You always had the hots for her and now you want to make a move."

He found the idea so titillating I couldn't bear to disappoint him.

"You got me. Come on. The worst that can happen is I get the phone slammed in my ear. The best is I get a date and tell you all about it. Give me the number."

He hesitated. "Angela Davis," I sang out.

"Oh, Christ. O.K. here it is. Five five five, two eight five four. Are you happy?"

"Delirious, darling. Ciao babe."

I hung up the phone and propped myself up on my elbows to contemplate the strange events of the day. I'd managed to do better detective work in an afternoon of lying around the house than I had in two days of running all over town, putting myself in harm's way. Maybe Nero Wolfe had the right idea. Stay home all day, grow orchids, eat great meals, and still solve murders. Of course, it only worked if you had a cook like Fritz and a legman like Archie.

"Hey Jerry," I called out. "You want to be my Archie?"

The only response I got to what must have sounded like a strange question was a few bars of "Sugar, Sugar" on the piano.

All I had to do was call Cleo Coltraine. Easy enough.

I noticed a tremor in my hand. There were plenty of things I could do first. I was getting hungry. Maybe it was time for some food. Jerry was still playing piano in the living room.

Options: make a difficult call to my sultry dream model in an attempt to bust her lover for murder or walk into the living room and finish a painful conversation with my husband.

I punched in the number. It led to a loft in the village where Gustave Klausman had his photography studio and living quarters. I listened to the ringing and realized I was holding my breath. After five rings, I was getting dizzy. I heard clicks and the electronic hiss that meant an answering machine was picking up, followed by Gustave's distinctively foreign accent.

"We're not here. Leave a message. We will call back. Make it good."

The message was disturbing on its own, but the attempt at humor pushed it into the realm of the bizarre, if it was supposed to be funny.

"This is Marti Hirsch. The message is for Cleo. Please call me. It's important. Here's my number." I gave it slowly and then repeated it. "I'm not sure how long I'll be here so give me a call. Bye-bye."

I hung up the phone and took a much needed deep breath. There was nothing to do but wait and hope. Time wasn't on my side, so I needed more than a little luck. If Gustave got the message first, Cleo would never call. That I was sure of. There might be other repercussions and those I didn't want to think about.

I propelled myself into the living room. It was late. I should have lit the menorah hours earlier. I went into the kitchen for a box of matches. My hunger led me to make an icebox inspection. The results were not promising. There were things in the freezer and sandwich fixings in the fridge, but nothing that would make a decent din-din. I discarded a white box that once contained

Chinese food and was now a science project.

"Jer, I could go for some moo-goo-gai-pan. You want anything?"

"Put me down for shrimp and bean sprouts."

I called in the order to Lee Chung's. They said it would arrive in twenty minutes. I communicated this to Jerry, who wondered out loud which would get there first, the police or the food.

"Very funny. Oh, by the way, were there any calls I should know about?"

"Elisa called. She was upset."

"Still thinks Daddy is out to kill her?"

"Thomas is talking about leaving the country. As soon as he gets Jana buried, he's taking off for the Virgin Islands. She doesn't want to go. She'd rather stay here."

"I knew she was uptight, but I didn't know she was stark raving nuts. She's got a chance to get out of this iceberg and she doesn't want to go? Maybe she's got a crush on you, sweetie pie. Either that or she doesn't want to leave pudge boy. For my stomach's sake, I hope it's you."

"She's scared."

"I've heard this already. So far the evidence isn't going with anything she's told me, except that her mother did get killed by a tourist who it turns out may or may not have been German. Maybe losing her beloved mummy was so traumatic that she went a little bonkers. You read too much Nancy Drew and you start seeing bodies in the attic."

"Is that what happened to you?"

"You know me better than that. I gave up on Nancy Drew in the middle of the fourth book. I figured out that nothing interesting was ever going to happen. I bought *I, the Jury,* and never looked back."

"I agree with you that Elisa is a little flaky, but you know Thomas Brinkham's a . . ."

For a guy from Williamsburg, Jerry was shy about stating his less pleasant opinions. Probably a trait acquired during years of parent-teacher conferences. I had no such qualms.

"Thomas Brinkham is a capitalist, male chauvinist, conniving piece of shit."

"Yeah."

"And he's a lousy father to boot, but I can only right one unrightable wrong at a time, and this week, it's the murder of Jana Crowley. Thomas is an arrogant prick, and I think he's involved in illegal activity, but it doesn't look like he's a killer."

I gave him a brief rundown of what I'd learned through my calls. The unpleasantness seemed to have been shelved for the time being.

Jerry looked disappointed.

"Darn."

"In a word. Any other calls?"

There was a pause. I knew Jerry was debating whether to tell me something.

"Jackie called."

"Oh yeah? Does Miss Vogel have any good news for me or has she been too busy lunching with Sy Newhouse?"

I was taking out on Jackie what wasn't her fault. She was still fighting for me. In a last-ditch effort to get my words into a publication of wider circulation than *New York Night*, I'd given her a stack of my short stories to try and sell in the magazine market. She agreed to try, although we both knew it was hopeless. The women's mags wanted bodice rippers and *The New Yorker* already had John Updike.

"She was calling for me. The guy who produced the Vicky Dell album is working on a movie. They're looking for some original songs and he showed them mine and . . ."

I felt like I had been kicked in the teeth with a steel

toed boot and knifed between the ribs at the same time.

"Your songs are going to be in movie!" I shouted. "That's wonderful! That's incredible!"

I kept making happy noises while trying to sort out my feelings. Jealousy. Surprise. Anger. And oh yeah, congratulations honey, your dream is coming true. I was amazed that he could have known for any amount of time and not told me immediately. I tried to imagine myself keeping a secret of that magnitude and then realized that I was.

"They want me to go out for a meeting."

"And leave me here," I said dully, remembering the last time Jerry had flown to L.A. and especially the return.

"I told them I wouldn't go anywhere without you, so they're kicking in for another ticket."

"That's nice."

"For tomorrow."

"Tomorrow?"

"Ten A.M. Eastern Airlines flying out of La Guardia."

"When are you supposed to come back? Because . . . I mean, I think I might be able to get this thing wrapped up tonight, but I'm not sure. And if I can't, then I can't just go running off to California."

"You have to do what's important to you," he said seriously.

"Exactly. I've got to get this killer." Then it hit me. "You're not coming back. And if I don't go tomorrow, it's going to be too late, isn't it?" I got up and went to the couch. Strudel was curled up on a cushion. She had her eyes closed, but I suspected she was awake and following the action like a child listening to Mommy and Daddy. "I can't believe this is happening. I can't believe you're leaving me like this." I couldn't believe I was talking like a some clinging, dependent housewife whose husband was abandoning her for a young floozy. "Jerry, this dialogue is piss-poor."

"Marti, I love you. I want you with me wherever I go."

"Then why are you saying I have to choose between being with you and solving this murder?"

"I'm not. Jana started taking you away from me the minute she showed up. I feel like she's still doing it."

"She's not. I swear. It's not even about Jana Crowley. It's getting back to who I am. I need to solve this one and then I swear I'll come to Hollywood and sit in the sun and write bad poetry about dead movie stars."

I was starting to cry. Jerry came over to the couch to wrap me up in his strong arms. He was wearing a Brooklyn College sweatshirt that was so old the gold letters were barely visible. Everything about him was soft. I was wearing nothing but my bathrobe and soft kisses started getting firmer.

"Marti."

"Yeah?"

"Things have to be different."

I started getting a sick feeling in the pit of my stomach.

"Like how?"

His voice told me this was serious and it meant trouble.

"We have to be more honest."

"We or I?" I said, pulling away. He sighed. Jerry's sighs could cut your heart out. "You got something you want to ask me about, Jerry? Let's hear it." I was a Brooklyn chick ready for a fight. It was all acting of course. I was terrified.

A loud ringing cut into our little drama. Telephonus interruptus. I ran for the phone.

"Hello."

"Is this Marti?"

I recognized Cleo's satin voice.

I WILL SURVIVE

"Yeah. Hi Cleo."

"Oh. You know it's me."

"Yes. I've been waiting for your call. I need to talk to you."

"It's about. You know. What you said the other night?"

"Right. I need to ask you some questions. It might help find out who killed Jana."

Her tortured syntax was contagious.

"Oh god. It's so awful."

"Can you talk?"

"No. Not here. We have to meet somewhere. Where he can't find me."

"Do you want to come to my place?"

"I can't."

I tried not to get frustrated. I used Jerry's "talking to not very bright children" voice.

"Where do you want to meet, Cleo?"

"I know. Let's go to Danceteria."

Five floors of noise and darkness. Not exactly conducive to what I had in mind, but if she felt safe there, so be it.

"It's kind of early for that, isn't it?"

"Not when I get there."

Whatever that meant.

"What floor?"

"I'll find you. What should I wear?" she asked seriously.

"Blue," I said without thinking.

"Yes, blue," she replied conspiratorially. "I'll see you."

"Bye."

I shook my head. Was she really dumb, or was she just high? If it was the smack, what was she like before she started taking it? I was firmly pro-drug and pro-legalization, but heroin had never held any interest for me in any form. I wouldn't even snort the stuff. I was a living argument against the "pot leads to heroin" argument. Pot may have led to acid, shrooms, peyote, mescaline, cocaine, Valium, Xanax, and Dexedrine, but never, ever, ever heroin.

I couldn't go to Danceteria in my bathrobe so I started looking for something to wear. My black spangly party dress was still lying on the bedroom floor. I held it up to the light. No stains, not too many wrinkles. I gave a sniff. Passable, especially with a little perfume. Tingle with the touch of Jean Naté. I groused a little as I put myself back into pantyhose and high heels. Why couldn't I solve this murder in jeans and a tee-shirt? Maybe because Jana Crowley wasn't a jeans and tee-shirt lady. I had to solve her murder on her terms.

Jerry saw me coming out of the bedroom in full attire.

"Where do you think your going?"

"Does my hair look awful?" I ran back into the bedroom to brush it. Jerry followed me.

"Marti, your hair looks fine."

"I think I'm actually getting used to this thing."

"You can't go out."

"Watch me."

"We were talking."

He was annoyed.

"We'll talk later," I snapped, getting annoyed right back.

"What if the cops come?"

"Tell 'em I'm at Danceteria. They can pick me up there."

"And if anybody else calls?"

"Same thing. I'm going to Danceteria. Anyone who wants me can find there. O.K.?"

I put the scented letter into my pocketbook and put on Jana's coat. I was almost at the door when I realized I had to march back and light the menorah. It was long past sundown and I didn't necessarily think that lighting the holiday candles and thanking God for giving us the

I WILL SURVIVE

festival of Chanukah was going to afford me any divine protection, but I didn't want to take unnecessary chances. Jerry watched all this with grim amusement.

"Fine," he said in a way that did not mean "fine."

My husband was mad at me. The cops were going to find out that I'd given them the slip again. I had no idea what I was going to do with a doped-up super-model. I was really on a roll.

I had the doorman call a cab for me. I got in and told the driver to take me to Danceteria.

I closed my eyes and tried to focus on what I would say to Cleo. Her beauty could get me tongue-tied and her stupidity could get me irritated. Neither of those approaches was going to work.

My mind started drifting. I kept seeing poor Jana lying on the floor. I still couldn't believe it had happened only two nights before. It was too bad I wasn't writing a book because this one would really be a doozie.

Fade in on dead body, I thought. Now there was an idea. Jerry was going to Hollywood. We'd patch up this little tiff and I'd get out there eventually. I was smelly fish in New York, but the L.A. Police Department had never heard of me. I could write a movie about this. They'd shoot it on location. Kirk Watson could play himself. I started giggling.

"Hey lady, we're here."

I opened my eyes. We were, in fact, there at West 13th. It was early, but there were still two limousines taking up space and a small crowd from the suburbs waiting to get in. You could tell they were from the suburbs because they didn't know it wasn't cool to be at a dance club in New York any time before midnight.

The girls in their drop-wasted skirts and preppie sweaters were also a giveaway. They'd get in, of course. Danceteria was more egalitarian than Studio 54 had been in its heyday, but if the outsiders knew what the inside club kids really thought of them, they'd run home in shame.

I looked at the meter. $7.60. I opened my wallet, prepared to give the driver a ten-dollar bill. It would be difficult since I discovered that I had only three dollars and fifteen cents.

"You're not going to believe this..."

"And I don't want to hear it either. Why don't I just call the cops right now."

"They'll be here soon anyway, but I really need to get in there."

"You ain't going nowhere, lady. I got better things to do than get ripped off by some bitch from the East Side. I got to make a living you know. I got a wife and three kids. You think you can just come in my cab and walk away without paying just because you come from up there in those big apartments—"

"Hey, hey, hey. I'm on your side. I'm a friend of the proletariat. I just happened to screw up. O.K.? Let's make a deal."

He turned around and gave a crude once-over.

"Not my type."

"Not what I meant anyway."

He wouldn't believe the coat was a real sealskin until I showed him the label from Dicker and Dicker of Beverly Hills. He went away happy and I got out freezing in the cold night air.

13

The next obstacle was the doorman, or rather doormen. Danceteria didn't go for the velvet rope that was so symbolic at Studio 54. Instead there was a chalk line that was unbreachable without the nod of one of two men who wore black tee-shirts over prominent muscles. I didn't have any more garments to barter so I was going to have to finesse the twelve-dollar cover fee. I recognized one of the two men. He'd been on the door the last time I was there with Marc. Come on brain, give me a name. Something with a *L*. Larry, Lenny, Louie. No, no, no . . . Lllllll . . .

"Hi Leo, remember me?"

He didn't. And then he did. He motioned me over the chalk line.

"Yeah. How ya doing."

"I'm O.K., and I'm in a jam. I need to get in and I got no money."

"Who are you again?"

"I'm a friend of Marc Rappaport's and I was also Jana Crowley's assistant. Maybe you don't recognize me without my clipboard."

"Yeah. That's it. I saw you in *New York Magazine*."

"I was blurry, but that was me. You've got a good eye."

"I'm an sculptor," he said proudly.

"Can you let me in?"

"Uh, I shouldn't. Everyone's supposed to pay. This ain't like 54 with the free publicity and the overpriced drinks."

"If Jana Crowley rose from the dead and were standing here in front of you right now you'd let her in."

"Well yeah."

"Have you had any showings yet?"

"No. Just in my studio."

"Let me in right now, Leo, or I swear you'll never show at any major gallery in this town."

"You can't."

"Oh yeah. Just see what I can get published in *Art Week*. Not to mention *New York Night*."

I threw that in for good measure, but he seemed to have heard of it.

"What do you want to go in so early for? There's hardly anybody in there."

"I hear you're so hairy you have to get your butthole waxed."

"All right. Go ahead."

He stamped my hand a little harder than necessary, but I was inside. He was right about the size of the crowd. "Tainted Love" was playing at a volume loud enough to make the fluid in your body vibrate, but there was nobody dancing on the first floor. I tried the second. One lonely couple gyrated. Or maybe it was two people who just happened to be dancing in proximity to each other. It's bad enough to be nostalgic for the music and dances of your youth. It's even worse when said youth was only three years earlier. Disco had practically disappeared and I missed it.

Three bucks wouldn't go far at the bar, but it would get me one ginger ale. I could always flirt for drinks but that was against my principles. I sneered at myself in a mirror behind the second floor bar. Principles. Yeah, right. Put the killer behind bars. Then talk to me about principles.

I nursed my ginger ale through "Bela Lugosi's Dead," "Games Without Frontiers," "Stand and Deliver," "Girls on Film," "Rapture," "Vienna." Those were the ones I recognized. Most of them I didn't. It was all synthesizers and angst.

No one offered to buy me a drink. No one asked me to dance. I tried to make myself visible in case Cleo Coltraine was having trouble remembering what I looked like.

The five floors of Danceteria were connected by stairways and elevators. It was hard to imagine Cleo doing three flights in stiletto heels so I kept an eye on the elevators. There were two of them side by side, rickety wooden death traps, operated by club girls who were inevitably clad in hooker regalia and had their hair bleached and then tinted to some outlandish hue.

My soda was gone, my feet were hurting, and I was getting a headache. Cleo was never going to show. She'd nodded out, or chickened out. Maybe her Svengali had intercepted her and taken her out with a silk curtain cord and I had another murder on my miserable excuse for a conscience. I was going home.

I made my way to the elevators and got in the first one to open its doors. The girl inside had hair the color and texture of cotton candy. I noticed a tear in her fishnet stockings through which a large chunk of meaty thigh bulged out. I had thought we were going down, but I was wrong. We went up one slow floor at a time, whether any passengers got on or not. After getting to the fifth floor, we made the same inchworm journey back down. We got a rider on the fourth floor.

He wore white spandex pants and a shirt with a pattern of fake bloodstains. His hair was died a silvery blond and moussed into hard little spikes and matched the metallic color painted onto his long nails. Obviously he never had to deal with a typewriter. He looked unwell. Even allowing for an emaciated frame and moon tan pallor, he still appeared on the verge of nausea. Either he'd imbibed too much alcohol for his slender body or he'd actually eaten the food on the premises.

Usually the elevator girl's reactions to the patrons were limited to sneering at their attire and haughtily refusing to answer questions, but this fellow was in such bad shape that our operator was forced to take notice. He had doubled over and she was probably afraid of an upchuck in the elevator. She decided to take preventive action. On the second floor, she opened the door and ran out with the sick boy. She left me alone in the elevator with the lever jammed in the open position.

The obvious thing to do was to just get out and take the stairs down to the first floor so I could leave. Another option was just to pull the lever and operate myself downward. It wasn't that difficult a procedure. Instead I stood in the elevator, leaning against the back wall, out of inertia and curiosity to see what would happen next.

A man emerged from the darkness. He was dressed in a regular business suit with a coat folded over his arm. He looked completely out of place. He must have gotten some serious sneering on the way in. There was something familiar about him. He peered into the elevator and took a quick stride into it. Then I recognized him.

"Hey Tony, what the hell are you doing here?"

He smiled his best "hello gorgeous" grin. Then he proceeded to use the hand that wasn't holding the coat to slap my face so hard, I fell across the side of the elevator. I felt a hot stinging start in my cheek. There was a particularly painful spot where his wedding ring had caught me. While I was trying to react, he assessed the lever system and closed the door with a fast, fluid motion.

"I've been looking for you, Marti," he said with a measured calm that terrified me. He turned to face me. I was cowering in the corner. There was no place to go. I figured he was going to beat the shit out of me and I couldn't think of anything to do about it.

"Do you know what happened to me today, Marti?" He added a verbal punch to the "ti" and followed it with a physical one to my nose. I could feel it starting to swell up. I fell to the floor in pain and tears.

He crouched to address me. "My wife left me. She actually packed a suitcase and left. She told me, what was it she said? She said she didn't want to be a laughingstock anymore. And she took my son. And do you know what he did, my son? My son laughed at me!"

I thought he was going to kick me or take another shot, but instead he stood up and started pacing the three-foot space to contemplate the injustice of it all. Through my fear and pain, I took a minute to think "good for you" to Paul. Maybe there was hope for the kid yet.

"But that was only the beginning. I got a call from the board of directors of the Simone School Foundations. They've heard some disturbing allegations about my personal life. They want me to step down as principal for an indefinite period. What do you think of that?"

I wasn't sure an answer was being asked for and I doubted I could put words together.

"What do you think of that?" He said more firmly.

I took a breath and tried to wipe my nose. It was too painful, but I was able to feel that I still had my glasses on.

"I think maybe being in this joint isn't the best thing for your reputation right now."

"My reputation," he enunciated with a sound between a sob and a wounded animal.

Blood from my nose had trickled down to my mouth. My whole face felt like a balloon that was about to pop. Pain and fear were competing for my attention, but the pain was much more compelling.

Are . . . are you going to kill me?"

"I should. You've destroyed my life."

"Did you kill Jana?"

"What?" He was truly shocked. I saw him shake his head in disbelief. "Why would I kill Jana? I loved her." His voice cracked. "I loved her." His weakness gave me strength. I started to stand.

"But she didn't love you. All she wanted from you was a good lay and you couldn't even give her that."

"You bitch." He grabbed me by the shoulders and pushed me down to the floor.

For a guy on the verge of disintegration, he still had strength and speed. I tried to push him away and found myself pinned to the filthy floor by his weight. He held me down with one hand while the other went for his pants.

The sound of his zipper was louder than anything else in the whole club.

He had his hands under my dress and was pulling down my panties and hose. They were big hands, pinching my thighs and buttocks in an obscene parody of caresses.

I could smell something roughly sweet and alcoholic on his breath. His unshaven chin grated roughly against my chin as he had the nerve to try and jam his tongue into my mouth. When I resisted, he smacked me again and overrode my screaming with a frenzy of profanity telling me what he was going to do to me and what a fucking bitch cunt I was.

I was face to face with the purest form of male aggression. The fight for equal pay and freedom of choice was really the fight against men who needed to dominate and humiliate and fuck women into submission. I was afraid for my body and my life, but I was not going to let it happen to me. I'd sold out a lot of ideals and dreams, but not this one. I had one weapon to use against Tony. Himself.

"Show me," I gasped.

"What?"

"I want to see it." I did it my best breathy, sexy voice, one part Marilyn Monroe, two parts Cleo Coltraine. "I want to see your big hard cock before you fuck me with it. It really turns me on to see it." He squinted and glared at me. "Come on, baby, please."

He pulled back to display himself. It looked like a small, lumpy potato. Nothing that would hurt a slender tampon user. I switched my voice to normal.

"Yeah, that's really impressive, Tony. An actual erection. O.K., let's get on with this. I'm a busy lady." He stared at me, too stunned to get violent. "Let's go, baby. You want to fuck? This is the time and the place. Before they come through that door with an ax or something. Are you going to give me the hot beef injection or what?" We both watched while he wilted like the flowers in a stop-motion Disney film.

I took the opportunity to get up and put myself back in order. Tony was kneeling on the floor, humiliated and exposed.

"Pull up your pants, Tony." I had my hand on the elevator lever. "Take a long vacation and get some therapy or some implants or something." I opened the door and walked out, leaving him to deal with the crowd that had been forming at the door, which now flooded into the small space around him.

I thought I was doing pretty well, except for my cheek and nose, but I found myself wobbling. Sitting down seemed like a good idea and the floor under me, a good a spot as any. I sat there listening to "Love Will Tear

Us Apart,'' and feeling dancers move around me. A voice seemed to come from very far.

"I've been looking for you."

"We've done this already, Tony," I muttered.

"Not Tony. Me. Cleo. I've been looking for you. Why are you down there?"

"Help me up."

I felt foolish asking her. She always appeared so frail, especially in her fashion shoots, which emphasized the swanlike splendor of her neck, but as she aided me in standing I could feel that her arms were strong, with well-defined muscles.

"What happened to you?"

"Bad dancing. Let's go talk. Can you stand me to a drink?"

"Sure. I'm sorry. I couldn't decide what to wear."

"I understand," I said, blinking at the sight of her.

The blue she had picked was electric. She shimmered in the darkness. She had topped off a shiny jumpsuit with a scarf in a darker blue. She worried at the scarf with her long nails, which were obvious fakes, but still amazing. She would have dispatched a buffoon like Tony Falzerano with a mere scratch of her talons.

She bought me a scotch. I used it on my nose. I hoped the alcohol would cauterize the bleeding and the ice would reduce the swelling. I couldn't drink the stuff, I might as well make some use of it.

"You look like her," Cleo whispered. I only heard her because she had brought her mouth right against my ear. The music was deafening. Picking Danceteria as a place to talk was something only a junkie could have thought was a good idea.

"What?"

"You look like her. Like Jana."

It was the nicest thing anyone had ever said to me, but it wasn't true. Except that I was wearing a dress that was nearly identical to the one Jana Crowley had been wearing the night she was murdered.

"Were you at the party?"

She shook her head no, but slowly, too slowly.

"We have to talk. Somewhere quiet."

"The roof."

"What are you, nuts?"

She shrugged and smiled. She got up and led me away. Crazy broad, I thought. For a junkie, she was in good shape. I was just as happy not to get back into an elevator, but four flights to the roof had me huffing and puffing. She didn't show the strain, even with those damn stiletto heels on her feet.

It was freezing up there. The wind was blowing and something wet was coming down. The fifth-floor speakers could be heard, although the music was muffled.

"It's just you and me up here, so tell me what you know about the murder."

She bit her lower lip and looked down.

"Do you think Gustave did it?" I asked, gently.

"Why?"

"Maybe he was in love with her."

"NO!" She stamped her foot.

I handed her the letter. She flicked her eyes over it and then crushed the paper and threw it away. The wind took it over and it went off the roof. I wasn't too worried about the evidence flying away. Sharon Warner had the rest of those letters. It was her reaction that was so disturbing. A petulant child in the body of a woman.

"*I'm* Liebchen. He's only supposed to call me that. Not her. Not that bitch. She was trying to take him away from me."

I couldn't believe what I was hearing.

"No, she wasn't."

"I know she was. I saw the stupid letters. I know she was calling him, having lunch."

I'd never known Jana and Gustave to have lunch together, and if she found him the least bit attractive, it was major news to me.

"Cleo. Tell me about Saturday night."

A gust of wind came through enhancing the chill. She didn't seem to notice.

"I heard him talking about the party. He didn't even tell me we were invited. He was on the phone making a date to see her."

This was too weird. I made up that guest list. It was strictly Simone School parents. Gustave and Cleo weren't invited. The disconnect was mind-boggling.

"I had to stop her."

"How were you going to do that?."

"I talked to Gustave. I told him I knew everything."

"Good move," I said sarcastically.

"He said it wasn't true, he told me I was crazy. I hate it when he says that. But I had the proof. I told him to just tell me the truth."

"And . . ."

Then he admitted it. He said it was all true. He was going to leave me alone. He said I wasn't beautiful to him anymore. He wanted her. He was going to make art with her. He said I was too stupid to be with a genius like him."

It sounded like Gustave was both a sadist and a liar.

"Bastard," I muttered.

"But it wasn't his fault. It was her fault. She said those things to him."

Women. Our own worst enemies.

"So you killed her?" I said, not wanting to believe, even as it seemed more and more obvious.

This couldn't be it. Cleo killed Jana because of Gustave, but there was nothing between Jana and Gustave except his sicko letters. Jana Crowley died for nothing.

I felt numb. Maybe that was just frostbite setting in.

Cleo gave me one of her camera looks. Lost and scared, but seductive at the same time. I looked into her

I WILL SURVIVE

eyes. Her arms were covered so I couldn't check for tracks, but it was all there in those little pinhole pupils. She knew who she was and where we were, but she was also high as the proverbial kite.

"Did you shoot up that night?"

"Sure."

It didn't mean anything to her.

"You need a good lawyer, honey. If you were on smack, they can't put you away. Well, they can, but not for as long as if you were straight."

I didn't know what the hell I was talking about. I shut up.

"I don't need a lawyer. He's taking care of it."

"Gustave? He knows?"

"Uh-huh. I told him. He's taking care of everything."

I was getting dizzy.

"Then why are you telling me?"

"I wanted you to know."

"Why? Listen to me, Cleo, this is not a game. I need to give you up to the cops."

It was so windy that I was shouting again.

"But it wasn't my fault," she said as though it were the most obvious thing in the world. "It was her fault. Are you mad at me? Please don't be mad."

My cheek still hurt. I had half a mind to hurl myself off the dangerously unrailed roof and provide a properly dramatic end to my embryonic script.

"I'm not mad at you, Cleo," I said truthfully. Shocked, stunned, and amazed, but not mad at the poor, deluded girl. Something in me actually wanted to take care of her.

"Can we be friends? I always wanted to be friends, but you were always around her and she was such a snob."

"Sure, we'll be friends. Let's go inside, O.K.? It's getting a little cold."

The music greeted us full blast as we came down the

stairs and back into the club. "Another One Bites the Dust" was playing. Cleo was so pleased with our talk that she wanted to dance. There was nothing to do but follow her.

The music switched to Roxy Music singing "Jealous Guy." This was as close as Danceteria got to a slow dance song. Some of the kids didn't know what to do with it. Cleo took off her blue silk scarf and put it around the back of my neck to pull me closer to her.

"You used this to kill Jana?" I asked.

She pulled me even closer.

"You like girls don't you?" she whispered.

"Some girls."

"You like me?" She giggled.

"I think you're beautiful," I said, honestly.

"Thanks." She beamed.

Cleo was paid large sums of money to look beautiful. I couldn't believe she needed the likes of me to bolster her confidence.

"If we're going to be friends, you have to tell me exactly what happened, O.K.?"

"When?"

"When you killed Jana."

"Oh that."

It didn't seem very important to her. I wondered just how crazy she was. Or was it crazy like a fox because I'd be her chief witness if she tried an insanity plea. Maybe I was the crazy one, spinning dizzily on the dance floor with her.

She started singing along with the record.

"I didn't mean to hurt you . . ."

"You did it with this scarf, didn't you?"

"*. . . I'm sorry that . . .* yeah, O.K. . . . I did."

"Tell me about it."

"At first I was just going to have a talk. You know, woman to woman. But then I thought, if she wants him she's not going to stop. And anyway he told me they were meant to be together and only death would keep them apart."

"He said that?"

She nodded.

"So I knew I'd have to kill her."

Premeditation. Even if she was smacked out of her gourd and nutty as a fruitcake.

"I got dressed up."

"Like you are now?"

"No. It was a powder-blue Chanel, with two-third sleeves and satin trim. I'll show it to you some time. It's the perfect dress for cocktails or dinner on the yacht."

That must have been the exact copy from the fashion spread in Vogue. It was nice to know she read something.

"And boots, right?"

Glenn had told me he'd heard heavy footsteps and thought they were boots.

"Dyed blue knee-length boots."

"What about the scarf?"

"Just something I had around. It matched."

"Because it's always nice to coordinate your murder weapon with the rest of your ensemble?"

She didn't get it.

"Did you know you were going to kill Jana with it?"

She tried to whistle along with the music and couldn't do it very well.

"I think so. Maybe. I don't know."

"How did you get past the doorman?"

"I told him I was going to the party."

So much for security.

"How did you find her in the laundry room? The party was being held in the penthouse."

"I know that. I went up. Someone told me she was down there."

"Who?"

"He was angry."

"Who?"

"He had a funny accent."

"British accent?"

"Yes."

We were practically embracing as I tried to keep hearing her over the speakers, which were back at full volume for "Fashion." I wondered if someone had spotted Cleo's fabulous presence and was playing the Bowie song as a tribute to her.

"Her husband? Thomas Brinkham told you about the laundry room?"

My head was pounding, or was it just the speakers?

"So I went down there and I heard her talking. She said she was going to leave her husband."

"Did you hear who she was talking to? Was it Gustave?"

"It . . . no . . . it wasn't. It was somebody else."

"Me?"

"No. I'd know your voice. I think she was with a guy."

"Then why . . ."

"Because I knew if she was leaving her husband, it meant she wanted Gustave."

"But what if she wanted someone else?"

"Slut."

"That's not what I mean."

She'd wrapped the scarf around my neck. It was so soft, it might have not been there at all. Yet a few sharp tugs and I could be as dead as Jana.

"So I waited a little bit and then I didn't hear anything. I went to see what was going on."

She must have heard the end of Jana's conversation with Glenn and then the beginning of their lovemaking. She'd come down the hall and her footsteps had interrupted them. If they'd managed to go all the way, maybe Glenn wouldn't have made a move and I wouldn't have . . .

I WILL SURVIVE   251

"She didn't even look at the door. She said, 'You're pathetic.' It was so cruel."

"But . . . but . . . she didn't know it was you."

According to Glenn, she thought it was Thomas. Thomas was pathetic.

"Of course she knew it was me. She was mean. She deserved to die."

"So you just strangled her?"

"Uh-huh."

"Just like that?"

"Yeah."

"Without saying anything?" I exploded.

She looked at me like I was crazy, which was certainly a possibility. Maybe my friend the killer was completely sane and I was the one who belonged in the loony bin.

"There was nothing to say. I just did it. Fast. You know?"

I tried to envision this for my movie. I figured it needed at least a few pithy insults hurled back and forth before the dirty deed was done, but maybe it would work in dramatic silence. Cleo coming in. Jana tossing off the "You're pathetic," meant for her soon-to-be-ex-husband. Cleo slipping the scarf around and pulling the ends into their deadly noose. Jana struggling because I know she was a fighter. Cleo not giving up, getting her strength from obsessive jealousy and drugs.

"When did you tell Gustave?"

"I didn't."

"But you said he knew."

"He told me he knew. When we heard it on the news. He just knew. He said I should keep my mouth shut and everything would be O.K."

"Did he act upset at all? I mean, you thought he was so crazy for her and all. If she's dead he would be freaking out, right? Cleo?"

She didn't like what I was saying and started dancing

away from me to "Don't You Want Me."

"Come back here, Cleo."

Suddenly the music went off. The silence was jolting. Confused muttering broke out everywhere. Then came a sputter of throat clearing on the speakers.

"This is the police. We have the club surrounded."

How nice, I thought. They've come to get Tony for assault and battery. They were late of course, but that was the NYPD for you.

"Miss Hirsch. Come to the first floor immediately and no one will get hurt."

They weren't there for Tony.

Cleo came running back to me.

"Marti. What's going on? Is it a publicity thing?"

"I don't think so. You want to go meet the cops?"

"Not really."

"The jig is up. Just tell them what happened. Then make sure you call Gustave. He'll take care of it."

"After I tell them?"

"That's right."

I wasn't sure what was more ludicrous. That I was saying it or that she was believing me.

"Do I have to?" she whined.

"Yes, you do. I'm your friend, remember?"

"I'm scared. Can I get a shot first?"

"Are you carrying?"

She didn't have a purse in her hand and I didn't see any telltale bulges where she could be stashing anything. Of course she had produced cash to buy me a drink so maybe she had a pouch, like an extremely well-dressed marsupial.

I hated to deprive her, but this would be an especially bad time for an bathroom O.D.

"Can it wait?" I asked seriously, like a mom trying to find out if her daughter could wait for a potty break.

"O.K.," she said with the same level of discomfort.

"Good girl. Gustave should have you out of there by midnight."

We took an elevator down. We arrived at the first floor in the middle of what looked like a cop convention. Boys in blue were everywhere with their weapons visible and walkie-talkies to make themselves feel important. I walked up to one and had Cleo tap him on the shoulder to get his attention.

"Take me to your leader," I said.

"Who are you?"

"I'm am the wanted woman," I intoned dramatically.

"You're Marti Hirsch?"

"Live and in color. Where's Johnny?"

"Detective Rostelli's at the door."

"Thanks champ. Come on Cleo."

We walked to the front entrance holding hands like the best friends we might have been in her dreams or even the lovers we might have been in mine.

Johnny was out there with his own walkie-talkie, looking like General Patton or General Custer, depending on your point of view. Police cars had brought 13th Street to a standstill. I couldn't see the reporters for all the strobes and sirens, but I knew the vermin were slithering somewhere in the darkness.

"Hey, Johnny. What's shaking?"

The sight of my face brought out his violent impulses. However there were witnesses and I wasn't trying to resist arrest, so he managed to restrain himself, especially when I introduced him to the glamorous vision of Cleo Coltraine.

"This is Cleo. She's the murderer. Here's her scarf. That's the murder weapon. It's a long story. Make sure you get her rights read loud and clear. She's a dope fiend, so be prepared for withdrawal symptoms in a few hours. That's if she's still in custody, but being as she's got great connections, I wouldn't count on that. By the way, I am flat broke. Since you've got the whole damn calvary here, could I hitch a ride with whichever car is heading in my direction?"

It wasn't that easy.

Johnny made me go to the police station. He was just being spiteful, if you ask me. I had to sit in a drafty hallway for a inordinately long period of time while they took Cleo's statement and did whatever it is that cops do to make the wheels of justice turn. I was still wearing that flimsy black thing, on which the sparkles were looking considerably less sparkly. It had acquired some gashes during the elevator incident.

A policewoman saw me shivering and took pity on me. She gave me a jacket, which I eventually realized was part of a police uniform. It made a fetching ensemble with my tattered finery.

I had to smile at the irony of wrapping myself in the colors of the NYPD. Then I remembered that I had turned Cleo over to the fuzz just to save my own ass and it wasn't so amusing.

Jana and I would never giggle through a movie together again or spend another sunlit afternoon in her studio, or exchange glances at an arty party. Cleo's insane jealousy had left a painful hole in my life.

Was that a good enough reason to betray a girl who had been made into an object by the fashion trade, been psychologically tortured by her lover, and was already carrying god only knows what psychic wounds that had led her to solace in the needle? It was especially hard to justify to myself when I knew I might have been capable of putting that silk around Jana's neck myself. Tainted love indeed. Could my script survive that kind of moral ambiguity? Could I?

I felt myself starting to drift off, even though I was still shivering with cold. Was that what Cleo felt like? Losing track of time. Feeling like a bit player in somebody else's nightmare?

Someone was roughly shaking my arm.

I WILL SURVIVE

"Wake up, Sleeping Beauty."

I had never felt less beautiful in my life, but Detective Rostelli wasn't Prince Charming either.

"Now what happens?" I asked, shaking off a yawn.

"Now you get out of my sight," he growled.

"Gee. Does this mean you don't love me anymore?"

Johnny shook his head in disgust. His normally brilliant blue eyes were dulled.

"The D.A. heard her story. She's under arrest and you're free to go. Now scram!"

"Wait a minute. Is she O.K.?"

"What do you care?"

I started to say, "I'm her friend," but I couldn't tell that lie to Johnny or to myself.

"Did she get through to Klausman? Does she have a lawyer?"

"There's been no answer. She started getting the shakes and gave the DA the whole thing without counsel."

"Is that going to stand up in court?"

"Who are you, the freaking public defender all of a sudden? The D.A. says it's kosher."

"Is she O.K.?"

I couldn't let it go. The thought of Cleo going through the shakes and sweats, heaving her guts out in a dirty cell surrounded by skid row drunks and Lincoln Tunnel whores, was more than I could stand.

Johnny stood there watching with his arms tightly crossed and lips pursed. I dropped the pretense of toughness.

"Johnny?"

He gave a short, irritated sigh and looked down.

"She started getting sick and they took her to New York Hospital. The D.A. says we can't have a big cover girl going cold turkey in the Tombs. I say why not, but no one listens. She's still under arrest, but they're taking care of her. You happy?"

"Yeah."

"Now get the hell the out of here."

"Gimme a ride," I said playfully.

"What?"

"Come on. You're a big hero. Larry will write a story about it. 'Fashion plate strangles art goddess. Smart cop makes great collar.' You owe me. Besides, we had such a good time driving together today, I just thought—"

"O.K., O.K., I'll give you a ride. Just shut up. Please."

"O.K., Daddy."

"I said shut up."

I shut up, but I couldn't help grinning. I had derived no pleasure from solving the murder. What good did it do to know that poor Cleo had killed Jana because she believed that Jana wanted her nutso Teutonic lover? The only consolation I could pull out of the evening was the fun of annoying Johnny Rostelli.

His revenge was to spend the whole drive filling me in about what had happened to the passengers of the car that went off the Harlem River Drive earlier that day. They were both dead. The girl, one Heather Davies, had expired due to the bullet that had entered the back of her neck through the rear window of the car during the chase.

She'd been lucky. It was Jesse Wilcox that Johnny was most interested in telling me about. He'd still been alive when the car went into the water, but didn't survive the water itself. The medical examiner reported death by drowning, which, as Johnny described with great enthusiasm, meant he died choking on his own vomit. Furthermore, the initial examination showed that "his backside was pretty messed up."

I tried to decode that. Back injury from the drop into the river? Whipping from his stay in jail? Or something else from his stay in jail. Maybe backside was a euphemism for something slightly lower than the back.

Was I supposed to feel sorry for either one of them?

What had happened to Jesse and Heather was truly hideous, but I didn't care. No more hiccupping horse laughs from him, no more of her unfunny funnies about the Knicks or the Nets.

They had been trying to kill me and they were destroyed. The murder was solved, even if it was a lousy solution.

Johnny stopped in front of the Lancaster. I couldn't resist a little more teasing.

"Is it really over between us?"

"Get out of my car. Get out of town."

He had pulled that "get out of town" stunt on me once before. It worked then because I was scared. It was three years later. He couldn't scare me anymore. If I left town, it was because I wanted to. I took a stab in the dark.

"You must have wanted me real bad back when I was fucking Doug."

His stricken glare was enough of an answer.

I got out of the car. A snowflake touched my face. The snow that had been missing for two months had arrived at last. It was very light. Not enough to qualify as a White Chanukah, but some kind of hope.

A strong feeling of vicious elation came to me in the darkness.

Schadenfreude. A good word. The delight and relief you feel when something bad happens to somebody else. The way my mom felt when a certain ingenue she detested broke her leg, back when Barbara Hirsch had been a chorus girl. Mom didn't get to be the lead à la *Forty-second Street*, but it was enough to see that other actress lose it. An evil feeling, but so delicious. A German word of course. Who knew evil better than the Germans? One German in particular. Or flying Dutchman or whatever the hell he was. Maybe Swiss. Gustave was a Swiss name, no? Gustave Trapp in *Lolita*.

I was standing in the snow, warmed by memories and word games, when I was interrupted by a rude car horn. I noticed that Johnny was still parked. He was waiting for me to go inside. Maybe he was concerned about my safety. I waved him away, but he stubbornly stayed. I couldn't let the poor guy sit there all night, so I went to the door to be greeted by one of our rotating, identical doormen.

"Hello Mrs. Barlow."

I sighed. Some battles would never be won.

"Hello . . ." I didn't know his name. I took a guess. "Jim?"

"Joe," he said smoothly. "Nice evening?" he asked. It was like talking to a Fisher-Price toy. He could only use the taped phrases that had been programmed into him. I looked like hell, was coming in after midnight wearing a police uniform jacket, and all he could do was ask if I had a nice evening.

"It was great."

"You missed some excitement."

"Right." I nodded absently and waited for the elevator. What excitement could I possibly have missed? I'd had enough excitement to last a lifetime. As much as I hated the idea of Johnny Rostelli thinking he could scare me into leaving the Big Apple, I really did need a rest. Los Angeles wouldn't be so bad. Swimming pools. Movie stars.

My mind was wandering back to *Schadenfreude*. Then another German word. *Danke schoen*. I started singing to myself. "Dah dah dah . . . all the joy and pain." Joy and pain. Life with Jerry.

I got on the elevator. I had to go up there and have it out. Tell the truth. Glenn, Topeka, the whole thing. It would be painful. I had to do it because the alternative was to walk away from Jerry and I couldn't do that. Superwoman turns out to be flash in pan. Might as well get it over with.

I WILL SURVIVE

Something was wrong.

Jerry was sitting on the couch. Strudel was perched sitting next to him. They both looked forlorn. Jerry didn't look up as I came in. He just sat there, with his head down staring at the floor. I got the impression he'd been crying. I had been gone an awfully long time without telling him exactly what I was doing. I couldn't be upset with him for being upset. I couldn't even be mad at him for telling Tony Falzerano where I was, since that was what I had said to do, even though I did say it in the heat of battle.

"Hi honey. I'm home," I started briskly. "Everything's taken care of. Cleo's confessed to the murder. She's in custody. I'm free to head out to the coast with you tomorrow and now we can have that little talk. I'm going to tell you everything. O.K.?"

He looked up at me slowly. He'd definitely been crying.

"I'm sorry it took so long. I'm sorry about everything, but it's all going to be different now. I'm going to be different. No more murders. A body could drop in the swimming pool by the bungalow and I would just call the police and go on with my writing. Isn't that what you want?"

"You don't know, do you."

"I don't know what?"

"Elisa's dead. Thomas killed her."

14

My first instinct was to run out the door and never come back. My second was the deep urge to get high. My third was to find out what the hell was going on.

"What the hell is going on?"

It sounded the same the second time.

Jerry was a wreck. He could barely talk. I sat down next to him on the couch. I put my arms around him.

"Marti, you have to do something."

Why me? I wondered.

"It's going to be O.K., honey. I am going to take care of it, but you've got to tell me what you know."

"Marti. I told her we'd take care of her. You told her."

It was like a knife through my heart. The night's meager victory felt like nothing but ashes. I'd been hit, nearly raped, and had to seriously compromise my own principles. None of it felt as sickenly rotten as this.

The final blow was the sight of Jerry starting to cry.

"Jerry!" I felt myself getting hysterical. Jerry had to be calm and strong, because that was his job. I was allowed to be crazy because Jerry was there to be the grown-up. If he was losing it, I had to be the strong one and I didn't know if I was up to the job.

I closed my eyes. I tried to find the Marti who had fought the cops during Vietnam, done six months on a kibbutz, and solved the David Price murder and the Dorothea Jones murder and written a book and knew who she was and what she believed in, no matter what kind of chaos was going on in or around her.

A certain Gloria Gaynor song came into my head. I let it play all the way through until I wasn't afraid or petrified anymore. I grew strong. I remembered how to get along. Those kids at Danceteria didn't know what they were missing. "Love Will Tear Us Apart" would never have that kind of power to strengthen and heal.

"I know this is really, really bad. And it looks like I fucked up big time. If he killed Elisa on my watch, I'm going to go up to that penthouse and pull out the large stick that he's got up his ass and personally shove it down his throat. It's just gonna be me and him and I'm gonna win."

The stunned misery on Jerry's face had melted into stunned amusement.

"What are you looking at?"

"Your Brooklyn accent."

"Hey!"

"And the fact that you're talking about using violence."

"Just tell me what happened?"

"I told you she called, right?"

I felt that pain in my stomach again. It was part guilt and part hunger. The half-eaten Chinese food was on the coffee table. I reached into a container of moo-goo-gai-pan and pulled out a water chestnut.

"She called and she was scared. You told me and I gave it the big brush-off because I was on my fox hunt."

"She called again after you left. She had tried to call Paul."

"That wouldn't have done any good. Rhonda took a hike and took Paul with her. I thought it was a giant step for womankind, but if Elisa couldn't find her buddy..."

"It was pretty bad. I tried to calm her down, but she was just hysterical. She said she was packing a bag and leaving, because Thomas was looking at her funny. She thought he knew she'd been telling us about him. I told her to come down here. She said she would. I waited and she never showed up."

There were a lot of phones in the apartment, and very little privacy. That's why Jana and I used the laundry room.

"I thought maybe she changed her mind," Jerry said miserably, drowning in his own guilt. "I lost track of time because the phone kept ringing. First the cops, then Tony. I wonder what he wanted?"

I sighed and gingerly touched my cheek.

"I'll tell you about it someday. What else happened?"

"I heard the sirens outside. I thought it was just the police coming to get you or bring you in or something. Then nothing else happened for a while. The next thing I know Detective Warner was knocking on my door with a funny look on her face."

"Funny?"

"It wasn't that funny. She said... she said that Elisa had committed suicide by jumping out the window."

"Oh my god!!! But you said Thomas killed her."

"He must have."

My own flippant words echoed back. "What's he going to do? Throw her out a window?"

"Give me some details. Which window?"

"Her bedroom."

I thought about the layout of the penthouse. Elisa's bedroom was located down the hall from Jana's studio. I'd never seen it, so I didn't know where the windows were or how difficult it would be to climb out or get pushed.

"Did Thomas call the cops?"

"He wasn't there."

"He killed her, but he wasn't there? You're not making sense."

"It doesn't make sense, Marti, but I know he did it."

"You sound like me."

"You mean it's catching?" He worked up a moment of mock horror before sinking back into the doldrums.

I finally got as much of the story as Jerry had from Sharon.

The body had been found on 65th street by an older woman and her poodle. Elisa was dead, having cracked her skull and bled to death from the fifteen-story fall. She was wearing a matching cream-colored skirt and sweater set, but no shoes. So far no one would admit to having heard or seen anything, although Detective Warner had her men conducting an apartment by apartment search of the Lancaster and any apartment house that could have had a possible view of the penthouse. Voyeurs with telescopes were especially sought.

Jerry had heard from Elisa at 9:30 P.M. The body was found at a little after 11 P.M. It was plenty of time for someone to have subdued the girl and heaved her out the window. It turned out that her father, the main suspect as far as Jerry was concerned, was out the whole time, and could be alibied, not just by the business associates he was dining with, but also by a slew of waiters and waitresses who had brought him food, drinks, and cigars. They had been handsomely and ostentatiously tipped for their services.

"He's good. He's damn good," I muttered. "Did he wave his magic money wand and get the press out of here too?"

"It was a mob for a while. I think they got him from the restaurant and then showed him the body here."

"How'd he take it?"

"Sharon said he was devastated."

"He's supposed to be in mourning. He should have been home clinging to his daughter, his only consolation in the world following the death of the wife he loved so much."

"You're making me sick."

"It makes me sick too, but don't you think that's at least how he should have played it? If he had to get out of the house to alibi himself while someone did the job on Elisa, then he must have known he was in the clear on Jana's death and been scared of what Elisa had on him."

"That he killed his first wife?"

"Which he didn't," I said glumly.

"Or Jana?"

"He didn't do that either."

"We're going in circles and he's up there laughing at us. What are we going to do?"

"Did Sharon give you any idea what the cops are thinking?"

"I told you. She said suicide."

"Suicide? Wait a minute. Why suicide?"

Jerry let out one of his deepest sighs.

"There was a note."

My arms were getting tired from being locked around Jerry. I had to get up and move around. I picked up the Chinese food and went into the kitchen for a spoon. I came back eating.

"There was a note?" I said, feigning calm. "Did you see it?"

"No. Detective Warner was really here to get information from me about the last time I heard from her and everything. When I started to ask questions, she said it was bad enough for one of us to be doing it."

"You should have pushed her anyway."

"I did. She told me the note was from Elisa's diary.

I WILL SURVIVE 265

It said she was depressed and lonely. Nobody cared about her and death was all around. Maybe she just lost hope."

"How could she lose hope if you were down here? I know I wouldn't." I nibbled on a piece of chicken. Something zinged in my head. "What did you say about the note?"

"That it was gloomy."

"No, where it was from."

"Her diary."

"On a page in her diary?"

"No. It was written in her diary but they found the page on her pillow."

"Torn out?" I asked.

"I guess so."

"No way."

"That's what Detective Warner told me."

"No. Uh-uh. I've kept a journal on and off since I was ten. You never rip anything out."

"Maybe you wouldn't have, but she did."

"Now you're believing the cop's version. No, no, no. She gets bummed. She can't find Paul. The world sucks. She feels like dying. She writes it all down for posterity and then she gets ready to come down here and cry on your shoulder or something. Whoever goes in there to kill her finds the diary. Those locks on those things aren't very good. Or maybe the key was there or something. Maybe it's out on the bed. I don't know the whole picture, but it sure looks like a suicide note and that makes the scene play ever so much better. Oh, when I get my hands on the son of a bitch, he is going to rue the day."

It was good talk. The only problem was I still didn't have all the pieces, and if I did, I couldn't see for the life of me how they fit together. There were too many stories. The soap opera that had left Jana dead in the laundry room didn't belong in the same script with Jesse and Heather careening around the city taking pot shots at me and ending up in the same morgue where a sad, pale teenager was lying with a cracked head, not to mention a once promising young man with eyes like summer skies who was a charred ruin.

At the rate things were going, Thomas Brinkham was going to be sitting on a beach, while I stood in the cold trying to explain this whole thing to Jana Crowley's parents.

"Why the hell didn't you go up there and confront him?" I yelled.

He didn't have an answer to a ridiculous question. He shook his head.

"You're the one who—"

"Goes out and does crazy things? Who's not afraid to have people hate my guts? Who fucks around?" It came out of my mouth without my knowing it was there. "Oh my god, Jerry. I'm sorry. I didn't mean to say that. I did say I was going to come in here and be honest but I didn't mean to hurt you. It was never about you. Do you want to know? I want to tell you the truth."

The murder was being preempted by our personal melodrama.

"You don't have to tell me anything. I already know."

"What? You know what?"

"I know about Topeka. The thing with Julie. And I know something happened last night."

"Who told you?"

"Nobody told me."

"Then how do you know?" My voice was cracking with fear.

"Because I love you," he said simply.

I couldn't take it. My mind couldn't process this. I ran into the bedroom and went to my jewelry box which mostly held cheap costume earrings and a few leftover Mardi Gras beads. It also had a razor blade and a tiny plastic bag with a small quantity of Colombia's best purchased from a certain Park Avenue "social worker."

I laid out the lines and did them quickly. It wasn't the easiest thing to do with a nose that was still swollen from contact with Tony Falzerano's fist, but the effects were worth it. The jolt came immediately in a straight line from my nose to my throat where that feeling of being clogged lingered for a second and then my whole body exploded into euphoric awareness. My eyes opened wide. The world felt big and bright.

I could handle Jerry. I could handle the murder. I could handle anything including making sure that there was no telltale powder showing in my nostrils, an unappealing look at best and one that was sure to trigger a ocean of disapproval from my darling hubby.

I strolled back into the living room.

"You know because you love me. Is that right?"

"Yeah," he said uncertainly.

"O.K.," I clenched a fist, digging my nails into the skin to steady my speeding thoughts and stop the shaking, "and you've never cheated on me, because I'd know."

"I would never do that to you."

"Exactly. Because I'd know. I love you, Jerry, you have to believe that. Love. It's all about love. Frank Polaris knew about Glenn, because he loved him."

"Frank and Glenn?" Jerry asked in total confusion.

"It'll be in the movie. Thomas didn't know about Jana because he didn't love her. He married her for her beauty and her name and maybe her money, but he didn't love her, so he didn't know there was another man."

"Marti, what are you talking about?"

Words were tumbling out of my mouth.

"Cleo was in love. Jana was in love. But Thomas wasn't. He just used love. He used other people's love.

Love. Love. Love." I was singing a Beatles song when I was interrupted by the phone.

All you need is love, I sang, at least I thought I was singing.

"Is this Marti?" said a confused voice on the other end.

"Marti Hirsch speaking."

"Hey, Marti. It's Larry, your favorite reporter." I managed to stop myself from telling him that my favorite reporter was Jimmy Breslin. "Amazing work on that Jana Crowley murder. Cleo Coltraine. I never saw that one coming. I was sure it was the husband. He's had a rough week huh? First his wife and now his kid? Poor guy."

"It's a tragedy," I said sincerely.

"You know what? You should be a reporter."

"Probably. You calling to offer me a job or get a quote?"

"Neither. I just wanted to give you the big thumbs-up. Way to go. Johnny gave me the whole thing. Front page tomorrow. Oh. One other thing. It probably doesn't matter anymore, but I finally got a call from that guy in England. Works for the *Times*. Well, he did some digging in the stacks. He didn't have anything different on the car accident, but he did have some information about the first Mrs. Brinkham's brother."

"Yeah?" I tried to sound interested. I couldn't see how it related to the case at hand but Larry had gone to the trouble of getting it, the least I could do was listen.

"Turns out he had a nice little art gallery in Chelsea, that's kind of like the Village here."

"I know that."

"Well anyway, he ran into trouble with Scotland Yard. He likes his girls a little younger than the legal age if you know what I mean. The secretary didn't press charges or anything because she wasn't that young or

I WILL SURVIVE

that innocent, but she did wind up dropping a dime on him for some financial irregularities."

"Irregularities?"

"Makes it sound like the money was constipated or something. Turns out he was ripping off artists left and right and doing money laundering on the side."

My hands was shaking. I looked down at my legs. They were shaking too. It wasn't just the coke either. This was it. I could feel it.

"What happened to him?"

"That's the funny part. He disappeared. This guy on the *Times* couldn't find anything after the initial arrest. Lots of charges, but no trial. The gallery closed and the brother just fell off the planet."

"And Scotland Yard never went after him?"

"If they did, they never found anything. There could have been some kind of payoff."

"That would have to be some fairly big bucks. Or pounds. Was this before or after Elizabeth had her encounter with German tourism?"

"A few months after. What do you think?"

"It's amazing, Larry."

"Yeah. That family has no luck."

"What was her maiden name again?"

"Winterwine. How could you forget a name like that?"

"That's right. Winterwine."

Winterwine. Wynn. Nicholas Wynn. I'd thought he was a pompous American trying to sound like an Englishman and doing badly. I hadn't guessed he was a slimy Limey trying to sound like an American. Now I knew why he would put up with piece of trash like Heather. She must have been younger than she looked although not much smarter. At least he had a way of keeping her mouth shut when he was alone with her. Did Jesse know? Of course he knew. It was almost pimping to have her in place so that he could use the gallery for his base of drug operations. I hoped his "backside" was an even bigger mess than Johnny had suggested.

"Marti. Are you still there, Marti?"

"Sorry, Larry. Just following a few stray thoughts."

"Well I have to go. I want to make sure this snow doesn't bump my page one."

"Bye, Larry. Thanks for everything."

"Don't mention it. And I mean that."

I hung up the phone. My mind felt like a time-warping jukebox. Love, love, love. Touch me baby, tainted love. Another one bites the dust. I should have changed the stupid lock . . .

"Marti."

"Huh?"

Jerry was trying to pull me back to reality.

"Do you want to tell me what's going on?"

"Yeah. It was a setup. It was a setup all along. Those fucking bastards set up poor Cleo. Don't you get it?"

"No, but then again, I'm not taking any drugs."

"Will you please lighten up. I'm high, but I'm right and I'm going up there right now to bust him."

"We'll go up," he said, bravely.

"No. I'll take care of it." I knew I sounded snotty, but I had the pictures in my mind and there was no way to communicate them.

"Marti. It's dangerous."

I came to the couch and sat on his lap.

"Do you still love me?"

"With every beat of my heart."

"Do you trust me?"

"I want to."

"And I want you to. I never wanted to hurt you."

"I must be crazy, but I actually believe that."

"Good. I'm going to go up there and get the truth out of Thomas Brinkham. He's the toughest one I've come up against yet and the best liar. He's not going to give it up and I don't have any way to tape him. All I can do is try and shame him into being honest. If he kills me, there's no way he can pass it off as anything but murder. Make sure the police know that. He won't be able to buy his way out of my death. Jana will know I've taken care of it. Maybe they have movie theaters in heaven."

"Marti, you can't—"

"Call the cops. Try and get Sharon. Tell her to get over here if she wants to wrap this whole thing up in a bright shiny ball. Then you go upstairs and stand by the door. If you hear me scream, do something."

"That's not much of a plan."

"You got a better one?"

"How about acting like a sane person and calling the cops, giving them the information, and letting them go in and make the arrest?"

"Because it's all theoretical and circumstantial. No one's going to believe it unless he either confesses or tries to kill me for confronting him with it."

"I must be crazy because that almost makes sense."

"I'm heading up. You get on the phone."

"Wait. What do you mean, I do 'something' if I hear you scream?"

"You know. Break down the door. Come to my rescue."

"Break down the door?" Jerry always was the practical one. I gave him the key. "How are you going to get in?"

"I'm going to knock. Paying a condolence call. Wouldn't want to intrude on his privacy," I improvised.

"Be careful."

"Be ready."

I couldn't stand to wait. I jogged up seven flights, high heels and all. I stopped at the top to catch my breath. I wanted to get rid of the globby feeling that coke leaves in the nasal passages. I swallowed hard. It drove any residual drug into my bloodstream, which helped me do something that my brain told me was dangerous and probably stupid. I knew I should listen to Jerry. Call the cops, be a good girl, play by the rules.

I couldn't do any of those things. This was the happening. The time, the place, and the girl. I was going to march in there and get the goods on Thomas Brinkham or die trying. I'd always had fantasies of dying young. At thirty-two, I was running out of time. Maybe Thomas was in there right now, packing. I couldn't let him hightail it to someplace warm and tropical while there were so many cold bodies with his fingerprints on them, even if none of the dirty deeds had been done with his own well-manicured hands.

Knock knock. Wait wait.

"Hello, Marti."

"Hi, Thomas."

It was strange to see him without a jacket. He was in a white monogrammed shirt with the sleeves rolled up. He had the same mask of anguish that he'd worn after I told him about Jana. He was smoking a cigarette and had a bottle of champagne with a glass on the table in the living room.

The blue lilacs were starting to wilt, but hadn't been removed from the room. The decorations were still in place. I almost expected to see Jake in the kitchen whipping up one more batch of latkes. There was an eerie quiet to the apartment. It wasn't so much the absence of life as the presence of death. Thomas Brinkham was death.

He was playing it cool. An outsider might have looked askance at champagne under the circumstances, but it was known to be the only alcoholic beverage that Mr. Brinkham consumed with any gusto.

The year that I taught Jana to love Shakespeare, she taught me to appreciate painting. She talked about how to read a picture. If I didn't know better, I would have read that Thomas Brinkham was a man whose wife and child had been snatched away, leaving him bereaved and bereft. He was slowly falling apart, trying to drink himself into insensibility to drown out the pain. A touching portrait indeed.

Bullshit. He was celebrating. In less than seventy-two hours, he had gotten rid of everyone who could possibly be a threat to him. If I'd pulled off something like that I'd be whooping it up myself. He was all alone with his joy.

"I came as soon as I heard about Elisa. I'm so sorry. Is there anything I can do?"

He shook his head slowly. He had that despair act down good.

"Join me?" he offered.

"O.K." He didn't know about my problem with alcohol. I didn't mention it. I faked a sip and felt a sting as the bubbles hit my sensitized nose.

"I should have seen it coming. How could I not know that my little girl was so upset?"

"You've had a lot on your mind."

"I know but . . . she's . . . she was so young. So much tragedy in her life."

"You mean about her mother."

"Yes . . . yes . . . she never got over that." His voice sounded thinner than ever. His eyes narrowed at me. "How do you know about that?" The mask was slipping. I could see the wariness taking over his face. For all his supposed pain, his hair was in its usual unmoving coif.

Up close, I could see his age, despite the hair coloring, the tan, and the work he'd had done on his face. His vanity could never have withstood the public embarrassment of his wife leaving him for a much younger man, and his beloved daughter fleeing in terror.

"I know a lot of things."

He gave me a sharp look and noticed that I was still wearing the police jacket.

"Have you made a sudden career move?"

"I stole it from a rookie."

"Excuse me?"

"Did you hear about Cleo Coltraine?"

"Yes. The officer phoned me. I still don't understand. Why on earth should she think that Jana was interested in . . . She hardly knew Gus . . . Mr. Klausman. It makes no sense. I'm sure the poor girl is insane. I know it makes me sound mad as well, but she needs help. Perhaps some sort of asylum, but not jail. Not if she's unbalanced. That wouldn't be right."

"Especially since you set her up to do it."

"My dear girl, what kind of rubbish is that?"

"Don't call me girl!" I snapped. "I took that shit because you were married to my best friend. Well I'm not taking it anymore."

"Maybe you'd best leave."

"Not just yet."

"I'll call the police."

"Be my guest. I can tell them about what really happened to your first wife."

He flinched, but then recovered. He poured himself another glass of champagne.

"Why should the police be concerned with a five-year-old traffic collision that happened to kill one beautiful woman who was an abysmal driver, especially when I was in Belgium at the time and the bloody accident happened in Kent?"

O.K., Marti, talk your way out of this one.

"Because I got the records of that accident from a friend at the *Times of London*. The other driver wasn't Dutch and he wasn't German. He was Swiss. And even though he was using a different name at the time, the picture that I saw bore a striking resemblance to our friend Gustave, Gus to you, Klausman."

This was the part where Thomas was supposed to either confess all or more likely accuse me of bluffing and thereby say something that would give the game away. He just sat there staring at me with an amused, contemptuous look that used to make me throw up when I saw him give it to Jana.

"You had a brand-new chunk of change to work with and you made it big over her dead body. That was cold, Thomas, but that's you all over, no matter how much time you spend in the Cayman Islands or Hong Kong. I could never figure out how Jana could stand to be close to you, because Jana was any number of things, but cold was not one of them."

"She knew what she was getting into."

"Are you calling my best friend a whore?"

"Are you calling my wife one?"

He gave his little hint of a smile. I nearly threw my champagne in his face. It was making my hand cold. I needed a place to put it down. There was a coaster right in front of me. It wasn't Thomas's because his glass was sitting on one and there was another one next to that. Three coasters.

I held on to my glass.

"Jana wanted it to work. If it didn't it wasn't her fault."

He gave me the look with a particularly nasty glint in his evil eye.

"I have to go to the airport in the morning and pick up Major Crowley. Maybe you'd like to go with me."

"Sure. I can tell them all about Glenn Doyle."

"Who?" he asked with a nonchalant tilt of his head. I noticed a tightening of the knuckles around his glass.

"The pretty boy on the canvas in Jana's studio. A sweet kid. A good actor. One hell of a lover. Probably much better than you."

He had to put his champagne glass down. It would have shattered in his hands.

"I fucked him the other night. Which, by the way, your darling wife never did. She tried to have an affair with Tony Falzerano, but that was kind of a flop."

Thomas didn't find that amusing. Of course he didn't know why it should be.

"But she loved Glenn. She was going to leave you. I know it. Glenn knew it. You didn't know because you didn't love her. You heard it from a guy named Frank Polaris. He's not in your league in the con department, but he did a number on me. He told me that he knew Glenn was destined to leave and made me believe that he accepted it without rancor, which I fell for."

It was embarrassing to realize what a schmuck I'd been on that one.

"He also told me that he made money by knowing what things were worth. He loved Glenn Doyle and he knew that Glenn was in love with someone else. He must have put a tail on him or just done a little snooping. He knew that information was worth something to you and came here to tell you about it."

His mouth was wide open. I could see the question "How do you know?" fighting with his desire not to give me anything incriminating.

"I was paying a social call on him this morning when I was interrupted the police. I asked Frank to take my baby home."

"What baby?"

"My little Strudel."

"The dog? That rat?"

"You're calling my dog a rat? Boy, are you pissing me off."

"No one's forcing you to stay here."

"Frank Polaris knew where to bring Strudel because he knew where I lived. He'd been here before to tell you what your wife was up to with his boyfriend. That really set things in motion." Even as I said it, I could see a million holes in my theory. If Thomas saw them, I was up a creek with no paddle in sight.

"This is getting quite tedious."

"Am I boring you? Hang on because this is where it gets downright diabolical. Once you figured out that she might actually pick up her marbles and leave, you had to do something about it."

"Make up your mind. One minute I'm a man without a heart and now you're accusing me of murderous jealousy."

"You didn't love her and I doubt you were particularly jealous, but you couldn't face the public humiliation of divorce. You knew she was having you investigated, right?

I saw his nostrils flare ever so slightly. "I know about the drug dealing and money laundering and she would have found out soon enough. In fact this might be a good time for Mr. Wynn to come out. Is he hiding in the kitchen?"

That caught him off guard. I wasn't sure if he picked up on the telltale coasters or not. I didn't need to give him all the answers.

"He's in the studio." Thomas raised his puny voice so that that he could be heard down the hall. "Come on out, Nicholas."

He appeared looking somewhat sheepish with an empty glass in his hand. He got a refill and lapped at it gratefully.

"How about Gus?"

He nodded.

"Herr Klausman, come out, come out wherever you are," I sang out.

He had a glass too.

I was getting nervous. Big win in the "Marti is smarter than everyone" department. Big loss by putting myself alone in a room with three men. Normally this wouldn't be a problem, but it wasn't every day that I was accusing three men of complicity in murder.

I sniffed. The edginess was still there, but the euphoria was wearing off. I knew there was a reason I never liked blow very much.

"So," I said with fake brightness, "where were we?"

Thomas was watching me with calculating intensity. Gustave and Nicholas were watching him. I could only hope that Jerry was, in fact, on the other side of the door, ready to move as soon as I screamed.

"Oh yeah. You had just found out that Jana was ready to leave you. That was unacceptable, of course. You didn't give a damn about her, but she couldn't drag your name through the mud."

I was fitting the pieces of the jigsaw puzzle together just seconds before the words formed in mouth.

"You were ready for that though. Your conspiracy was started long before you needed it. The three of you are quite a combo. I've been underestimating you for a long time, Thomas. I thought you only got rich by screwing people. You must be a fucking genius to have hatched this plot."

He might have wanted to accept the compliment, but he was too cagey for any acknowledgment.

"And I know you came up with it, because it certainly wasn't this clown," I said, turning to Nicholas. "I mean really. You get your brother-in-law to buy you out of trouble in London and then you come here and start the same thing all over again?"

"But that was for him—" he blurted out, eliciting a glare. "Actually, I meant your amorous habits, not the money laundering. I mean, I know you like them young but that one? Is a piece of American trailer trash the next best thing to a Cockney waif? How could you stand the sound of her voice?"

His pale skin was reddened by a blush that reached the tips of his ears.

"Actually, I don't want to know."

"She was sixteen," he whispered.

"That's not legal in the state of New York. Did you know that?"

"Don't say another word," snapped Thomas.

I kept working on Nicholas, who seemed to be the weakest link.

"So you had a nice little scam going on down there at Art Attack. I assume you were getting a piece of the drug action and running that through the gallery too. When the bust came, you let your mistress and her repulsive darling take the fall. Did you tell them that I called the cops or did they come to that conclusion on their own?"

Thomas let out a snort of a laugh.

"I would never call the cops on a drug dealer, you idiot."

He stood up threateningly. Now I was surrounded by three standing men. I remained sitting. It was a frightening position to be in, but I wasn't sure how well my legs would hold up if I tried to stand.

The cut on my cheek was starting to sting again. I wondered if this man would sense the pain and attack me in the same place. My eyes were drawn to his heavy gold ring. Then he seemed to relax with a shrug. He lit another Dunhill.

"It doesn't matter."

"Well it does to me. Because they thought I did it, and that's why they wanted to kill me. You like to make people your tools without them realizing it. If they wind up dead or in jail, that's not your problem, is it? Like poor Cleo." I looked at Gustave. "How could you do that to her?"

He looked more undead than ever. What had she seen in him anyway? I thought my ego had taken a few dents over the years, but I would never have been desperate enough to kill out of jealousy. Certainly not over this squat man, with his broad pale face, receding hairline, and livery lips.

"You never had any interest in Jana Crowley. Those letters were for Cleo's benefit. It was all planned." I turned back to Thomas. "You never really trusted Jana, and as soon as you knew about Glenn you pushed the plan into high gear."

Gustave and Nicholas were coming closer to the couch.

"What the hell did you whisper in her ear?" I asked Gustave. "You created her and made yourself the center of her world and then you made her think you'd leave her for Jana. A few overheard conversations that never really happened. A letter left where she could see it. An invitation you never got from me. You knew she'd fall over the edge eventually. It didn't even have to be at the party, it just had to be before Jana could leave her rotten husband. You bastard. You three bastards. The only thing you didn't count on was me surviving to catch you at it. The cops would have been happy with a confession and it would be over. Well it's not over. I've got you!"

I stood up to announce it again.

"I've got you!"

"Really?" Thomas took a deep drag from his cigarette. The heat from it came close to my already burning cheek. I looked around again. Three men, two or at least one of whom had probably propelled Elisa out the window. Too close. Shit, shit, shit.

Take care of it.

"You wouldn't want to do anything stupid like hurting me, because I already told this all to the cops. I'm wired you know. They're taping this whole thing. In fact they're outside the door right now."

Thomas gave Nicholas a signal. He went to the front door and gave a long look through the peephole. He shook his head.

"Would you care to show me this listening device

that's on your person? Take off that ridiculous jacket and let's take a look." He put a hand on my shoulder and I flinched. He reached inside my jacket and ran a cool hand over my chest with an unnecessary squeeze of my right breast. I felt more sexually threatened than I had when Tony Falzerano had my panties down and my legs spread.

I started screaming.

It was a louder scream than had come out of me either at the fire or during the car chase. It was a sound that came from the absolute conviction that I was about to die and the pain of knowing that it had happened out of stupidity.

Nothing happened. Jerry did not come through the door. The police were nowhere to be seen. I was dead.

Thomas grasped my left arm firmly. Nicholas and Gustave were moving closer. I'd never had a real fight in my life. The technique for dealing with cops during demonstrations was similar to the one for surviving a nuclear attract. Duck and cover didn't seem like an effective tactic at this particular moment. I remembered one particular time, the big event in Sacramento when I was filmed giving the finger to then Governor Reagan. The camera had missed the moment a few seconds later when a particularly belligerent state policeman tried to take away my STOP THE WAR sign. I'd been wearing heavy boots that day and the kick that I aimed without thinking about it landed somewhere that caused the cop to crumple into a heap. I was arrested by the next pig in line, but it was a satisfying moment in the quest for peace. I didn't know if strappy high heels would be as effective as those sturdy army surplus boots, but I had to try.

Nicholas was still between the door and the couch so I took that moment to heave the drink I was still holding into Gustave Klausman's face and aim my right foot between the legs of Thomas Brinkham with every ounce of energy I could derive from fear, hatred, anger, pain, and drugs. It was enough.

"Bi-itch."

This second syllable went into a register that even his high-pitched voice had never spoken in before. He dropped the cigarette, and the lit end touched my arm before falling to the floor.

"Ow."

The added pain gave me the unknown ability to hit Gustave Klausman when he recovered and tried to come at me. I wasn't sure if I had made a fist or just slapped him hard. Whatever I did it made my own hand sting, but it bought me enough time to vault over the table, kicking over the rest of the expensive stuff in the process.

Nicholas was still too close to the door, so I sprinted down out of the living room and down the hall. I ran into the studio and locked the door. The lights were off, but I could see the blue eyes and golden cowlick of Glenn Doyle shimmering in the darkness.

I was alone in the room with ghosts of the dead. Jana and Glenn. I hoped they were together in some lover's heaven reading Shakespeare to each other. Jesse and Heather. They were sleazy, pathetic losers, but since I thought the threesome of evil was heading down the corridor to do away with me, I found a moment to hope there was a good place for them too.

There was banging on the door. I checked the window. Getting out would be a tight squeeze. It opened and a blast of cold air came rushing in. Even if I got out, I didn't know if there was a way off the roof besides the fast drop method. They could say I'd cracked up and followed Elisa' s example. Elisa, whom I had let down so badly. I deserved to die for that alone.

"Break it down," I heard Thomas say. His voice had dropped back to its normal light tenor, but there was a new tension in it. If he got his hands on me, I was going

I WILL SURVIVE

to pay for that kick. I heard a body slamming against the door and prepared to take my chances on the roof.

Then I heard the unmistakable sound of a large-caliber weapon with the safety off.

"Right there, pal. All three of you. Nice little party you've got going on here. Thanks for inviting me. Ya know, you should never doubt the word of a lady."

Who the hell was that? It didn't sound like Johnny or any other cop I knew. Where was Sharon? For that matter, where the hell was Jerry? What was going on out there?

A bunch of heavy footsteps came running down the corridor.

"Take em' away. Right now it's murder, plus we're going to have a bunch of conspiracy charges, some financial stuff for the Feds, drugs for the DEA, and maybe statutory on that guy, so make sure he has some nice roommates in his cell."

"Oh no," I heard Nicholas whimpering.

Gustave was expelling a blast of obscenity that covered at least three languages as far as I could tell.

Thomas Brinkham limited himself to a flat warning.

"You're making a rather large mistake. Do you have any idea who I am?"

"I know all about it. Do you know who I am?"

"I have no idea."

I listened breathlessly, hoping to find out myself. Why did that voice sound so familiar? It sounded just like . . . No. It couldn't be.

"I'm the guy who knows all the crap you've done and is going to make sure you pay for it."

"Is this a shakedown, is that what all this is about? Really, you needn't be quite so melodramatic about it. I'm sure we can . . . ooooohh!"

"Add attempted bribery to that list. Make sure you get some treatment on that before you lock him up."

Footsteps and curses went in the opposite direction.

All was quiet. There was a gentle rapping at the door.

"Ms. Hirsch? It's all right. You're safe."

The last time I'd heard that voice I'd been shivering at the 72nd Street entrance to Central Park.

I opened the door.

"Kirk Watson. Long time no see."

"I been busy." He shrugged.

"So I see. You want to tell me about it?"

"That depends."

"You owe me the truth."

"Some of it anyway."

"Was it all lies? I heard about you back in the Sixties. You weren't working for the man then, were you?"

"Not at first. About fifteen years."

"Why? You had it all, man. It was perfect."

"You gotta grow up sometime."

"Well I don't," I said angrily. "How could you?"

"Don't bother thanking me for saving your life just now."

"Yeah. Muchas gracias. How'd you find me anyway? I told Jerry to call the cops, but I was expecting the regular fuzz, not whatever bunch of letters you're working for."

"That's real funny. I wanted to ask how you found out about the bug. I thought it was pretty well hidden in there."

"In where?"

"You look pretty good in uniform." He had a smile that I didn't like at all, but I found myself unable to look away. His hair seemed redder in the light of the hall than it had that cold afternoon in the park.

I looked at the police jacket I was wearing. I felt a wave a nausea and struggled to get out of the garment so I could throw it at him. He caught it with a laugh.

"You throw like a girl."

"Very funny. What if I'd taken it off?"

He shrugged.

"I might be dead!" I exploded, overlooking the fact that I had been perfectly willing to sacrifice myself for the cause.

"The situation was even more dangerous than you think."

"How is that possible?"

"One Chuck Camaro, in the employ of Samuel Rubinstein and Associates, CPA, was found dead in Kowloon Harbour, Hong Kong, this morning. Presumed dead about forty-eight hours. You were right. Brinkham knew the wife was on to him."

"So, you guys are everywhere, huh?"

"We're around. Like me. I was recruited because of my position and reputation. No one would ever believe I could be working for the law."

"Does Harvey know?"

"Nah."

"Good. It would break his heart. It's practically breaking mine. I should have known you were full of shit. That whole Thai whore thing. Keiko's a Japanese name. You must have made that up for my benefit."

"No. That part was true."

"Like I can believe anything you say. Why should you have been interested in me anyway?"

"Purely accidental to tell you the truth. We've had an eye on Winterwine and Brinkham for a couple of years, but it's the kind of thing that's hard to pin down. The people I work for act as a liaison between agencies of different governments, but we don't have actual power to prosecute. We just collect information and make sure that the perps get brought to the right people."

"So Thomas could still buy his way out of this."

"Not this time. Not with FBI, CIA, DEA and Scotland Yard involved."

"None of this is real. I'm having a cocaine-induced dream and you're telling me that you're James Bond, Matt Helm, and both Men from UNCLE wrapped up in one."

"I did that silly interview to help bolster the cover. That was how I found out about your connection to Art Attack."

"Did you turn in Jesse Wilcox and Heather Davies?"

There was a pause. He peered into the dark studio. He walked in and sat down on the bed. He was wearing his trench coat over a suit. I sat in the dark next to him.

"Whoever did it made quite a bit of trouble by putting everybody involved on edge. I was working in Mexico when the news came about Jana Crowley. We figured Brinkham had something to do with it, but we couldn't put the whole thing together. You did that for us."

"You've been tailing me."

"In this town? Let's just say we've been keeping tabs."

"How many of my friends were involved?"

"Never count on friends. We try to use enemies. Your doormen here don't think a lot of you."

"How about Johnny?"

"Who? Oh, Detective Rostelli. We looked at his psychological profiles. Not a good risk."

"Were you close enough to save Glenn? I mean what good is a super spy organization if you can't stop two idiots from hitting a guy with a car and sending him through a plate-glass window?"

"That was the night I came back from Mexico. I don't think I could have stopped it if I'd been standing there. I'm sorry, Marti. I know it was tough. But all of them are going to pay. Doesn't that make it better?"

I looked at Glenn. Could there be forgiveness in those eyes? He had to forgive me before I forgave anyone else. All the victims had to be taken care of.

"What happens to Cleo?"

"She did confess to murder."

"But . . ."

"I know. I'll do my best."

"That's a hell of a promise, Kirk. Is that even your name?"

"You don't need to know that. Unless..."

"Unless what?"

"You've proven to be incredibly resourceful. We already know about David Price and Dorothea Jones. As an amateur, you've done better than a lot of people who get paid for it. Imagine what you could do with some training and backup."

I stood and looked at him with shock and disgust.

"Look, whoever you are, whatever your name is and whatever bizarre organization you work for. You can tell them to take a flying leap to the moon. You can tell them I would sooner eat my own vomit than go to work for or do anything involved in law enforcement. Hell, do you know I'm probably still high on cocaine right now?"

He smiled at me and nodded. I looked in his eyes. Was he high himself? He was the legendary drug procurer, after all.

"You want some drug-crazed pinko-Commie feminist tree hugger running around with your guns? I think not."

He shrugged and stood up.

"Where's my husband?"

"He's under guard in your apartment until I deliver you safely. That's a very cute dog you've got there, by the way."

"Thanks."

He accompanied me out of the penthouse. Once we were in the elevator, he made friendly conversation.

"What are your plans?"

"Getting out of this town. Going to California. Sitting in the sun. Writing a screenplay with an ending that no one will fucking believe."

"They'd better not," He said ominously, and I realized that to Kirk Watson, there was no polite conversation, only interrogation.

I walked into my apartment and into the arms of my husband. I was never so happy to see anyone in my life. Strudel yapped loudly and scampered to my feet.

"Are you O.K.?" he asked, embracing me tightly, while the dog jumped up and down between us, wanting to be included.

"Are *you* O.K.?" I responded urgently. "Did these goons do anything to you?"

"No. They did finish off our Chinese food, though. Who's that?" he said, looking over my shoulder.

"Jerry, say hello and good-bye to Kirk Watson."

Kirk took the hint and left followed by his minions, who didn't actually look like goons or thugs. One was a college-boy type with sandy hair and a vanilla-pudding face. The other was a woman of approximately my age. She had a short blond bob with bangs. I wondered if she had a leg holster with a gun under the skirt.

The door closed behind the blond woman.

I fell into Jerry's arms.

"It's over," I said.

But it wasn't. Not quite.

15

Nothing is ever easy.

The light fluffy snow I had felt my on arm and been so happy about was the beginning a full-fledged snow storm. By the time we called our cab, there were three inches on the ground and the city was tied up in knots. California was more desirable than ever but harder to get to. We got to La Guardia half an hour late, but it didn't matter. Our flight was delayed at least two hours.

We sat down amid the cluster of potential vacationers who were now a disgruntled mob ready to attack the uniformed bearers of bad news. The snow was still falling. The talk was of whether this storm would match the intensity of the one the January before. That was the snow I had come back to New York in. This was the snow that was trying to stop me from leaving.

I tried to be calm. I thought about the night before. Jerry and I had stayed up talking. We had so much to sort out, so many ghosts hanging over us, especially Elisa's. Jerry was shattered by our failure to protect her.

He couldn't fathom cruelty like Thomas Brinkham's.

"How could he kill his own daughter?"

I could explain the motive, but that didn't answer the question.

We also had a long-overdue conversation about Jana Crowley. It was frightening to admit how much of my love had been going to her when it should have been going to Jerry. I apologized to him over and over. He apologized to me for ways he felt he had let me down.

And we talked about Glenn. I'm pretty sure I'm going to heaven because having that conversation was doing my time in hell.

We were both exhausted, but ready to start another chapter together. I left behind the rest of my cocaine, weed and all prescription bottles. The flight delay was giving me a case of the nerves, but I'd just have to deal with that.

Strudel was in her travel crate. I wasn't about to subject her to the baggage compartment again. I was going to keep all my promises. We were huddled around our bags like a family of refugees. We should have had a goat instead of a pure-bred dachshund.

I pulled out a notebook from my handbag and tried to start my screenplay.

"Fade in on dead body."

I closed my eyes. Three days. It had all happened in three days, the longest three days of my life.

"Ms. Hirsch." I didn't bother to open my eyes. I recognized the voice.

"Go away Kirk."

"But I came to give you a bon voyage present."

I love presents. I stood up.

The well-modulated female voice came over the loudspeaker.

"Ladies and gentlemen, Eastern Airlines flight 221 to Cleveland with continuing service to Los Angeles International is now boarding. We apologize for the inconvenience. We've gotten a break in the storm. We'd like to board and get you out of here as quickly as possible.

Will all first-class passengers as well as parents with small children or anyone else who needs extra time to board please do so now."

Jerry also stood up. He had the dog carrier in one hand, a suitcase in the other.

Kirk reached into the inner pocket of his suit jacket and pulled out something. He handed me three photographs. I was holding the mug shots of Thomas Brinkham, Gustave Klausman, and Nicholas Winterwine. For some reason, I touched my own nose and cheek. Nothing hurt anymore.

"Eastern Airlines now asks the business-class passengers to board flight 221."

There was something else in my hand. Tucked between two of the pictures was a nickel bag of weed. I palmed it quickly, hoping Jerry hadn't seen.

"Are you trying to get my ass busted?"

"You could sail into LAX with a kilo of smack and an Uzi and they wouldn't stop you."

"If I need an Uzi, I'll let you know. What do you want?"

"I'm restating my offer of last night."

"At this time, we'd like to invite all passengers for flight 221 to board. We'd like to leave as soon as possible."

"Marti, we have to go." Jerry was getting impatient.

"Go ahead, I'll be right with you. I have something important to say to this guy."

He went looking worried.

As soon he was out of earshot, I delivered my message.

"Fuck off."

"The pay is great. You can travel. Fringe benefits."

He raised an eyebrow toward the weed.

"And die," I spat, turning away. I started walking to the line of people shuffling toward the jetway door.

"We could help you with your publishing problem."

I stopped dead in my tracks.

"What?"

"We did some digging. I spent the night reading your book about the Price thing. You're style's a bit overwrought, but I think Mortimer and Sweeney could be convinced to rethink their position."

I couldn't breathe as I stared at his arrogant, cocksure grin. It had to be demonic temptation. He had red hair, after all. The line was getting shorter. Jerry was urgently waving at me.

"It would make a great cover. Almost as good as mine. In fact, we might find ourselves working together."

I looked at the pot. I looked at Kirk.

Self-knowledge can be brutal. If I worked with, around, or near Kirk Watson, we'd end up in bed. I could see us standing up in a dark foreign alley doing it against the wall despite the cozy bed back at the hotel room. I could see my bare legs and his trench coat.

I looked at the line. Jerry was walking backward, still urging me toward him.

"It's now or never."

What do you think, Jana?

I didn't get an answer. I'd taken care of it and she didn't need to haunt me anymore.

I looked at Jerry and Struedel and a future of peace and happiness that I wanted to believe I deserved.

I gave Kirk back his pot and his pictures and ran toward the receding figure of my husband and our dog. I made it into the plane just as they were announcing the closing of the doors. I was panting as we took our seats. California, here we come.

After all, everyone has to grow up sometime.

Nationally Bestselling Author of the Peter Decker and Rina Lazarus Novels

Faye Kellerman

"Faye Kellerman is a master of mystery."
Cleveland Plain Dealer

JUSTICE
72498-7/$6.99 US/$8.99 Can

L.A.P.D. Homicide Detective Peter Decker and his wife and confidante Rina Lazarus have a daughter of their own. So the savage murder of a popular high school girl on prom night strikes home . . . very hard.

SANCTUARY
72497-9/$6.99 US/$8.99 Can

PRAYERS FOR THE DEAD
72624-6/$6.99 US/$8.99 Can

SERPENT'S TOOTH
72625-4/$7.50 US/$10.50 Can

MOON MUSIC
72626-2/$7.50 US/$9.99 Can

THE RITUAL BATH
73266-1/$6.99 US/$8.99 Can

Buy these books at your local bookstore or use this coupon for ordering:

Mail to: Avon Books, Dept BP, Box 767, Rte 2, Dresden, TN 38225   G
Please send me the book(s) I have checked above.
❏ My check or money order—no cash or CODs please—for $_____ is enclosed (please add $1.50 per order to cover postage and handling—Canadian residents add 7% GST). U.S. residents make checks payable to Avon Books; Canada residents make checks payable to Hearst Book Group of Canada.
❏ Charge my VISA/MC Acct#_____ Exp Date_____
Minimum credit card order is two books or $7.50 (please add postage and handling charge of $1.50 per order—Canadian residents add 7% GST). For faster service, call 1-800-762-0779. Prices and numbers are subject to change without notice. Please allow six to eight weeks for delivery.
Name_____
Address_____
City_____ State/Zip_____
Telephone No._____   FK 0599

Explore Uncharted Terrains of Mystery
with *Anna Pigeon, Parks Ranger* by

NEVADA BARR

TRACK OF THE CAT 72164-3/$6.50 US/$8.50 Can
National parks ranger Anna Pigeon must hunt down the killer of a fellow ranger in the Southwestern wilderness—and it looks as if the trail might lead her to a two-legged beast.

A SUPERIOR DEATH 72362-X/$6.99 US/$8.99 Can
Anna must leave the serene backcountry to investigate a fresh corpse found on a submerged shipwreck at the bottom of Lake Superior.

ILL WIND 72363-8/$6.99 US/$8.99 Can

FIRE STORM 72528-7/$6.99 US/$8.99 Can

ENDANGERED SPECIES
72583-5/$6.99 US/$8.99 Can

BLIND DESCENT 72826-5/$6.99 US/$8.99 Can

Buy these books at your local bookstore or use this coupon for ordering:

Mail to: Avon Books, Dept BP, Box 767, Rte 2, Dresden, TN 38225   G
Please send me the book(s) I have checked above.
❑ My check or money order—no cash or CODs please—for $_____is enclosed (please add $1.50 per order to cover postage and handling—Canadian residents add 7% GST). U.S. residents make checks payable to Avon Books; Canada residents make checks payable to Hearst Book Group of Canada.
❑ Charge my VISA/MC Acct#_____Exp Date_____
Minimum credit card order is two books or $7.50 (please add postage and handling charge of $1.50 per order—Canadian residents add 7% GST). For faster service, call 1-800-762-0779. Prices and numbers are subject to change without notice. Please allow six to eight weeks for delivery.
Name_____
Address_____
City_____State/Zip_____
Telephone No._____   BAR 0399

Discover the
Deadly Side of Baltimore
with the Tess Monaghan Mysteries
by Agatha and Edgar Award-Winning
Author
LAURA LIPPMAN

BALTIMORE BLUES
78875-6/$5.99 US/$7.99 Can

Until her newspaper crashed and burned, Tess Monaghan was a damn good reporter who knew her hometown intimately. Now she's willing to take any freelance job—including a bit of unorthodox snooping for her rowing buddy, Darryl "Rock" Paxton.

CHARM CITY
78876-4/$6.50 US/$8.99 Can

BUTCHER'S HILL
79846-8/$5.99 US/$7.99 Can

IN BIG TROUBLE
79847-6/$6.50 US/$8.50 Can

Buy these books at your local bookstore or use this coupon for ordering:

Mail to: Avon Books, Dept BP, Box 767, Rte 2, Dresden, TN 38225   G
Please send me the book(s) I have checked above.
❑ My check or money order—no cash or CODs please—for $_____ is enclosed (please add $1.50 per order to cover postage and handling—Canadian residents add 7% GST). U.S. residents make checks payable to Avon Books; Canada residents make checks payable to Hearst Book Group of Canada.
❑ Charge my VISA/MC Acct#_____Exp Date_____
Minimum credit card order is two books or $7.50 (please add postage and handling charge of $1.50 per order—Canadian residents add 7% GST). For faster service, call 1-800-762-0779. Prices and numbers are subject to change without notice. Please allow six to eight weeks for delivery.
Name_____
Address_____
City_____State/Zip_____
Telephone No._____   LL 0699

E. J. Pugh Mysteries by
SUSAN ROGERS COOPER

"One of today's finest mystery writers"
Carolyn Hart

A CROOKED LITTLE HOUSE
79469-1/$5.99 US/$7.99 Can

HOME AGAIN, HOME AGAIN
78156-5/$5.99 US/$7.99 Can

HICKORY DICKORY STALK
78155-7/$5.50 US/$7.50 Can

ONE, TWO, WHAT DID DADDY DO?
78417-3/$5.50 US/$7.50 Can

THERE WAS A LITTLE GIRL
79468-3/$5.50 US/$7.50 Can

And Coming Soon

NOT IN MY BACKYARD
80532-4/$5.99 US/$7.99 Can

Buy these books at your local bookstore or use this coupon for ordering:

Mail to: Avon Books, Dept BP, Box 767, Rte 2, Dresden, TN 38225   G
Please send me the book(s) I have checked above.
❏ My check or money order—no cash or CODs please—for $_____is enclosed (please add $1.50 per order to cover postage and handling—Canadian residents add 7% GST). U.S. residents make checks payable to Avon Books; Canada residents make checks payable to Hearst Book Group of Canada.
❏ Charge my VISA/MC Acct#_____Exp Date_____
Minimum credit card order is two books or $7.50 (please add postage and handling charge of $1.50 per order—Canadian residents add 7% GST). For faster service, call 1-800-762-0779. Prices and numbers are subject to change without notice. Please allow six to eight weeks for delivery.
Name_____
Address_____
City_____State/Zip_____
Telephone No._____

SRC 0799

www.avonbooks.com/twilight

•

Visit Twilight Lane for all the scoop
on free drawings and premiums

•

Look up your favorite sleuth in
Detective Data.

•

Subscribe to our monthly
e-mail newsletter for all the buzz
on upcoming mysteries.

•

Browse through our list
of books and read chapter
excerpts and reviews.

•

The Joanna Brady Mysteries by National Bestselling Author

J.A. JANCE

An assassin's bullet shattered Joanna Brady's world, leaving her policeman husband to die in the Arizona desert. But the young widow fought back the only way she knew how: by bringing the killers to justice . . . and winning herself a job as Cochise County Sheriff.

DESERT HEAT
76545-4/$3.99 US/$3.99 Can

TOMBSTONE COURAGE
76546-2/$6.99 US/$8.99 Can

SHOOT/DON'T SHOOT
76548-9/$6.50 US/$8.50 Can

DEAD TO RIGHTS
72432-4/$6.99 US/$8.99 Can

SKELETON CANYON
72433-2/$6.99 US/$8.99 Can

RATTLESNAKE CROSSING
79247-8/$6.99 US/$8.99 Can

——————— And in Hardcover ———————

OUTLAW MOUNTAIN
97500-9/$24.00 US/$35.00 Can

Buy these books at your local bookstore or use this coupon for ordering:
Mail to: Avon Books, Dept BP, Box 767, Rte 2, Dresden, TN 38225   G
Please send me the book(s) I have checked above.
❏ My check or money order—no cash or CODs please—for $_____is enclosed (please add $1.50 per order to cover postage and handling—Canadian residents add 7% GST). U.S. residents make checks payable to Avon Books; Canada residents make checks payable to Hearst Book Group of Canada.
❏ Charge my VISA/MC Acct#_____Exp Date_____
Minimum credit card order is two books or $7.50 (please add postage and handling charge of $1.50 per order—Canadian residents add 7% GST). For faster service, call 1-800-762-0779. Prices and numbers are subject to change without notice. Please allow six to eight weeks for delivery.
Name_____
Address_____
City_____State/Zip_____
Telephone No._____ JB 0499